What people are saying about …

FIVE DAYS IN SKYE

"Sweet and scathing, lush and intimate.… This story has guts and heart as well as the depth and heat necessary to satisfy any romance reader's palate."

—USA Today

"From page one, *Five Days in Skye* captured my imagination and every minute of my pleasure-reading time. With enviable finesse, author Carla Laureano weaves romance, hope, healing, and faith into a spunky and sparkling tale that made me sorry to say good-bye to the characters and the alluring Isle of Skye. I look forward to reading more from this author."

Tamara Leigh, author of *Splitting Harriet* and *The Unveiling,* book one in the Age of Faith series

"After reading *Five Days in Skye,* I wanted to pack my bags and catch the first flight to Scotland to discover Skye for myself. In her debut novel, Carla Laureano brought Skye alive with vivid detail, drew me into the main characters' budding romance, and kept me turning the pages late into the night. I'm looking forward to more books from Carla!"

Beth K. Vogt, author of *Catch a Falling Star* and *Wish You Were Here*

"*Five Days in Skye* swept me away to Scotland! Against the craggy beauty of the Isle of Skye, author Carla Laureano weaves a story of love between an American businesswoman and a Scottish celebrity chef. Fans of the movie *The Holiday* are sure to enjoy this contemporary romance. Laureano's voice is deft, seamless, and wonderfully accomplished. An exciting newcomer to the world of Christian fiction!"

Becky Wade, author of *My Stubborn Heart* and *Undeniably Yours*

Five Days in Skye

Five Days in Skye

Carla Laureano

David C Cook

transforming lives together

FIVE DAYS IN SKYE
Published by David C Cook
4050 Lee Vance View
Colorado Springs, CO 80918 U.S.A.

David C Cook Distribution Canada
55 Woodslee Avenue, Paris, Ontario, Canada N3L 3E5

David C Cook U.K., Kingsway Communications
Eastbourne, East Sussex BN23 6NT, England

The graphic circle C logo is a registered trademark of David C Cook.

This story is a work of fiction. Characters and events are the product of the author's
imagination. Any resemblance to any person, living or dead, is coincidental.

LCCN 2015937219
ISBN 978-0-7814-1307-7
eISBN 978-1-4347-0701-7

The Team: John Blase, Tonya Osterhouse, Nick Lee, Tiffany Thomas, Karen Athen
Cover Design: Amy Konyndyk
Cover Photo: Shutterstock

Printed in the United States of America

Second Edition 2015

1 2 3 4 5 6 7 8 9 10

033015

For Rey, my hero and best friend.
No fictional tale could ever compare
to our real-life love story.

ACKNOWLEDGMENTS

My deepest thanks to:

Katherine Goodman, Eisley Jacobs, Cindy R. Wilson, and Vicki Severson, my fellow Writing on the Ledge group members, who waded through dozens of incarnations of characters, plots, and openings and told me when I finally got it right. Special thanks to Eisley, who talked me off more than one ledge during the writing process.

Amy Drown, who helped "Scottish-ize" my dialogue, demanded nightly chapter installments during the revision process to keep me on track, and then read it all over again. You've got a lot of editing/brainstorming hours in the bank, my friend.

Jill Cooper, James's biggest fan and my most vocal cheerleader. I promise I'll do my best to get Gerard if there's ever a movie version, even though I'm still partial to Henry.

Lisa Tawn Bergren, for being the voice of reason and experience when I needed it most.

Alastair Cunningham of Scottish Clans and Castles, whose recommendation sent me to the Isle of Skye years ago and inadvertently started me on my own new adventures. Thank you for helping me with Scottish travel and culture. I hope I got it right!

The entire David C Cook team, who takes speed and efficiency to a scary level. You all amaze me!

My brilliant and exceedingly patient husband, Rey, for not complaining when I work late, melt down, or daydream when I should be listening. Thank you for knowing that the most romantic gestures to a writing mom are washing dishes and taking the kids out for ice cream.

My two favorite little guys in the world for letting Mom "just finish this one paragraph" and thinking it's cool that I write really long books.

My mom and dad, who taught me to work hard and follow my dreams. Without your encouragement and countless hours of babysitting, this book would never have been written.

Last but certainly not least, my loving heavenly Father. Thank You for giving me the desires of my heart. Any good I accomplish is solely because of Your grace and mercy.

Chapter One

At least they couldn't fire her.

Andrea Sullivan propped her elbows on the bar and buried her head in her hands. How had things gone wrong so quickly? One minute she'd been on the verge of closing a half-million-dollar deal. The next, she'd nearly broken her hand on the jaw of a client who thought her company's offerings extended to favors she had no intention of delivering. Three years of working her way up the ranks toward VP of Sales all down the tubes because one man couldn't keep his hands to himself.

No, her company certainly wouldn't risk an ugly, public legal battle. They didn't have to. Her boss had other, more subtle means of showing his displeasure.

As punishments went, Scotland was a big one.

"What's so terrible about Scotland?"

Andrea jerked her head up and met the bartender's gaze. Had she said that aloud?

The man's eyes crinkled at the corners as he ran a towel along the polished mahogany surface of the bar, evidently amused by her slip. Round faced and topped with a thinning mop of dishwater-blond hair, he looked as stereotypically English as the London pub in which he tended bar.

She let out a long breath, her shoulders slumping. "Scotland's cold, it's miserable, and the food is horrible."

"Oh, it's not so bad as all that, is it?" His expression turned from amused to sympathetic. "Take in some countryside, tour a castle or two, maybe some high street shopping …"

"This is a business trip. Trust me. My dream vacation involves sunshine and umbrella drinks on the beach, not rain and fog in some backwater village."

If she'd only managed to keep her temper in check, she'd have been spending the next week in the tropics with the promise of a fat commission and a guaranteed promotion, not serving time in Scotland babysitting a celebrity client who suddenly wanted to dabble in the hotel business.

James MacDonald.

She'd never heard of the man. Then again, she didn't own a television. She spent so much time on the road, she wasn't even sure why she owned an apartment. She seemed to be the only one on the planet, however, who hadn't heard of the Scottish celebrity chef. Half a dozen restaurants, four cookbooks, his own television show. Even her taxi driver had been able to name MacDonald's three London restaurants without hesitation.

Andrea toyed with her half-filled wine glass, watching the golden liquid slosh around the bowl. "I should be on my way to Tahiti right now, not sitting in a pub drinking a rather mediocre glass of wine."

"That's because you go to Paris to drink wine," a deep male voice said over her shoulder. "You come to London to drink ale."

Andrea straightened as a man leaned against the bar beside her. He was tall and broad shouldered, dressed in a pair of dark slacks and a business shirt, the collar unbuttoned and sleeves rolled up to show off muscular forearms. Dark hair worn a little too long, brilliant blue eyes, handsome face. Handsome enough she took a second look and immediately wished she hadn't been so obvious about it. His grin made her heart do things it was certainly not intended to do.

She couldn't prevent the corners of her mouth from twitching up in a smile. "Now you tell me."

He glanced at the bartender. "Get me a 90 Shilling, and whatever light's on draft for the lady." He looked back at her. "We can't have you leaving London thinking that pathetic chardonnay is the best we have to offer."

"That's very thoughtful." She offered her hand. "I'm Andrea."

"Mac." He held her hand just a moment too long while he studied her face. Her stomach made a peculiar little leap. She quelled it ruthlessly and drew her fingers from his grasp while he slid onto the barstool beside her.

"Now tell me why you're sitting here instead of on what sounds like a brilliant holiday in the South Pacific."

Because my temper finally got me into more trouble than I could talk my way out of. Aloud she said, "I'm doing research on the owner of this pub."

"Ah, the illustrious Mr. MacDonald. Brilliant chef, but not the full quid from what I hear." The sparkle returned to those devastating blue eyes, and she had the feeling she was the butt of a private joke.

Andrea couldn't pass up the opportunity to gather some local gossip. She plowed onward. "You know him?"

"That depends on why you're asking. Is it business, or is your enquiry of a personal nature?"

"Business. I'm supposed to meet him in Inverness tomorrow, and I'm looking for a little background."

"Are you always so unprepared for meetings?"

Andrea bristled. "Of course not. I only got the call from my office a few hours ago. I'm now fortifying myself for a long night of web browsing back at the hotel."

"I can see that. Well, I'd say this pub is a pretty good reflection of him. Comfortable, slightly sophisticated. Best selection of locally brewed beers in England and some truly inspired food."

Andrea looked around. Typical decor, lots of wood and brass, dim lighting. Stained glass and leather accents. Upscale but not uptight. Welcoming but not sloppy.

"Middle of the road," she murmured. "But that still doesn't tell me much about the man."

"And why do you need to know so much about him?"

The bartender returned with Andrea's drink and poured Mac's from the bottle into a glass, watching them as if they were his evening's entertainment.

"My job requires rapport," she said. "I can't convince someone we're right for the project if I don't know what he's looking for. I can't win him over if I don't know which buttons to push."

"Hmm." He sipped his ale, his eyes dancing over the rim of the glass.

Was he laughing at her? "What?"

"I've just never heard a woman worry about which buttons to push when she's wearing a skirt that short and heels that high."

Heat crept up Andrea's neck and into her cheeks as she tugged down her suit skirt. It wasn't as if she were wearing a miniskirt. The length was perfectly modest when she wasn't sitting on a barstool. The heels were admittedly less conservative, but she wore them for height, not for looks. Then she realized he was watching her with a satisfied smile. She had taken the bait. Who exactly did he think he was?

She stilled her fidgeting and fixed him with a direct stare. "I could close a deal in jeans and tennis shoes. I just don't like being unprepared. Besides, I'm used to dealing with hotel groups with hundreds of properties, not celebrities with nothing better to do than play innkeeper."

"So MacDonald's a dilettante?" He swiveled on the stool and leaned back against the bar, arms crossed over his chest. Repressed laughter flashed in his expression.

"Frankly, I don't know the first thing about him. I've never seen his show, I certainly don't cook, and I can't fathom why anyone with a successful career in London would want to open a hotel on the Isle of Skye."

"Now that just sounds like bigotry. We Scots have an over-abundance of national pride."

Andrea's cheeks heated again. How could she not have noticed? His accent, while refined, had a distinct Scottish burr. She was really off her game if she had failed to pick up something that obvious. Still, he had needled her about both her clothing and her professionalism, and she had to pry the apology from her lips. "I didn't mean to be rude."

He waved a hand in dismissal. "You've got bigger problems, if you know so little about your client. Though you'll do fine if you avoid the pejoratives about his native land. I do think you have one thing in common."

"What's that?"

"You both think work is a terrible reason to cancel a trip to Tahiti."

A reluctant smile crept onto her face. "I can drink to that."

"*Slàinte*, Andrea." He clinked his glass to hers, took a long pull of the ale, and hopped off the stool. "I should get going now. I would suggest you do the same, Ms. Sullivan. You've got a long day ahead of you tomorrow."

She blinked at him. "How did you—"

"Night, Ben. Her drinks are on the house."

"Night, James."

Mac—or the man pretending to be Mac—winked at her and sauntered out of the pub.

"That was … He was …"

Ben seemed to be fighting a smile. "Mr. MacDonald, yes. I daresay that's the first time not only has a woman *not* fallen all over him, she's actually insulted him to his face."

Andrea's heart sank to the soles of her Jimmy Choos. "I think I'm going to be sick."

"I wouldn't worry too much. I rather think he liked you."

Right. She glanced back at the door, but James MacDonald had already gone. Why, oh why, did this happen now? She had to hook this account if she had any hope of getting back into her boss's good graces, and now she'd be spending the next few days trying to placate a celebrity ego.

She'd never been particularly proficient at groveling.

Andrea hopped off the stool and reached for her purse before she remembered Mr. MacDonald had taken care of her bill. She found a couple of one-pound coins in her change purse and set them on the bar as a tip, even though Ben had done nothing to signal her impending disaster. Would it really have been so difficult to give her a shake of the head, a raised eyebrow? But of course he'd stay out of the matter when his boss was involved.

"Thank you, Ben." *For nothing.*

"Good night, Andrea." He slipped the coins beneath the bar and added, "Don't think too badly of Mr. MacDonald. He's a good man, beneath it all."

Andrea forced a smile and hiked her handbag onto her shoulder, then escaped onto the dark London street. At nine o'clock on a Sunday evening, traffic had tapered off, and the usual haze of diesel fumes faded into the musty scent of damp concrete. She made a left and strode toward the Ladbroke Grove tube station, irritation speeding her steps.

How many times had she lectured her junior account managers on the importance of maintaining professionalism at all times? Every contact was a prospective client or referral. She'd just proved her own point in a particularly embarrassing manner.

Not that she excused James MacDonald for his role in this debacle. She knew his type. Wealthy, good-looking, famous. He expected women to fall at his feet, and God forbid one had a mind of her own. She'd probably be dodging his advances for the next three days while she tried to convince him she was more than a pretty face. He was lucky she hadn't smacked him for commenting on her clothing in the bar.

Truthfully, she hadn't been in much shape to do anything but put her foot firmly in her mouth. It had been years since she'd let a man rattle her, and it had taken only a smile and a lingering hand-shake to do it. Heaven help her.

She only made it a few blocks from the pub before the stiletto pumps began to rub blisters on her heels. She gave up on her plans of an indignant walk to the tube station and raised a hand to the first black cab she saw. She climbed into the rear and gave the driver her destination.

She could salvage this. She'd spend the rest of her evening with her laptop, finding out everything she could about the man. From here on, she would act with the utmost professionalism. She hadn't gotten this close to VP through years of seven-day weeks and gru-eling round-the-clock hours to blow it now. Her boss may have given her this assignment as some backhanded punishment—after all, it had been years since he'd wasted her on a barely five-figure deal—but there had to be some sort of cachet to landing a celebrity client like James MacDonald. Surely she could turn it into bigger accounts. But first she had to repair the damage she'd done with her big mouth.

The cab pulled up beside the imposing Victorian brick edifice of the Kensington Court Hotel. Andrea paid the driver and climbed out with a wince, once again regretting her choice in footwear. She limped into the richly decorated lobby and rode the lift to her fourth-floor room.

The lush carpeting muffled her footsteps to a whisper when she let herself in. She certainly couldn't complain about her accommoda-tions. She had stayed in the hotel dozens of times over the years, and each room was impeccably decorated in its own style. Her current space featured an enormous tester bed, framed by blue silk brocade draperies that spilled from a gilded corona above the headboard. She gingerly eased off her shoes, sank onto the luxurious mattress, and heaved a sigh.

She was tired, and not the kind of tired a good night's sleep in a fluffy bed could solve.

She lay there for a long moment, then threw a glance at the clock and calculated back five hours. Her sister should just be getting supper ready in Ohio. She pulled her cell phone from her pocket and dialed.

Becky answered on the fifth ring. "Andy! Why are you calling me? Aren't you supposed to be on a plane right now?" Something sizzled in the background, punctuated by a child's scream.

"Did I call at a bad time?"

"No more than usual. I'm frying up some chicken for dinner—Hannah! Leave the cat alone!"

Andrea smiled. Becky was almost eight years older than Andrea, and she had three children: a nine-year-old son and three-year-old twins, a boy and a girl. "I can call back later—"

"David! Don't hit your sister! I'm sorry, what were you saying? Aren't you supposed to be on your way to Tahiti?"

"Change of plans. Michael booked me a consultation with some celebrity client while I'm here. I'm flying to Scotland tomorrow."

"And you're okay with that?"

"I'd rather be in Tahiti, for sure."

"No, I meant—"

"I know what you meant. I'm okay. What's one more, right?"

"Oh, I don't know, the difference between a luxury vacation and a padded room, maybe?"

Andrea chuckled despite herself. Even from Ohio, Becky couldn't resist the urge to mother her. "It's my job. What am I going to do, say no?"

"That's exactly what you say. 'Michael, I've planned this vacation for over a year. Find someone else to do it.'"

"I know." The smile faded from Andrea's face. Had it not been for the disastrous outcome of her last appointment in London, she would have said exactly that. She'd gotten away with plenty of attitude in the past based on her unmatched sales record, but in this business, she was only as good as her last deal. "I'll be fine. Really. I'm meeting a client in Inverness tomorrow, and then we're driving to Skye. I should be back in New York on Wednesday."

"Maybe you should take a few days off while you're in Scotland. Your vacation is blown anyway."

"I don't think that's such a good idea. I'm staying at the client's hotel."

"Who's the client?"

Andrea paused. "James MacDonald."

The squeal that emanated from the speaker belonged to a teenage girl, not a thirty-eight-year-old mother of three. Andrea held the phone several inches from her ear until she was sure her eardrums were safe.

"And here I thought your job was completely boring!"

"Strictly business, Becks. I've got less than two days to put together a proposal, and he doesn't seem like the easiest client to deal with. It's going to be a long trip."

"I bet you don't even know who he is," Becky said reprovingly.

"Oh, I know who he is." *A self-absorbed celebrity with the sexiest smile I've ever seen.* She yanked her mind back from that precipice before she could slip over. "I need to do some research for my meeting now. I'll call you from Skye."

"All right, have fun," Becky said in a singsong voice. Andrea could practically hear her grin from four thousand miles away. "I expect an autograph, by the way."

Not likely. "Love you, Becks. Give the kids a kiss for me."

Andrea clicked off the line and pressed her fingertips to her eyes, trying to calm the urgent thrumming of her heart. The last thing she needed was to think of her client in anything but a professional fashion. Men like MacDonald were predators—any sign of weakness and she'd never be able to shake him. She knew all too well what could happen if she succumbed to an ill-advised attraction. She'd been there once, and she wasn't going back there again.

"Strictly business." The steadiness of her voice in the quiet room reassured her. She took a deep breath and levered herself up off the bed. Enough procrastinating. She still had work to do.

Andrea slipped out of her suit jacket and skirt, hung them carefully in the closet, and ensconced herself in a luxurious hotel robe. Then she chose an obscure Dussek piano concerto from her phone as mood music and dragged her laptop onto her legs.

"*James MacDonald chef,*" she typed into the search box, and waited. Page after page of results appeared: restaurant reviews, interviews, television listings. Andrea clicked through to his official website first and quickly read through his bio. Born in Portree, Isle of Skye, schooled in Scotland. Completed a degree in business at the University of Edinburgh, followed by culinary training at Leiths School of Food and Wine in London. A long list of assistant- and sous-chef positions at some of London's most prestigious eateries culminated in his first restaurant, a gastropub in Notting Hill. That first location was quickly followed by smaller, more focused restaurants in Knightsbridge and Covent Garden, then Cardiff, Edinburgh, and Glasgow.

Last year he had been invited to prepare his take on traditional English food for the prime minister. A few months ago he had been named a member of the Order of the British Empire for his philanthropic work with at-risk youth.

She blinked at the screen. Wonderful. She'd just insulted a member of a British chivalric order. That was a distinction not many women could claim.

Andrea moved on to the newspaper articles, all of which called him the standard-bearer for nouveau-British cuisine, then scanned a Wiki page listing each of his six restaurants. All of them had received starred reviews in the Michelin Red Guide. The Hart and the Hound, the flagship pub she'd just visited, received one of only a dozen two-star ratings in Britain.

She should have bypassed the wine and ordered dinner instead.

MacDonald couldn't have accomplished all that by age thirty-five without a sharp mind and plenty of talent. Somehow that just stirred up her irritation. She'd half-expected to find evidence he had simply ridden his looks and charm to success, but every detail pointed to hard work and sacrifice. For heaven's sake, the man had even established a vocational cooking program for secondary-school dropouts.

"The perfect man," she muttered. "Just ask him."

She scrolled through the search results until gossip sites began to appear. Photos of MacDonald with a string of beautiful women—models, actresses, dancers—at exclusive parties and club openings. So he was that sort. Never with the same woman twice.

Great. Her hand still hurt after the encounter with the last wannabe Don Juan. Now she had to spend the next three days trying to get James MacDonald's signature on a contract while keeping things strictly professional. The fact he'd already turned her into a blithering idiot once didn't bode well for her quick thinking.

But she'd manage. She had to. She hadn't come this close to achieving her goals just to let a man get in her way.

Chapter Two

Ian was a dead man.

James gave the cab driver his South Kensington address and settled back against the seat. It was just like the man to make a unilateral decision without consulting him. James might be the president and CEO of a multimillion-pound culinary empire, but his older brother still seemed to think he needed guidance. Ian hadn't even given him the courtesy of a full day's notice.

A reluctant smile tipped up one side of James's mouth. He must not have read his brother's email very thoroughly in his annoyance, because he'd been under the impression he was to meet an Andrew Sullivan at Inverness Airport tomorrow. Even after he'd realized his mistake, it had taken a few moments to reconcile the Irish name with the saucy, auburn-haired beauty at the bar.

No, *saucy* was an understatement. She was a firecracker in spiked heels. Dancer's body, fine-boned face, full lips. Perhaps not conventionally pretty, but exotic. Every time she moved, he'd caught the faintest hint of an Oriental perfume, so subtle it made him want to move closer to find out if he'd imagined it.

For one mad second, he'd actually considered trying it.

Probably best he hadn't. The flash of irritation in those gorgeous caramel-colored eyes said she was used to being in control of every situation and she didn't appreciate being treated like an object. Or even a woman. Still, he hadn't imagined the current of attraction between them, and he certainly wasn't going to pass up the chance to explore it.

Maybe he'd let Ian live after all.

James dug out his mobile phone from his trousers pocket and dialed his assistant. The glare from the streetlights crawled across the tinted rear windows of the cab while the line rang. He didn't even wait for her greeting after she picked up. "Good, you're home."

"It's nine o'clock on a Sunday evening, James," came Bridget's dry voice. "Where else would I be?"

He smiled. The fifty-something Londoner had been his personal assistant for years, and her voice had never wavered from its half-bored tone. She was efficient, though, and she possessed an uncanny way of anticipating his needs before he ever thought of them. "I need to change my Inverness flight to 10:00 a.m."

"That's why God invented the Internet, James."

"You changed my password on the airline's site. I can't access my account."

Silence stretched until the clacking of keys indicated she was seated at her computer. "All right, you said ten o'clock, Gatwick to Inverness?"

"Yes, thank you."

"What happened? I thought you weren't leaving London until tomorrow night."

"Ian's consultant happened."

"Oh, that."

"You knew? You might have tipped me off."

"Well, I assumed he'd told you." More clacking. Then the sound stopped, and he could almost hear her hesitation. "Don't be too hard on Ian. He's doing what he thinks is best. You did make him COO of your company for a reason."

"For the restaurants. Not for this."

"He's your brother. You might cut him some slack."

"You might mind your own business."

Bridget chuckled. "If you hadn't noticed, you are my business. And you're all set for tomorrow. I emailed you the change confirmation and your password. Oh, and Madeline needs to move the filming of the promos. I'll call you in the morning when I know all the details."

"Thanks, Bridge. What would I do without you?"

"God only knows. Good night, James."

James clicked off the line and sighed as the cab turned onto Exhibition Road toward the Kensington museums. When had this business gone from being about cooking to press releases, book signings, and after-parties? Some days he wished he could just slip on his chef's whites and spend an evening in the kitchen. But there were always appearances and promos demanding his attention, not to mention the travel it took to ensure his managing chefs were upholding his vision for each individual restaurant. At what point had he become a brand instead of a man?

Ian certainly couldn't separate the two. The hotel on Skye was supposed to be about family, about a return to the things that had been important to his father before James got caught up in all ... this. Instead his brother wanted to treat it like just another business venture, apparently one James couldn't be trusted to take seriously. Otherwise Ian wouldn't have felt the need to spring the consultant on him the night before his flight back to Scotland.

The cab pulled up outside an elegant five-story Victorian just off the main street. Unlike the restaurant's trendy Notting Hill location, which buzzed with foot traffic almost every hour of the night, this upmarket residential district rarely saw activity after sundown. It may not be the solitude of Skye, but at least here he could draw a deep breath at the end of a long day.

James let himself into the building's colonnaded front entrance and paused to collect yesterday's mail from the post boxes located on one wall of the vestibule. He flipped through the stacks of envelopes—bills, adverts, more bills—until he came to an envelope addressed to him in a flowery, feminine hand. He tucked the rest of the mail under one arm and slid his thumb beneath the flap as he started up the four flights of stairs to his penthouse flat. Who would send a letter here? Most of his friends knew the surest way to get something into his hands was to send it to his office.

He pulled out a battered newspaper clipping with a sticky note affixed to the top, but the lighting in the stairway was too dim to read it. He shoved it back into the envelope and jogged up the remaining steps to the top-floor landing of his flat. He punched a six-digit entry code into the keypad, and the high-tech lock disengaged with a metallic click. Modern conveniences in a historic building. Had to love the contrast.

The door shut with a soft hiss and a click of the lock engaging behind him as he stepped into his foyer. He took the envelope with the newspaper clipping and tossed the rest of the mail onto the entry table without looking. They skidded across the polished surface onto the floor. He didn't bother to go back for them, eyes already scanning the unfamiliar handwriting on the sticky note.

James, I'll owe you forever for the introduction! I hope you'll come see the show when we open in June.

He peeled the note off the clipping to reveal the headline: "Cast announced for new West End production of *Top Hat*." Down below, a line had been circled in red pen: "The role of Dale Tremont, originally played by Ginger Rogers in the 1935 film of the same name, will be performed by talented Welsh newcomer Olivia Carey."

"Good on you, Olivia." He'd be in Scotland on opening night, but he'd have Bridget send flowers to the theater. An absurdly showy bouquet of roses would do—yellow, not red. The last thing he wanted was to send mixed signals about his intentions. He'd been very clear about the arrangement. He got a beautiful young woman to accompany him to the necessary events. She got exposure in the press and access to people she'd never have met otherwise. They both won, and no hearts had to get involved.

James dropped the clipping onto the countertop and jerked the refrigerator door open, perusing the contents with better humor than they deserved. Just a half-carton of eggs, some milk that looked dangerously close to the expiry date, and a couple of bottles of Guinness. He really should look into one of those grocery-delivery services. He never could remember to go to the supermarket when he returned to London.

He retrieved an open box of Weetabix from an equally bare cupboard and plopped a shredded wheat biscuit into a bowl. He sniffed suspiciously at the milk before drenching the cereal with it. Lovely. Prize-winning chef, and here he was eating cereal for dinner. If he hadn't taken the joke with Ms. Sullivan so far, he might have talked her into enjoying a pleasant meal with him in the pub. It certainly sounded more appealing than his empty flat.

He kicked off his shoes by the counter and carried his bowl into his impeccably decorated reception room, where he flopped onto a sleek leather sofa. He put his feet up on the glass coffee table and clicked on the enormous television. It was the one concession he'd wrung from his designer. A man needed an obscenely large plasma screen on which to watch sports.

He scanned through his recordings with the remote and found the London evening news. He clicked it on and settled back to eat his pathetic dinner while he watched tonight's report—a petrol spill on the M1 motorway, a bomb threat at the Israeli embassy, a fare hike for the Underground. Then a story made him sit straight up in his seat. He set his bowl aside on the sofa and turned up the volume.

"—award-winning actress Cassandra Sinclair was married to fellow actor Philip Kane in a private ceremony on Mykonos today—"

James stared at the television as it flashed paparazzi shots of a smiling Cassandra in a short wedding dress, her arm linked with the handsome English actor. His chest spasmed, momentarily blocking off his air. His pulse pounded in his ears so loudly he almost missed the newscaster's next words.

"—also known for her very public relationship and subsequent breakup with former fiancé, Scottish television personality and restaurateur, James MacDonald."

He swallowed hard and clicked off the television. Married? After less than two years and to the man she'd left him for? Dampness spread across the thigh of his trousers, and he looked down to find he'd tipped his bowl on its side. He righted it, then stood and strode back to the kitchen, his appetite gone. The remainder of the cereal went into the rubbish bin, the bowl in the sink.

He braced his palms against the countertop and dropped his chin to his chest. It shouldn't bother him. He didn't want her back. Not after her lies, and certainly not after the humiliation of finding out she'd been having an affair with Kane the entire time they'd been engaged. It was just a shock, finding out about her marriage on television along with millions of other viewers. Not even the courtesy of a warning after he'd so carefully kept the reason for the breakup out of the press in order to save her squeaky-clean image.

Not tonight. He'd already let Cassie poison enough of his life. He wouldn't let her spoil the lovely glow left from his encounter with Ian's spunky consultant. He drew himself up and briskly washed the bowl and spoon, then set them in the drainer to dry.

Tomorrow he was going home. And it certainly wouldn't hurt to have the lively Ms. Sullivan with him.

Chapter Three

Andrea woke to the moody chords of Rachmaninoff's "Second Piano Concerto," her heart pounding. She grabbed her cell phone from the nightstand and shut off the alarm with trembling hands. Panic rushed in with the silence when the pitch-black room gave no hint to her location. New York? Chicago? London?

London. She was in London. She fell back against her pillows, clutching the phone. This was the worst part of the job, waking up not knowing where she was. This month had been particularly bad, coming off a string of appointments without the advantage of decompressing in her apartment in between.

Andrea's heart slowly returned to its normal rhythm, but it was too late to stop the familiar knot of anxiety from tightening in the pit of her stomach. She clicked on the lamp by the bed and squinted in the harsh glare as she fumbled to dial room service. She'd be calm enough to eat by the time her breakfast arrived, but it would take a straight shot of caffeine to the bloodstream before she'd be ready to do battle.

Irish oatmeal with fresh berries and two cups of strong coffee improved her mood considerably, as did a hot shower. She was in the middle of blow-drying her hair when the room phone rang. She raced to the nightstand and jerked the handset off the cradle.

"Ms. Sullivan," the desk clerk said in her polite London clip, "your car has arrived."

"My what?"

"Your airport transfer. It's waiting for you outside."

"I didn't …" MacDonald. Of course. He would send a car, just to prove he knew where she was staying. "Thank you. I'll be down in a few minutes."

Andrea returned to the bathroom and flipped the hair dryer back on. She had three hours until her flight left. The car could wait. Once she'd straightened and smoothed her shoulder-length bob into place, she shoved her brush and cosmetics bag into her carry-on and took one last look in the full-length bathroom mirror.

She'd chosen her most conservative outfit today, a subtle gray tweed pantsuit with a ruffled peplum jacket and a lilac silk blouse. She still wore towering heels, but she'd abandoned last night's scarlet platforms for a stunning pair of Louboutin peep-toe pumps. She checked herself over and smiled. Feminine armor. Clients might pay more attention to her looks than her business sense at times, but she wouldn't let them force her to dress like a man just to prove she could work like one.

As she turned away from the mirror, the gold cross resting at her collarbone caught her eye. Her fingers drifted to the necklace, and she rubbed the cool metal pendant between her fingers. The symbol felt like a lie now. What would her mother think if she could see what she'd become? Would she be proud of what Andrea had made of herself? Or would she be disappointed that a piece of jewelry was all she retained of her past?

Andrea drew in a deep breath and forced down the unproductive thoughts. Her mother was gone, and whatever hopes she'd had for her daughter had gone with her. Maybe it was for the best. It would have broken her heart to see her younger child abandon the beliefs that had sustained her through her own trials.

She straightened her jacket, extended the handle of her rolling suitcase, and mentally prepared herself for what awaited her. Today was the day she would turn this whole mess around. She'd close this deal, and then she'd be back on the fast track to promotion. She could forget this whole disaster in London and move on with her orderly, predictable life.

The bill had already been settled by credit card, so Andrea breezed through the lobby downstairs, her carry-on bag whirring across the marble floor behind her. The doorman opened the glass door for her, and she stepped outside to find a black sedan at the curb, a uniformed driver waiting casually by the rear bumper.

He strode toward her with a polite nod. "Ms. Sullivan, may I take your bag?"

Andrea handed it to him with a smile and followed him to the curb. Then the car's back door opened, and James MacDonald stepped out, wearing a broad smile. "Good morning."

She faltered, her smile slipping at the sudden lurch in her chest. Somehow it had never occurred to her that he would be in the car— the car she had kept waiting for twenty-five minutes.

There went her plan to use the trip to the airport to prepare her pitch. There would be no thought-gathering now, not when those thoughts solely consisted of how attractive he looked in his impeccably tailored charcoal suit and crisp white shirt. Rather than dwell on those details, she focused on the two paper cups he held. "You brought coffee?"

"Call it a peace offering." He held one out. "After a long night of research, I figured you'd take yours black."

"Clever." He *would* rub in last night's faux pas. Still, she took the offered cup—no doubt already cold—while the driver placed her suitcase in the trunk of the sedan.

James stepped out of her way and gestured toward the car. "Shall we?"

She slid into the backseat, and he closed the door behind her before circling around to the other side. She settled her shoulder bag on the floor next to her feet and laid her wool overcoat on the seat between them.

The rear of the car seemed roomy enough until he climbed in the other side and shut the door behind him. She slid away an inch or two and jerked her head to indicate the vehicle. "Yours?"

"Hired. I don't keep a car in London."

"And I suppose you know my flight the same way you knew my hotel?"

He flashed a grin. "I'm very efficient."

Andrea sipped her tepid coffee and looked out the window as the sedan pulled away from the curb. She'd have to stay on guard against that smile. He used it like a weapon, and no doubt it slew females by the dozens. She'd already fallen victim to it once. "So, Mr. MacDonald, tell me what you have planned for us today."

"Mr. MacDonald? Are we so formal? I thought we were on a first-name basis now, after I complimented your legs."

She whipped her head toward him and then cursed herself for letting him catch her off guard again. "If I recall, you noticed my skirt and my shoes. Legs were never mentioned."

"They were implied. Just like you implied I was a self-indulgent playboy."

"You *are* a self-indulgent playboy." The words came out before she could think better of them. She softened her tone and added, "But that has nothing to do with your business sense. I did my research. You don't get to this place in life at thirty-five without hard work and vision. It's impressive."

Surprise flickered across his face. "Thank you."

"You're welcome. Now, you didn't answer my question. This would go a lot more smoothly if I knew exactly what you expected from me."

"This was Ian's idea. Frankly, I've no idea what you're doing here."

Andrea blinked. "Who's Ian?"

"My chief operations officer. He owns a one-third interest in the hotel, and he took it upon himself to set this up."

Andrea's heart sank. Great. No wonder James was so resistant to treating her like a colleague. "If you don't want me here, why go to all this effort?"

"I didn't say I didn't want you here." The twinkle in his eye raised warning flags. "I just said it was Ian's idea. Why don't you tell me exactly what you hope to accomplish?"

She straightened in the seat and smoothed her jacket. No chance she would let some internal corporate power struggle ruin this for her. "Morrison Hospitality Consulting is a boutique firm specializing in unique, historic properties. Our clients rank among the most impressive hoteliers in the world, including Excelsior Properties and Hôtel du Soleil, but we also work with other smaller, more focused—"

"I know all that," James said. "I read the website last night. I want to know why *you* are here. You, specifically."

Very well, she could deal with straightforward. "I'm here to evaluate your hotel's needs, from infrastructure to marketing and competitive analysis. Before I leave, I'll provide a detailed proposal for the areas in which I think we can help you. I'm awarded 90 percent of the projects I bid on, and my accounts see a minimum 55 percent increase in revenue within nine months. In the eight years I've been in the industry, I've never had a client go out of business."

"So if we contracted your company, you would be the one doing the work?"

She searched his expression, wondering if there was more to that question, but he seemed serious. "I work out of New York, but I would be your account manager, yes. It's my job to make sure our team in London accomplishes what we lay out in the next two days and to ensure your revenue goals are being met."

Now his expression turned guarded, the perpetual half smile fading. "I'm not in this for the money. This is a personal project."

Andrea nodded and swallowed her response, but she hadn't gotten this far in her career by questioning her gut. "May I speak frankly?"

"Please."

"You obviously know how to run a restaurant. But a hotel is another venture entirely. Most fail within the first five years, many within the first two years. If you're serious, you need us. Your COO chose us because we're the best. And out of all Morrison's account managers, *I'm* the best. So if this is all just some bed-and-breakfast fantasy, you might as well tell me now, before this becomes a colossal waste of my time. And yours."

James held her eyes for a long moment, appraising, as if he were trying to see deep inside her. She struggled to keep her breathing even and just barely managed to avoid shifting under his gaze. Then he smiled again, and it felt like the seat had dropped out from beneath her. "All right, I'll give you a shot. If only to prove I'm not a dilettante."

She nodded. "Fair enough. That's all I ask."

The twinkle returned, a sure sign he was preparing another onslaught of charm, but before he could speak, his phone rang. He shot her an apologetic glance and answered briskly, a smile creasing his face. "Hello, Bridget."

Bridget? A girlfriend, maybe? A man like him would never be single for long. Which, of course, made his flirting all the more unsettling.

"No, that's fine. I'll be back in London at the end of the month. Just change my flight to Cardiff from eight to three."

Not a girlfriend, then. His assistant. Not that it was her business anyway.

She leaned back into the plush leather seat and watched him arrange his month, his tablet balanced on one knee, notebook on the other, phone braced against his ear. His overflowing schedule eased some of her concern. James MacDonald might like to tease and flirt, but he was serious about his career and the management of his business. He couldn't fail to recognize the value she and her company brought to his project as long as she could keep their relationship on friendly, professional terms.

When he hung up, Andrea said, "I'm curious. Why Skye? Why not Edinburgh or Glasgow or Inverness?"

"When we arrive, you'll understand." His phone rang in his hand again and back to his ear it went. "James."

Andrea pulled a small notebook from her purse and jotted down a few thoughts on how to pitch her company—*time sensitive, capable, turnkey*—while James rearranged his schedule yet again in order to fly to Canada to judge a televised cooking competition.

He hung up his phone as the driver pulled up to Gatwick's North Terminal. "Sorry for that." He fixed his intense blue stare on her, the businessman gone and the charmer firmly back in place. "There's no mobile signal at the hotel. Once we arrive, you will have my full and undivided attention."

It sounded like a promise, but the wicked glint in his eye told her she'd be safer taking it as a threat.

Chapter Four

Andrea Sullivan was handling him.

James followed her through the sliding doors into the terminal. It was subtle, of course, and she was good at it. Most women would have put up an icy shield against him, but she'd probably realized he would see it as a dare. Instead she was cordial, professional, and straightforward, brushing aside his flirtation with the skill of a woman used to being in complete control of every situation.

As much as he hated to admit it, Ian had chosen well. He had no doubt Andrea could do what she claimed. And maybe it wouldn't be such a terrible idea to have an outside perspective on the hotel. It had been closed for over a year now, and his last look at the books had shown it hadn't been as profitable as it should have been under his father's management. He had a vision for what it could become. He simply didn't have the time to implement it. Some outside help could ease his overburdened schedule.

They passed directly through security, where they both underwent the usual dance of pocket-emptying, scanners, and baggage checks with the bored calm of frequent fliers. Andrea shrugged out of her suit jacket, stepped out of her pumps, and laid them precisely beneath her coat in the bins on the conveyor belt. She absently ran her fingers through her hair and walked to the scanner in her bare feet.

How did she do that? He was used to the overt sensuality of the women he dated, perfect figures displayed in body-skimming dresses, their movements calculated to draw the eye of every man in the room. Beautiful and yet somehow plastic. Two-dimensional. Andrea Sullivan, on the other hand, wore a conservative business suit and still managed to make her most mundane gestures worthy of lingering over.

"Sir?" The security officer looked at him impatiently, and he hurriedly put his belt, keys, and watch into the bin on the conveyor. She was definitely a distraction. He reined in his imagination while the scanner did its work. Flirting was one thing. Entertaining thoughts of more was entirely another. Besides, he had plenty of practice admiring beautiful things from afar. Paintings at the National Gallery, for example. He'd never had the urge to caress a Rembrandt.

He chuckled at the thought of attempting to kiss Andrea, just to be dragged off by security. Unfortunately that brought him around to topics he was trying to avoid.

By the time he passed through the security barrier, she'd already put herself back together and was waiting for him with one hand on her rolling case.

"Ready?" James tucked his keys into his pocket and fastened his watch. He followed her gaze to his wrist. "Don't worry. We're on time."

A smile played at the corners of her mouth. "I should have known it wouldn't be a Rolex."

He glanced down at the timepiece, a moderately expensive Breitling in stainless steel. "What? You don't approve?"

Her eyes flicked down him and then back up. "It's exquisite. Just ... telling."

Telling? What exactly did that mean? "Considering we barely know one another, you seem to have some particularly strong opinions about me."

She met his eye. "Oh, I know you."

"Why don't you tell me, then?" He smiled and lifted his eyebrows in challenge.

"Fine." She studied him openly. "I think you're the youngest in the family. Always looking for attention, always trying to prove yourself. But you'd want to do it your own way. Something like banking or law would be too boring and too respectable. Now that you've made it, you don't like to do what others would expect. Custom suit, but no tie. Breitling watch, not Rolex or Omega. I'm sure you could afford to live anywhere you want in the city, but since you'd be expected to live in a hip district, you'd pick something quiet and elegant. Mayfair. Belgravia, maybe. A flat, though. Anything more would require too much upkeep when you're on the road."

He stared at her, unsettled by how close she'd come to the truth. Of course, some of it she could have come by last night in her Internet research, but her tone said she was speaking off the cuff. She did read people well. "So this is how you establish a rapport with your client? By dissecting him piece by piece?"

Her mouth opened and snapped closed again. A shadow of regret—or was it embarrassment?—passed over her face. "Am I wrong?"

He let the silence stretch, and only the slight press of her lips hinted at her discomfort. He rescued her. "No, you're not far off. Except I live in South Kensington."

"Close enough."

"I suppose it is." He stole a look at her while they moved toward the departure concourse. Its complement of restaurants and duty-free shops rivaled a high street for variety and expense, but Andrea didn't give them a second look as they proceeded to their gate. She seemed entirely too satisfied with her evaluation of him. Time to shake her up a bit.

"My turn now."

Alarm flashed over her face. "For what?"

"To play our little guessing game." He grinned and gave her a blatant once-over. "Let me see. You grew up someplace rural, probably barely middle class, and you haven't quite gotten used to having money or living in the city. You're the only woman at your firm, at least at your level, which makes you feel vulnerable. The men say you only got this far because of your looks, and you resent it, just not enough to wear dowdy shoes or hide your figure. No, I take that back. You dress in open defiance of the stereotype, because, as you say, you could close a deal in jeans and trainers. How am I doing so far?"

"Pretty close." She dipped her head, but she didn't look at him. "I grew up in a small town in Ohio. How did you guess?"

He softened. "Because you made a point of mentioning my suit, and you treat those six-hundred quid shoes of yours like you remember every hour of work it took to earn them. You don't take things for granted." *Like you assume I do.*

She nodded, a faint tinge of pink coloring her cheeks. He hadn't meant to embarrass her. He had actually meant it as a compliment. Then she threw a look in his direction. "How do you know how much my shoes cost?"

"I spend a lot of time with women. I recognize Louboutins when I see them." *And Cassie owned a couple dozen pairs.* He knew how it felt to be walked on by those red-lacquered soles—metaphorically speaking. He quickly shifted the direction of the conversation. "How many of these do you do each month?"

"This is my ninth one in thirty days."

"And I thought I traveled a lot. From how many of those did you walk away with a signed contract?"

"Five. Two more are working their way through legal."

"Very impressive."

"I told you, I'm the best." The glint in her eye was a clear challenge.

Oh, he'd unsettled her all right. She hated showing vulnerability and talking about her past made her feel exposed. Interesting. "What happened to the eighth then?"

"He offered to trade a contract for certain favors. My reply might have been less than diplomatic."

"Meaning?"

The pink in her cheeks deepened. "I hit him."

"Where?"

"In the elevator."

James chuckled. "I mean, where on his body?"

"Oh. The jaw." She held up her hand ruefully. The faint marks of a new bruise shadowed her knuckles.

A startled laugh escaped James's lips. "Well done! Remind me not to become acquainted with your left hook."

"That's entirely up to you, isn't it?" She threw him a mischievous glance, and he breathed a sigh of relief that they were back on comfortable footing. Though why it should matter to him …

"Wait." James's hand shot out and grasped her upper arm before he had time to think about the wisdom of the action.

Andrea jerked to a halt, spinning to face him. He blinked and let go before she could take a swing at him. That client of hers must have been completely daft not to see the danger in that expression. He inclined his head to his right. "You missed our gate."

She glanced up at the sign, and the tension drained from her posture. "Oh. I'm sorry. It's just … after the last time …"

The client had really spooked her. James had figured the man had just propositioned her, but maybe it had been more. Had he tried to force himself on her?

If that were the case, he deserved far worse than a bruised jaw.

He realized they were still standing too close to one another on the concourse walkway. In her high-heeled pumps, she could nearly look him in the eye, and that sensual perfume enveloped him again. Amber. Sandalwood. A hint of vanilla, perhaps?

The distraction made him lower his tone, speak more quietly than he intended. "I assure you. I am very capable of keeping my personal and professional interests separate."

Their gazes met and held, and she froze, not even a breath breaking her stillness. James didn't dare move. He couldn't have even if he wanted to.

Then she lowered her eyes and stepped past him. "Good. Please see that you do."

James exhaled and watched her walk back toward the gate lounge, stride clipped by the high heels, spine straight. For the first time, he wondered if he might have promised more than he could deliver.

Chapter Five

Inverness may have been the unofficial capital of the Scottish Highlands, but its airport more closely resembled an industrial-styled chain store than a terminal. Andrea stepped from the plane onto the rolling staircase and tugged the collar of her wool jacket closed against the wind. London had already begun to show a hint of spring warmth, but here the air held a crisp bite despite the bright sunshine. Had she known she was coming to Scotland, she would have packed more appropriate clothing.

"Allow me." James took her carry-on and edged past her down the steps. She dug in the pocket of her coat for her sunglasses and slid them on against the glare of the afternoon sun. The dark lenses shielded her eyes and, she hoped, her expression.

James had been perfectly cordial, even gentlemanly, since that odd, intense moment in the airport. He'd spent the short flight looking over what appeared to be financial statements on his tablet while Andrea distractedly worked a crossword puzzle. Other than to offer a six-letter word for *ponderous*, he'd spoken little, but she'd still felt his gaze slide over her when he thought she wasn't looking.

His suddenly serious demeanor was all the more disconcerting because she suspected it was unusual, at least where women were concerned.

She carefully navigated the narrow steps to the tarmac, where James waited with the handle of her case extended. She took her suitcase with a nod and followed him across the short expanse of asphalt to the terminal entry.

The interior of the low-slung building was compact, with a few rows of blue-upholstered chairs beside each of the handful of gates, freestanding shops cluttering the center aisle.

"Do we need to rent a car?" she asked.

He slowed as they approached the information desk and produced a parking stub from his inside jacket pocket. "I left mine. It's a fair way to Skye. Too far for a taxi."

The redhead behind the desk brightened as he approached. "Mr. MacDonald. Welcome back to Scotland."

"Thanks, Marcie." Andrea couldn't tell if he actually remembered her or if he had just sneaked a surreptitious look at her name tag. "How's the weather been the last couple of weeks?"

Marcie shrugged and gave him a coy smile. "It's Scotland. Rainy." She swiped his credit card and handed it back to him, her eyes deliberately finding his.

Andrea barely resisted the urge to roll her eyes. The woman couldn't be sending out clearer signals if she'd been waving semaphore flags. Not that Andrea cared. Why should it matter that women fell all over James MacDonald wherever he went? It wasn't as if she planned on joining their ranks. If anything, it just proved idle flirtation was as natural as breathing for him. Except he didn't seem to be returning the flirtation with more than his usual friendly manner, which was obviously just fine with Marcie.

James finished up the transaction, and Andrea fell into step beside him as they walked out the front entrance to the parking lot, the wheels of their cases humming on the uneven asphalt. She had been so distracted by her client's charms—or rather, the effort of not falling under them—she hadn't given much thought to what came next. "My office said you'd arranged a room at the hotel. Does that mean the renovations are finished?"

"Not the main house. But there are three self-catering cottages on the property. We completed them first so we'd have a place to stay when we came to check on the work."

"Good. How long is the drive?"

"Three hours, give or take."

"Give or take what?"

"Speed. Weather. Sheep."

"Sheep?" Her eyebrows flew up.

"It is Scotland, after all. They're a complete menace outside the city." He cast her a curious look. "I assumed you'd been here before. Or is your dislike of Scotland strictly a matter of principle?"

"I've just been to Glasgow, and I don't remember anything involving sheep."

"Glasgow and the Highlands are two entirely different things." He stopped abruptly. "Here we are."

"Where?" Andrea looked around the nearly empty lot, but she saw no vehicle she would have expected him to drive.

He dug his keys from his pocket and threw her that half smile as he unlocked a battered green Subaru wagon. "Disappointed?"

"No. But I admit, I didn't see this one coming."

"I'd never leave a nice car at an airport for weeks." He popped the hatch and loaded their suitcases in the back. "Besides, the roads here can get pretty bad in the winter."

He slammed the hatch with a rattle of the license plate and then opened the passenger side for her. When they were both settled in the car, he asked, "Are you hungry?"

She was, but she hardly wanted to do something as social as have lunch with him. Besides, she only had thirty-six hours to concoct a proposal that would sell her company's services to a somewhat disinterested client.

Well, he's interested. Just not in the same thing I'm proposing.

She gave a little internal laugh. Then she noticed his quizzical look and realized she still hadn't answered his question. "I'm fine. I'd rather get started on the proposal tonight if I can."

"Suit yourself. If you change your mind, I probably have something in the glove box."

As he put the car in drive and exited the long-term lot, Andrea popped the latch on the glove compartment, more interested in what the contents might tell about her client than in finding a snack. All in all, it was disturbingly tidy. A packet of road maps, a pair of lined leather gloves, and an unopened bag of organic trail mix. Barely worth the effort of looking. So he didn't like to get lost, his hands got cold in the winter, and he was health conscious. Hardly illuminating. She closed the compartment with a click.

"What were you expecting to find?" His voice hummed with barely repressed amusement.

Dang. She needed to stop being so transparent. He'd been far too smug about his lucky guesses in the airport. She looked at him over the top edge of her sunglasses. "Oh, I don't know. Unpaid parking tickets? Little black book?"

"I'm disappointed. I thought you'd at least give me credit for being smart enough not to leave that sort of thing in the car." He grinned, and she almost felt relieved. Playful was much preferable to … smoldering.

She fixed her gaze out the window while he drove toward Inverness proper, then turned south onto the A82. Andrea relaxed into the seat and watched thick patches of trees and open fields fly by. She rarely got the opportunity to break free of the noise and activity of the city, to be surrounded by nature. The few times she had gone home to Ohio, she'd been struck by the broad expansiveness of the land, a sort of freshness. By contrast, Scotland felt old. Maybe it was just her awareness of its long history of conflict and warfare, its old, majestic structures and even older ruins, but even the trees felt more deeply rooted here.

Signs of civilization thinned as they skirted a broad lake, its edge choked with greenery and mountains rising sharply beyond. "What is that?"

James glanced out her window. "That's Loch Ness."

"As in the Loch Ness monster?"

"One and the same. We can stop in Drumnadrochit if you'd like. Urquhart Castle is worth a look, and the view's spectacular from the ruins."

She was sorely tempted to take him up on the offer, but this wasn't a pleasure trip. She was here to close a business deal, and the more firmly she kept that in mind, the better off she'd be. "Thanks, but I really need to get to work."

"That makes it difficult for me, then. Less than two days to change your mind about an entire country, and I can't even show you its historic treasures."

"You take this very personally, don't you?"

"How else should I take it? You seem to have rather strong feelings on the subject."

"There's nothing particularly wrong with Scotland," she admitted. "It was just supposed to be my first vacation in three years. Have you ever been to Tahiti?"

"Tahiti? No. Bali. Fiji. The Philippines. Trust me, I understand the appeal of a tropical holiday after a long winter. Why didn't you just say no?"

"Say no to the illustrious James MacDonald? I wouldn't dream of it."

He laughed, and she couldn't deny she found the sound appealing. Deep, warm, free. It twined itself into her middle and radiated warmth into her chest. She tamped the feeling down. That response was just the sort of distraction she didn't need.

"You had no idea who I was. That much was obvious last night. Why didn't you just say you were taking time off? With your sales record, I doubt you'd get sacked."

"No, probably not. Passed over for promotion, maybe. I've worked too hard and too long for a chance at VP to throw it away over a vacation."

"So I'm standing between you and a corner office? That puts a bit of pressure on me."

Maybe she shouldn't have been so frank about her objectives. Somehow, her mouth always seemed to run away with her where he was concerned. "I hope it doesn't put pressure on me."

"I already told you, I compartmentalize well. Tell me, *Ms. Sullivan*, how did you get into the business in the first place?"

No harm in answering that question. He could pick up almost as much from reading her biography on Morrison's website. "I worked in pharmaceutical sales to put myself through my MBA at Cornell, but it was too hard to keep up with classes when I traveled. One of my professors mentioned a market research position at Morrison, I got the job, and you can guess the rest."

"Somehow I wouldn't have pegged you for a researcher."

"Me neither. But I was good at it. I also worked in creative in London for six months before I decided I'd rather gouge my eyes out than sit in an office and write copy for one more second. By that time I knew so much of the business, Michael—Mr. Halloran—figured I was better out front anyway."

"You're their closer."

It was exactly what she was. She handled the largest and most difficult clients, because she never walked away without the deal. Until recently. She wasn't about to admit it to him, though. "Something like that. How about you? Did you always want to be a chef?"

"Not always. I wanted to drive grand prix cars for a while. At some point I may have conceived a plan to swim the English Channel."

"Seriously."

"I am being serious. But yes, my aunt taught me how to cook at a very young age, and I loved it. My mother, of course, wanted me to do something 'useful.' So I suffered through my business studies until I'd finally had enough and went to culinary school."

"Your mother doesn't like what you do for a living?" Andrea asked in surprise.

"Oh no. Quid pro quo. You can't start questioning me about my mother unless you give me something that's not on your CV."

"Not going to happen." Andrea crossed her legs and planted her hands firmly in her lap.

"You can start small. Your favorite color. Your favorite movie. Favorite television program."

She almost refused, but that was just silly. It wasn't as if he were asking her to spill her deepest secrets. "All right. Purple, *North by Northwest*, and I don't own a TV. Your turn."

"Hang on a moment. I want to explore this. We'll ignore the fact that purple is a very girlish color for someone like you, though you wear it well. Why would you choose a movie that's over sixty years old as your favorite?"

"That wasn't the deal. You asked, I answered. Now, why doesn't your mother like what you do for a living?"

James made a face. "She wanted me to follow in my brother's footsteps and become a lawyer. Or an investment consultant. Or anything respectable. In her mind, cooking in a restaurant is one step above being a servant. Owning said restaurant is only marginally better. Your turn, answer the question."

Andrea hesitated. Delving into personal matters with a client was never a good idea, but James didn't seem the type to let it go. Besides, if she was going to make this deal happen, they needed to venture beyond flirtation and insults.

"I grew up in a little town near Dayton, Ohio," she said finally. "It was small. No stoplights or fast food chains. We had this old art deco movie theater on Main Street that only showed one new movie a month. The rest of the time, they played classic films: Greta Garbo, Bing Crosby, Cary Grant. I loved them. I saved my allowance so I could just sit and watch for hours after school. I was usually the only person under the age of fifty in there, but I was hooked."

"Why?"

She remembered hunkering down in the threadbare red seats, transfixed by the flickering black-and-white images on the screen. "I don't know. They were clever and sophisticated and sometimes a little naughty without being vulgar. No one I knew talked like that. They seemed so glamorous. To a small-town girl ..." She broke off, heat rising to her cheeks. "I know that probably sounds ridiculous."

"Not at all. Skye is not exactly the cultural center of the UK, you know."

He didn't seem inclined to elaborate, so she let it go. Instead she studied him as he drove. One hand rested easily on the steering wheel, the other moving from the seat beside him only when he needed to shift. In London, he had practically radiated energy. Now his intensity was muted to a soft glow.

How much of the flirtatious wit was the real him, and how much was just the public persona? It wasn't as if he were a movie star, drawing paparazzi to him every time he stepped outside—they'd made it through two airports without anyone doing more than a curious double take—yet his frequent appearances in the gossip pages suggested he purposely sought the spotlight.

She dragged her eyes away from him and looked out her window. She was spending far too much time analyzing the man when she should be focused on the business owner. At least James seemed comfortable with silence. She'd figured he'd want to flirt and tease the entire drive to Skye.

Andrea lost track of time, soaking in the rapid changes of scenery: open country, enormous lochs, and patches of forest that reminded her of home. The land finally gave way to a tangle of trees as the road climbed upward into the craggy hill. Storm clouds mounded overhead, spattering the windshield in a half-hearted attempt at rain, and mist hung over the higher peaks in the distance.

"Look. We're approaching Glen Shiel."

Andrea pulled her attention back to the road, which now wound downward into a valley, rounded mountains sloping sharply up on either side of them. Green had begun to overtake the brown, but snow still capped the top of the ridge. Wide swaths of evergreens stretched along the side of the road and jutted up the mountainside. There was something both desolate and breathtakingly beautiful about the scene.

The road curved along the edge of a loch and climbed back into mountains. When they emerged again from between the hills, Andrea gaped at the water spread out before them, twisting between the mountains in craggy inlets and shorelines. Below, just off the shore, rose a stunning stone castle.

"Eilean Donan," James said. "The most photographed castle in Scotland. You're sure you don't want to stop? I don't mind."

"No," Andrea said, but she heard the reluctance in her voice. "We have work to do."

"I am going to wear you down, you realize."

It won't take much. How long had it been since she'd laced up her hiking boots and strapped on a pack simply to spend a day surrounded by the quiet of nature like she had as a child? Three years? More? The promotion to senior account manager meant weekends in the office or on planes, not exploring her favorite spots in the Hudson River Valley or on Breakneck Ridge. Long summer days and mountain sunsets were just distant memories.

They emerged from the mountains and descended toward the water. Andrea took note of the whitewashed buildings on either side of the road as they passed through a tiny town that reminded her of a New England fishing village. Then the graceful concrete arch of the Skye Bridge lay before them, stretching over the short span of water and framing a lighthouse just beyond.

James pressed a button and rolled the front windows down.

"What are you doing?"

This time his smile made him look downright boyish. "You can't tell me you don't love salt air."

"I suppose I do." Andrea inhaled the tang of salt and the earthy scent of peat beneath. When they proceeded over the wide multilane bridge, she allowed herself to peer out the window at the water.

"I've got you now. Don't try to deny it."

A smiled stretched across her face. "It's spectacular. I'm beginning to understand why you decided on Skye."

"Just wait, love. You haven't seen anything yet."

"Love?" She shot him an exasperated look.

He frowned, taken aback. "It's just an expression. Like—"

"—sweetheart, honey, pumpkin."

"I swear to you, I have never used *pumpkin* as a term of endearment for anyone over the age of ten, nor will I."

She scowled at him.

"I'm sorry. I didn't mean to offend you. I thought we were having a nice friendly conversation. It just slipped out."

His abashed expression summoned a twinge of guilt. Maybe she was being too sensitive. She just despised the diminutives men used for her. Too often they felt like subtle put-downs, a way of minimizing her position. But James didn't seem to have meant anything of the sort.

She quickly changed the subject before she could embarrass herself further. "You grew up here on Skye?"

"Until I was twelve," James said. "Then I went to boarding school in Edinburgh."

"Why?"

"My parents were divorced. I got myself into so much mischief after my mother left, she was sure I'd turn into a delinquent. I didn't want to go back to England with her, so we compromised on an independent school in Scotland."

"I can't imagine leaving home at twelve."

James shrugged. "I enjoyed myself. Of course, I wasn't the most serious of students. I got tossed from my first two schools anyway."

"I don't believe that. You don't get into the University of Edinburgh without good grades."

"Oh, I earned high marks. I just spent as much time in the headmaster's office as I did in class." His mouth curved upward, secretive, mischievous. "I had a rather unfortunate propensity for practical jokes."

"Which, apparently, you have not lost."

"Perhaps not." He made a face. "Do I owe you an apology for last night? I couldn't resist."

Andrea sighed. "No. I should have been better prepared."

"If you'd been prepared, you'd have been perfectly polite. Maybe you would've felt you needed to flatter my ego. Trust me, Andrea, I get enough of that as it is."

"Yes, it must be terrible to have women fawn all over you."

He glanced over long enough to catch her eye. "Do *you* enjoy turning the head of every man who gets within ten feet of you? Tell me the truth."

Heat rushed back to her cheeks, though she couldn't quite say why. Of course men looked. They looked at all moderately attractive women. It wasn't as if it meant anything. "It depends on the man, I suppose."

"Is that right?" Something in the way his gaze slid over her before it returned to the road made her heart trip. The flush deepened. Out of the corner of her eye, she saw him smile. Blast him. He'd noticed, and he knew why.

She closed her eyes and tried to ignore the sinking feeling in her gut. In the course of a three-hour drive, she'd managed to destroy her only chance of keeping things on a strictly professional level. James was intelligent enough to recognize the effect he had on her, involuntary as it was. If she'd been playing poker, she would have just tipped her hand.

Well done, Andrea. Well done.

Chapter Six

For someone used to being in charge, Andrea Sullivan blushed more than any woman he'd ever met.

Not that he minded. There was a fine line between assertive and brash, and so many of the women he'd met took a giant leap over it. James suppressed his smile. Andrea might be opinionated, but there were apparently some things she couldn't plan or control.

He slowed as he made the turn onto the road that led down the Sleat peninsula toward Isleornsay. His heart lifted at the familiar stretch of asphalt, bordered by dry grasses and patches of evergreens. He may have lived the last twenty years of his life in London, but Skye would always be home. Even his lingering irritation toward Ian faded as he took in the slant of sunlight through the clouds, the rapidly moving shadows on the rolling hills.

After a few minutes, he turned onto a pitted road, the Subaru's spongy suspension magnifying every bump and roll in the macadam surface. He'd have to remember to have the car looked at. Apparently the previous winter had taken its toll on the vehicle.

They rounded the bend, and the water stretched out before them, a gleaming, protected bay of blue dotted with tiny islands.

A backdrop of mountains framed Isle Ornsay, the larger island in the Sound of Sleat from which the village had drawn its name. The isle's charming lighthouse stood sentinel in the bay, a slender column rising from the craggy island, a splash of white against the dark scenery. James may have grown up here, but he was struck by the spot's wild beauty every time he returned.

"This is the village of Isleornsay," James said. "Those mountains across the water are the mainland."

A surprised smile spread over Andrea's face. He stole glances at her, gauging her reaction as he navigated the rough road into the gravel lot and pulled up before the main house. "This is the hotel. Welcome to the MacDonald Guest House."

Andrea opened her door before he could do it for her and stepped out. James paused in his own open door and folded his arms atop the car's roof, watching as she took in the hotel and the picturesque bay in the background. The smile hadn't yet left her face.

He followed her gaze to the main structure. The lines of the original Hebridean croft house remained, though it had been updated and expanded over the years to a two-story whitewashed stone building with a shingled roof and many tiny, multipaned windows set into its sides. Several smaller buildings stood nearby and wild grasses and spring flowers spread around it in a riot of early color. Even closed up and in dire need of attention, it still spoke of warmth and welcome. He had missed it.

"I've never seen any place like this," Andrea murmured.

"It's breathtaking," he agreed. "Even to me. Come, let me show you to your room."

He retrieved her bag from the back of the car and led the way toward three small freestanding stone cottages that faced the sound. Built a few decades before, they had been designed to blend with the main house, even though they were more open and expansive than the isle's traditional cottages. He flipped through the keys on his key ring to find the proper one. "The cottages aren't quite finished. It may not be what you're accustomed to, but they're comfortable enough."

He unlocked the red-painted door of the farthest cottage, set Andrea's suitcase inside the door, and stepped aside for her to enter before him.

She brushed past him and looked around. "Nice." She walked slowly through the kitchenette, trailing a finger along the stone countertops, checking the interiors of the hand-finished cabinets. The woman who blushed at the slightest innuendo was gone, the executive in her place. "I assume you'll be providing dishes and cookware?"

"Yes. As I said, we're not quite done yet." His stomach gave a twist. He hadn't been this nervous since the first time a reviewer stepped inside the Hart and the Hound. That was ridiculous, though. He was the client. She was the one who needed to impress him.

Except he had taken a personal interest in the renovations. He'd consulted a designer, but most of the choices had been his, from the hand-planed wood floor to the antique bed tucked into the niche on the back wall. Andrea paused by the bed, rubbing the edge of the fluffy duvet between her fingers.

"Checking the thread count?" That was a phrase he'd never thought he'd hear from his own mouth. A man really shouldn't know a thing like thread count existed.

She didn't say anything, just shot him an unreadable look and continued into the small sitting area with its two slipcovered armchairs and colorful rag rug.

He couldn't stand the silence. He moved to a door beside the niche that housed the bed and opened it. "This is the bathroom."

Andrea strode across the room and peeked through the narrow doorway. The corners of her mouth edged up. "Now this is a bathroom."

She brushed past him, her shoulder grazing his chest and leaving a trail of her perfume behind. Vanilla. Definitely.

"I hear the way to a woman's heart is a claw-foot bathtub and a sparkly chandelier."

Her eyes rose to the dainty antique fixture hanging from the vaulted ceiling, then returned to the other details—the subway tiles on the walls, the fluffy towels. "The chandelier is a nice touch, I'll admit. But you had me at the heated towel rack."

He chuckled as she turned to exit the bathroom, but he stayed where he was, shoulder against the door frame. A cheap ploy, maybe, but since she wouldn't willingly get near him any other way … He was gratified to see that this time her step faltered at the contact. She hurried past him into the open space at the center of the room.

"So? What's the verdict?"

"It's lovely." She took another sweep of the room, her eyes lit with appreciation. "Both rustic and elegant. Peaceful yet sophisticated. I can't imagine a better setting for a romantic getaway." She met his gaze and added quickly, "Which is how we'd probably want to market the cottages."

"Of course." If his slight smile hinted at something other than agreement, he couldn't be held responsible, could he? He glanced at his watch. "It's after four. I should be getting up to the house to start supper."

"I don't understand."

"My aunt's house up the road. My sister, Serena, is visiting for the week. I promised I'd make supper."

"Oh." Andrea blinked, obviously taken aback. "I'd hoped we'd be able to see the main house tonight."

"We can see it in the morning. The electricity's off while the house is being rewired, and the plasterboard is falling off the walls. It's a hazard."

"Fair enough. I guess I'll see you in the morning, then." She retrieved her suitcase and rolled it toward the wardrobe. "What time should I be ready?"

She really thought he would leave her to her own devices without a car? Was her opinion of him that low? "Don't be ridiculous. You're coming with me."

Alarm flashed over her face. "Oh no. I couldn't. It's a family thing. I wouldn't presume—"

"Andrea, there are no restaurants within walking distance. I'd lend you the car, but I don't like the idea of you driving these roads after dark. I insist." When she still hesitated, he added, "There's some big-shot chef cooking tonight. It might just be rumor, but I hear he's pretty good."

She repressed a smile. "When you put it that way, I can hardly say no."

He shouldn't feel so relieved she'd relented without an argument, but so far she seemed to think he was a poseur, a celebrity constructed on paper and video. Some part of him wanted her to appreciate why he'd become so popular.

Not that he could take full credit for it. His success had come too easily—his hard work and talent not withstanding—to not believe in divine intervention. Opportunities had fallen into his lap, chances most men only dreamed about.

He ushered her back out the door and into the car for the short ride to his aunt's house, a modern clapboard structure facing the bay, painted the ubiquitous white of Skye. The storm shutters had gotten a new coat of gray paint since his last visit, and window boxes promised colorful blooms to come during the island's warmer months. The garden plot already lay tilled and ready for planting, a square of dark earth on the far side of the gravel drive.

James parked behind Serena's dusty red Vauxhall before he noticed the vintage Austin-Healey in front of it. His heart plummeted to his stomach and churned there for a minute. Perfect. Just what he needed—a confrontation in front of Andrea. For one second, he considered putting the car into reverse and heading back to the hotel, but he'd promised Aunt Muriel and Serena he'd make dinner. He couldn't let his brother run him off. He'd never hear the end of how he'd broken his promise.

"Something wrong?" Andrea asked.

"Not at all." James released his white-knuckle grip on the steering wheel. He got out of the car and circled to open her door for her. "This was the house I was raised in."

Andrea lingered by the car to take in the panoramic view of the water, the brisk wind whipping her hair into her face. "It looks like a lovely place to grow up.

"It was. Peaceful. Of course, to a young boy, peaceful means boring."

She huddled deeper into her coat. "Small-town girl, remember?"

"Right. Come. Let's get out of the cold." He gestured for her to follow him up the path to the front door. The door was unlocked as usual. He opened it and stepped aside for her to enter, then followed her into the wood-paneled reception room.

Old-fashioned oak furniture mingled with floral upholstery, and diaphanous lace curtains filtered light from the windows. An upright piano cluttered with family pictures dominated one wall, some turning pink or yellow with age. In his thirty-five years, those photos were the only thing that had ever changed.

Andrea turned toward him. "It's sweet. It reminds me a little of my grandparents' house in Indiana."

"A bit of a time capsule, I realize." He raised his voice. "Auntie? Serena? I'm here."

A blur of pink streaked through the doorway and launched itself at him. "Uncle Jamie!"

"Oof." James caught the exuberant six-year-old before she could knock him into the piano bench. "Who's this? I only have one niece, and she's just a little thing!"

The little girl giggled, showing the gap in her smile. "It's me, Emmy!"

"Minus a couple of teeth." James crushed her to him in a bear hug and threw her over his shoulder. She squealed as he jostled her around and pretended to drop her. "Where's your mum? Where's Granny? Quick, before I have to shake it out of you!"

"I'm here." Serena appeared in the doorway, his one-year-old nephew propped on one hip. She looked as pretty and put-together as usual, but the cropped pixie hairdo was new, as were the dark smudges beneath her eyes. She looked between him and Andrea, and a questioning smile formed on her lips.

James jumped in before she could voice her assumptions. "Serena, this is Andrea Sullivan, our hospitality consultant. Andrea, this is my sister, Serena."

Serena juggled the baby onto her other hip in order to thrust out a hand. "Andrea, pleased to meet you. Welcome to Skye. What do you think?"

Andrea shook Serena's hand. "It's stunning. James wouldn't tell me why he chose Skye for the hotel, but I understand now that I see it with my own eyes."

"I miss it," Serena said wistfully. "But at least I have a good excuse to visit, and the kids love it. Well, Emmy does. Max's too young to notice yet."

"Your children are beautiful." Andrea's voice wavered, and her forehead creased slightly. James frowned as well. What had he missed? He might not know her well, but that was not a woman's usual reaction when faced with a baby.

"Jamie."

James's muscles seized for a moment, and his blood pressure spiked. He kept his expression neutral as he turned to the man in the doorway. "Ian. I didn't realize we had a wake to attend."

"I beg your pardon?"

Not likely. Ian had never begged anyone's pardon. Told James what he should be sorry for, maybe, but never apologized on his own. James's reply came out tighter, harder than he intended. "The only thing that can get you to Scotland is a funeral. I'd assumed someone had died."

Ian didn't even flicker an eyelash at the jab. James shouldn't have expected anything less. Ian never betrayed weakness, always remained in control. Even his perfectly pressed chinos wouldn't dare wrinkle on his body.

"It's a pleasure to see you, too, Jamie. I'm just here to attend to our investment."

"Right. Investment." James glanced at Andrea. "As you've no doubt guessed, this is my brother, Ian MacDonald. Ian, Andrea Sullivan."

"Welcome, Andrea." Ian strode toward her, hand outstretched, and shook her hand. "Thank you for making the trip from London at the last minute."

"It's my pleasure, truly." Andrea smiled at Ian, and James felt the slightest pang of … irritation. Surely it couldn't be jealousy.

"Here, let me take your coat." Ian moved smoothly behind Andrea and slipped his hands beneath the lapels to ease it off her shoulders.

No, James was most definitely annoyed now. Leave it to his brother to make him feel thoughtless and ungracious thirty seconds after he walked into a room.

"Jamie, dear."

James nearly sighed in relief at his aunt's timely arrival. He crossed the room and kissed her on both cheeks. "Hello, Aunt Muriel. You look beautiful." He'd never seen her anything but impeccably turned out, today in a pair of pressed trousers and a lightweight jumper.

Muriel chuckled, put her arms around him, and squeezed. "Dear boy, finally. When Ian said you'd be coming early, I'd hoped you were going to be here for church this morning. Who is this lovely young lady?"

"Andrea Sullivan, ma'am." Andrea stepped forward and offered her hand. "I'm a consultant. I'm here to look at the hotel with James."

"Welcome, Andrea." Muriel turned her stern gaze on her two nephews. "I hope you two can manage to get along for a few days. I won't have you bickering."

James thrust his hands into his pockets. "No bickering."

Ian raised an eyebrow, clearly challenging him.

Muriel's iron tone brooked no further discussion. "It's high time you two began acting like adults."

This was exactly what James had hoped to avoid. He was all too aware of Andrea watching the exchange. "I'm sure Ian and I can put our differences aside for a couple of days."

Muriel frowned, apparently not pleased with the implication that hostilities would resume immediately after. She turned to Andrea. "Do you like Italian food?"

"Of course," Andrea said. "I love Italian."

"Good. We picked up everything on your list this morning, Jamie. It's waiting in the kitchen."

He could take a hint. "I should get started, then. Andrea, fancy being my sous-chef for the evening?"

"As long as I don't have to do anything more complicated than boil water."

"That means it's just you and me, Em." Ian knelt down and turned his back to the little girl. "Hop on. We'll go find something to do outside until your uncle calls us for dinner."

Emmy wrapped her arms and legs around Ian, and he headed for the door. He smiled warmly at Andrea as he passed. "Back in a bit."

Andrea returned the smile, and the knot in James's gut tightened another degree. He'd always gone to great lengths not to compete directly with his brother. Not in school. Not in sports. Certainly not with women. He'd be daft to think Ian hadn't already guessed his interest in Andrea and decided to show him up as a matter of principle. These things just never ended well. If he won, Ian could never let it go. If he lost, he'd never let James forget it. Just more proof his older brother had rotten timing.

This time James wasn't in the mood to back down.

Chapter Seven

Being in the same room with the MacDonald men was like standing in a demilitarized zone. It seemed safe and cordial until someone got trigger-happy and started sniping. Even with Ian's departure, the tension in the living room remained so thick Andrea thought she might trip over it on the way to the kitchen.

Ian MacDonald was not what she had expected, either as James's brother or as his chief operations officer. For one thing he looked more like an athlete than a lawyer, lean and broad shouldered, dressed casually in a cabled sweater and khakis. And he was nearly as good-looking as his younger brother, which was saying something. Taken with their ethereally pretty sister, it was obvious the MacDonald children had gotten more than their fair share of looks from the family gene pool.

The enmity between the two men, however, took her by surprise. What on earth had happened that they couldn't even stay in the same room together? And why did Ian remain an officer of James's company if they'd had such a drastic falling-out?

She followed James through the attached dining room into a small kitchen. "May I ask what that was all about?"

James grimaced. "Old, ugly business. He didn't tell me he was coming, because he assumed I wouldn't put in an appearance if he did."

"Would you have?"

"Probably not." He cast a glance over his shoulder at her and gave her a crooked grin. "Then again, that was before I laid eyes on his consultant."

And back to business as usual. "Nice change of subject."

"I thought so."

"What can I do, then?" Andrea leaned against the counter and watched him gather ingredients from various cabinets.

"You can pour." James opened the pantry and came out with a bottle of red wine, followed by four glasses and a corkscrew. He popped the cork and set the bottle back on the counter, then frowned. "Serena! You raided my wine cellar again!"

Serena ducked into the room and gave James an exasperated look. "Do you mind? I just put Max down. And yes, I raided your wine collection in the cottage. You've been holding out on us."

"That's because you don't know Syrah from Chianti," he said, his tone affectionate. He glanced at Andrea. "Or so she claims. She managed to find my best bottle of reserve Cabernet, which I am very sure I hid in the back."

"I know how you think. You're not just going to stock your cupboard with a collection of ten-quid Chablis. They had to be decoys."

Andrea picked up the bottle and filled the four glasses with a flourish. Then she raised her own. "To a sister who isn't fooled by the decoys, then."

"Well said, Andrea." Serena grinned and clinked her glass against Andrea's. "Now I'm going to go enjoy the quiet. Give a shout if you need me."

Andrea turned to James as Serena exited the kitchen. "What else can I help with?"

"Since you already boasted about your water-boiling skills, you can fill the stockpot under the sink."

Andrea chuckled and found an enameled stockpot in the cupboard, then filled it with hot water and carried it to the stove. "This cooking thing is easier than I thought."

"You're a natural. I can do the rest, though. Have a seat and enjoy your wine."

Andrea slid onto a barstool at the island, shrugged off her suit jacket, and placed it neatly on the stool beside her. They'd strayed far enough from business matters for one day. Time to get back on point. "Tell me about the dining room you'll have in the hotel."

"The concept will be similar to my other restaurants in Scotland." James doused the pan on the burner with a healthy dose of olive oil and then began dicing an onion across from her on the island. "Locally sourced, heavy on the seafood, some grass-fed beef and lamb. A limited menu and no more than ten tables, I think."

Andrea watched his expert movements with the knife, fascinated. She'd probably chop off a finger if she tried to work that fast, but he'd done it so often, he didn't seem to give it a thought. The tension melted from him as he performed the familiar movements, the lines of his face softening.

"You want visitors to have a taste of the real Skye," she said. "Do you expect mostly tourists?"

"In the summer, yes, though the restaurant will probably draw as many locals as hotel guests. There are a number of excellent restaurants on Sleat, but they tend toward traditional. I want to do something a little fresher." He scraped the diced onion from the cutting board into the pan. Immediately the kitchen filled with a heavenly aroma.

Andrea inhaled appreciatively and leaned forward onto her elbows while she watched him score and scald tomatoes for the sauce. She'd wondered more than once how someone made the leap from chef to celebrity, but now she understood. Handsome, masculine, and capable was a lethal combination. Add in the appealing Scottish accent, and it was no wonder women fell at James's feet.

She watched him for a few more seconds, reluctant to broach the subject they really needed to discuss. "It would be helpful for me to understand the situation with you and Ian. As it relates to the hotel, of course."

A muscle in his jaw twitched, but he nodded. "When our father died, he left this house to Aunt Muriel and the hotel to the three of us."

"Then Serena's an equal partner?"

"She was. She said she couldn't be as involved in the renovations as Ian and me, but I really think she didn't want to play peacemaker the whole time. I bought out her share last year."

"So why is Ian here if he doesn't have a controlling share? It seems to me you could do whatever you wanted."

James turned, wiping his hands on a dish towel. "I could, but I wouldn't. He may be a sorry git at times, but he's still my brother."

"So both you and Ian need to sign off on this proposal? He wouldn't refuse out of spite, would he?"

"Of course not. Regardless of how we may feel about each other, his business sense is sound. I wouldn't have kept him on as an officer of the company if I didn't believe he'd make the right decisions."

Andrea couldn't even begin to understand the dynamic between them. Brothers who couldn't stand the sight of one another yet still maintained enough trust to remain in business? Apparently James compartmentalized as well as he claimed. She doubted she could stay so objective. What in the world could have driven such a wedge into their relationship?

But that wasn't her concern. She hopped off the stool. "I'm going to go sit down out there. Call me if you need your sous-chef back."

"I will," he said. "You boil water brilliantly."

"Glad to be of service."

His laugh followed her out, and she took a gulp of her wine to control her own lingering smile.

The living room was empty except for Serena, who stretched out lengthwise on the rose-flowered sofa, her feet propped up on the arm and her eyes closed. Andrea halted in the doorway. The woman looked exhausted. The last thing she wanted to do was disturb her few moments of peace.

Serena opened her eyes and turned her head just as Andrea was planning her hasty retreat. "Come, have a seat. I was just resting my eyes." She swung her legs to the floor and patted the cushion next to her.

"Are you sure? With a little one, you could probably do with some alone time."

"I'd really rather have some adult conversation. And don't say I can get that from my brothers, because as you can see, they turn into little boys in each other's presence."

Andrea navigated around a scatter of blocks to sit on the sofa. "I'd noticed. Are they always like that?"

"To some degree." Serena reached for her wine glass, which rested on a side table. "I've never seen two people so completely opposite in temperament. And when you consider they didn't really grow up together …"

"What do you mean?" Andrea asked before she could think better of it. She really shouldn't be asking such personal questions. It wasn't as if this were a social visit. But Serena was so welcoming, and she seemed genuinely eager to talk.

"There's almost five years between Ian and James. When our parents divorced, Ian was already headed off to Eton. James was barely eight. That was the last time any of us really lived under the same roof."

Interesting. Ian had attended the most exclusive boys' school in the UK, but James had refused to follow in his footsteps and had attended school in Scotland instead.

Andrea tried to steer the conversation to lighter topics. "You seem close to them both, though."

"They're good uncles, and Emmy especially adores them. She needs that now." Serena threw her a bare smile. "My husband died over a year ago."

"I'm sorry." This was definitely treading on topics Andrea didn't want to discuss with a complete stranger, but Serena wanted to talk. She forced herself to ask, "What happened?"

"Heart attack. He was on a business trip when it happened. He was only forty-two."

"I'm so sorry." What else could she say? No wonder Serena looked so exhausted. She would have been pregnant with Max when her husband died, leaving her to raise the children alone. The thought shuddered through Andrea, twisting her stomach. That might have been her if things had turned out differently.

Andrea took a drink of her wine and thought about how to turn the direction of the conversation. She was saved when the front door banged open, followed by a rush of cold air and a rosy-cheeked girl.

"Look, Mum. See what we found!" Emmy rushed over to the sofa and opened her hand to reveal a clutch of tiny, sandy seashells. Andrea moved her expensive shoes out of reach of the girl's damp sneakers just as Emmy turned to her. "Did you see, Andrea?"

"Ms. Sullivan," Serena corrected immediately, but Andrea shook her head.

"Andrea's fine. And they're lovely. What are you going to do with them?"

"Put them in a jar with some sand so I can take the beach home," Emmy said immediately.

"Not your typical business trip, is it?"

Andrea looked up from Emmy's treasures as Ian seated himself in an armchair on the other side of the coffee table, one long leg crossed ankle to knee over the other. "No, not so far."

"That's Skye for you." The wry twist of his mouth brought to mind his brother. "A family welcome whether you want it or not."

"Ian," Serena said reprovingly.

He shrugged. "I didn't say it was a bad thing. I just meant the situation's more informal than Ms. Sullivan probably expected."

"Call her Andrea, Uncle Ian," Emmy said.

Ian met Andrea's eyes over the girl's head. "Andrea, then. Don't worry. We'll get down to work tomorrow."

"Will you be joining us for the walk-through in the morning, then?"

"No. I have plans. I thought we might discuss your observations over lunch tomorrow. I'm staying in Broadford."

Andrea studied him for a moment. If it had been James speaking, she would think there was a hidden agenda behind the invitation, but Ian just stared back at her, his expression placid, unreadable. That was the biggest difference between the brothers, she decided. With James, she always had a pretty good idea what he was thinking, and it generally wasn't business. Ian, on the other hand, was a complete blank.

"I'll let you work the schedule out with James," she said finally. "But it's fine with me."

He nodded and turned his attention to his niece. "So, Em, I hear you've been taking piano lessons. Want to demonstrate?"

Her face lit up, and she jumped to her feet, scattering seashells over the coffee table. Andrea leaped forward to scoop them up before they rolled off the table. Emmy skidded by on her way to the piano and shoved the fall board carelessly back from the keys with a thud. Andrea winced.

"Come watch me, Andrea!"

Serena held out her hands for the newly corralled seashells. Andrea stood and skirted the coffee table, smoothing the wrinkles from her slacks as she went. Emmy placed her hands awkwardly on the keys and began a halting rendition of "Ode to Joy," her feet swinging beneath the piano bench as she played.

When she finished, Ian and Serena clapped lightly. "Very nice," Andrea said with a nod. "What else can you play?"

"That's it except for scales." Emmy wrinkled her nose. "They're boring."

Andrea smiled down at her. She remembered how she felt at Emmy's age, plodding away at simple sheet music. "I agree. But the more you learn, the more skills you have to make it interesting."

"Do you play, Andrea?" Serena asked.

Her pulse sped up at the question. She could lie, of course, but after the woman had been so honest with her, it hardly seemed right. "Some."

"Play something, Andrea!" Emmy hopped off the bench to make room for her.

She glanced between Serena and Ian. He lifted a shoulder. "You might as well. She's not going to stop asking until you do."

Stupid, stupid, the voice in her head whispered. She didn't play in public anymore. But "Ode to Joy" hardly qualified as playing, and the pleading look Emmy shot her made it hard to refuse.

"All right." Andrea pulled the bench farther back and settled herself so her feet comfortably touched the pedals. Then she placed her hands on the keys and began to play a very calm, respectable version of the choral piece.

Emmy was right. It was boring. She glanced at the little girl's unimpressed expression. Apparently this sedate arrangement wasn't enough to convince her that piano could be fun. Andrea bit her lip. Why not?

She started into her own interpretation of the piece, upping the tempo, throwing in triplets and changing chords to arpeggios, playing with the notes around the central motif until it only barely resembled the original. A smile spread across her face, and she had to stifle a laugh. If this didn't convince the little girl music could be fun, there wasn't much else she could do.

Suddenly she realized the room had gone still and every eye was fixed on her. Ian stood to one side of the piano, Emmy backed up against him, her eyes wide and sparkling. Andrea broke off abruptly, and her smile faded.

"Very impressive."

James's voice drew Andrea's eye to the doorway where he leaned, a towel in hand. His expression made her heart skip.

She had to swallow before she could manage an answer. "I don't play much anymore."

"You should," Ian said quietly. "You're very talented."

The brothers exchanged a glance above her head she didn't understand. Whatever was behind the look, though, she knew she didn't like being the object of it.

Chapter Eight

James called the family to dinner while he set out the food on the small oak dining table, though he gave it only half a mind. Just when he thought Andrea couldn't surprise him, she did something completely unexpected.

Where had she learned to play piano like that? It wasn't the playing of someone who merely remembered her childhood music lessons. The variations she had spun off Emmy's simple melody had felt completely improvisational, and her smile hinted at pure, unabashed delight. It reminded him of how he felt when he had nothing to do but experiment in the kitchen, testing new recipes and trying out unusual flavors.

Muriel had arranged everyone around the table when he returned with the first of the dinner plates. He was pleased to see she'd left him a seat beside Andrea, though that was dulled slightly by the fact that Ian sat directly across from her. He set the first plates before Muriel and Andrea.

"Fresh fettuccini with a traditional tomato and basil sauce," he said, as if he were reading from one of his menus. "Caprese salad, of course. And Serena's legendary garlic knots."

"Hardly legendary." Serena rolled her eyes.

"You should have been a baker, sis." Serena had a touch with breads and cakes he envied. He had never been able to get his baked goods to come out right, but then again, unless he was writing a cookbook, he rarely measured ingredients. Baking was far too precise for his taste.

Once he brought the rest of the plates to the table with a second bottle of wine, Muriel looked to his brother. "Ian, will you bless the meal?"

James stole a glance at Andrea from the corner of his eye, wondering what she thought of the gesture. She just bowed her head and folded her hands, but whether out of respect for their traditions or her own reverence, he couldn't tell.

Ian prayed simply and quickly. "Almighty Father, thank You for Your blessings of health, family, and fellowship. Amen."

The rest of them echoed Ian's closing, including Andrea. James waited for her reaction while she took her first bite.

Her eyebrows flew up. "Are you sure Italian isn't your specialty? This is amazing."

He looked across the table at Muriel. "Auntie loves Italian food. I always make it when I come to Skye."

"You two have always been close?"

"Aunt Muriel raised us," Serena said, bouncing Max on her knee. "When our parents divorced, Mum moved back to London, and Auntie came to stay with Dad. She just forgot to leave."

Muriel chuckled. "What did I have to go back to? Besides, heaven only knows what Jamie would have gotten up to without supervision." She leaned toward Andrea with a conspiratorial expression.

"Ian was always the responsible one. Serena, the quiet one. Jamie, on the other hand, good Lord help us, is responsible for every bit of gray hair you see now."

"That's not fair," James protested. "Ian and Serena got up to their fair share of trouble. They just always blamed it on me."

"We did not!" Serena laughed and reflexively moved a milk glass out of the way of Emmy's elbow. "You didn't need any help from us. Do you remember the time you wrapped the parish minister's car in cling film?"

"You didn't!" Andrea said.

James rubbed his forehead ruefully. He'd forgotten about that one. "To my everlasting shame, I did. Now, to be truthful, it was a dare, and I never could resist a dare. I'm fairly certain Reverend Stewart told me I was going straight to hell for my wickedness. He still hasn't forgiven me."

"No," Serena said. "He hasn't forgiven you for spiking the communion chalice with hot sauce."

James smiled sheepishly. That one he remembered clearly. Not his proudest moment. It really was a miracle he'd not grown up to be a delinquent after all. "Another dare. Let's say I had an uneasy relationship with organized religion as a boy. Auntie thinks I'm a heathen."

"Nonsense." Muriel caught Andrea's eye. "Don't let him fool you. He's a good Christian man, no matter what he says. He and the parish church just clashed a bit over his high-spiritedness when he was a child."

"As he did with every headmaster he ever had," Serena said, snickering.

Ian glanced at Andrea, then quickly lowered his gaze back to his plate.

What was that all about? James wondered. Trying to judge her reaction to his youthful indiscretions? Or trying to convey his disapproval over the fact Muriel still made excuses for him?

Andrea delicately lowered her fork to her plate. "What about you, Ian? Serena says you attended school in London. And James mentioned you were a lawyer?"

"Yes. I practiced as a solicitor for several years before I took the job with Jamie."

"What kind of law?"

"Corporate, mostly contract law."

Serena rolled her eyes. "Ian earned first honors at Cambridge, quite an accomplishment considering he spent most of his time on the river, rowing. Not that he'd ever mention it."

Ian didn't need to. Their mother liked to spread the news of her favored son far and wide. Not a single one of their family members or acquaintances had lacked the details of Ian's academic and athletic accomplishments.

"You row?" Andrea's gaze swept over Ian, as if she were trying to reconcile the information with what she saw before her. Or maybe she was just admiring him. It wouldn't be the first time. It wasn't as if his brother needed any help with women, when he chose to pay them attention.

"I do," he said with a shrug. "Or I did. I retired almost ten years ago."

"Ian was on the GB team for eleven years," Serena said. "He won, what, four gold medals in the world championships?"

Ian didn't look up. "Five."

"Wow," Andrea said. "That's … very impressive."

James pushed down a twinge of something that, this time, he couldn't pass off as anything but jealousy. Amazing how being in the same room with Ian could make him feel fifteen again, afraid to bring a girl home to meet his family in case she decided she fancied his accomplished, athletic older brother instead. It had happened, though admittedly not in recent years.

The silence stretched, but before it could become any more uncomfortable, Muriel asked, "What about you, Andrea? Where are you from originally?"

"A very small town in Ohio."

"With a movie house and no signal lights." James glanced at her and was rewarded with a tiny smile before she answered his aunt.

"I did my undergrad work at NYU and then my MBA at Cornell. I've lived in some part of New York ever since. Right now I live in Manhattan."

"Are you married?" Muriel asked bluntly. "Engaged? Seeing someone?"

Andrea made a choked sound and brought her napkin to her lips. James patted her on the back, and she took a swift drink from her water glass. Finally she said, "I'm single."

"Why is that? You're a lovely woman. What, twenty-nine?"

"Thirty-one."

"It's long past time for you to settle down, don't you think?"

Andrea shot a wide-eyed look at James, obviously pleading with him to intervene. She was looking to the wrong quarter for help in this area. "Yes, Andrea, why is it you haven't settled down?"

She looked at Ian, who didn't seem inclined to intervene either. She met James's eyes again, a dangerous glint in her own. "Well, I travel so much for work, the only men I meet are clients. And most of them are self-serving egomaniacs, so you can imagine it puts a cramp in my social life."

A laugh burst out of him and quickly turned to a cough. He reached for his own water glass. That was the second time she'd surprised him tonight. Not that it should have. He'd already gotten a glimpse of her wickedly sharp tongue in the pub.

Muriel nodded, her expression satisfied. "I like a woman who speaks her piece. Mind yourself with this one, Jamie. She's not one to be trifled with."

"Yes, I'm beginning to see that." James shot her a sideways glance, and she just smiled sweetly. *Touché*. If she thought she'd put him off, though, she was sorely mistaken. She might try to deny she had any interest in him, but she couldn't hide the fact she held her breath whenever he got within a foot of her. He couldn't help but take the words as an open challenge.

At the end of the meal, Andrea brushed off Aunt Muriel's protests and collected the dishes to take to the kitchen. Ian rose to assist, but James gave him a terse shake of his head and gathered the empty wine glasses. For once, his brother actually obeyed and lowered himself back to his chair.

When James entered, Andrea was rinsing the dishes and stacking them neatly in the sink.

"Do I need to apologize for my family yet?"

Andrea threw a glance at him over her shoulder. "They're great."

"Are we speaking about the same family?" He laughed at her reproving look. "No, they are. I always forget how much I miss them until I come home." Most of them, at least.

He leaned past her to place the wine glasses in the sink, purposely brushing her arm. She shifted away from him and scrubbed the dish with renewed vigor.

No. Definitely not immune to him.

When she finished washing the last plate, she shut off the water and turned to him. "Can I help with anything else?"

James poured hot water from the electric kettle into the cafetière, which he'd already filled with ground coffee. "You can take this and the cups to the table. I'll be out with dessert in a moment."

He took out the containers of gelato from the freezer and began scooping perfect globes of the dessert into glass dishes while Andrea took the cafetière to the dining room. When she returned for the coffee cups, the stack tilted precariously, and he automatically reached out to steady them. She froze when his hands closed over hers.

"Got them now?" He let his fingers brush over the back of her hands before he released them. She swallowed, her tongue darting out to moisten her lips. He smiled.

A flush instantly spread up her neck to her cheeks, and she turned quickly with a rattle of china. His grin widened. She might be determined to put him in his place, but he was definitely going to get the last laugh.

When he brought their dessert out a few minutes later—perfect globes of gelato, garnished with lacy, anise-flavored cookies and sprigs of mint—Andrea was talking to his sister about Emmy's piano lessons. She barely acknowledged his presence, her body turned slightly toward Serena so she didn't have to look at him when he reclaimed his seat beside her.

After dessert, Aunt Muriel waved off Andrea's second attempt to clear the table. "Serena and I can manage these. It was lovely meeting you, dear." The older woman kissed her on the cheek. "You'll be joining us for breakfast, won't you?"

Andrea shot a questioning glance at James. When he nodded, she said, "I'd love to."

Emmy popped out of her chair and gave Andrea a quick hug around the waist. A startled expression, then something deeper, more painful, surfaced on her face.

"Will you teach me to play something new tomorrow, Andrea?"

"Emmy, she doesn't want to spend all her time at the piano," James said.

Emmy's lip quivered. Andrea gently disentangled herself. "Of course I will. Let me think about what to teach you, all right?"

Serena smiled over Emmy's head, jiggling Max on her hip. "Thank you, Andrea. It was nice to meet you."

"Likewise."

James retrieved Andrea's coat and held it for her while she slipped it on.

"I've asked Andrea to have lunch with me tomorrow to discuss her proposal," Ian said. "Will you be done by one o'clock?"

James tensed, but he nodded. "I'll drive her. Broadford Hotel?"

Ian looked like he wanted to argue, but he just reached into the pocket of his trousers. He extended a business card to Andrea with two fingers. "My mobile number is at the bottom if you need to reach me tomorrow."

"Thank you. I'll see you then." She gave him a slight smile and then extended it to the rest of the family. "Good night, everyone."

James ushered her out the door and down the gravel path to the car. Already, the temperature had dropped, and their breath puffed out in white clouds around them. He breathed the damp air deeply, welcoming the freedom from the tension inside. He opened the car door for her, waited for her to settle herself into the seat, and then shut it firmly behind her.

"Dinner was wonderful," she said when he climbed into the driver's seat. "I can't remember the last time I enjoyed a meal so much."

"Thank you." He studied her face, cast alternately in shadow and light, trying to decide if she meant it or was merely being polite. Her vague smile gave away nothing. He put the car in reverse and backed down the drive.

They didn't talk on the short ride back to the hotel, but at least now it was a comfortable silence. She'd apparently decided to forgive him for his earlier teasing, and as much as he liked to see that spark of annoyance, he was glad to be on level terms again.

He delivered her to the door of her cottage and unlocked it, then leaned past her to flip on the light switch inside. He slid a key off his key ring and pressed it into her hand. "Good night, Andrea. I'll see you in the morning."

"Good night." She stepped inside, but she didn't close the door immediately. He felt her eyes on him as he walked away. He didn't turn. He just slipped his hands into his pockets and listened until he heard the soft click of the door close behind her.

He exhaled his held breath, then retrieved his suitcase from the back of the car and crossed the lot to his own cottage. He let himself in and flipped on the light switch. It was as sparsely decorated as Andrea's, but a basket of fruit sat on the table, and a quick glance at the refrigerator showed it had been stocked with the basics: milk, bread, cold cuts. Bless Muriel. Even now, she was looking out for him.

He turned on the television while he unpacked his carry-on bag. Since the hotel was still under construction and he was the only one to occupy the space, he always left the essentials in the wardrobe: jeans, a heavy coat, casual shirts, workout wear. It saved him the trouble of checking baggage, especially when he flew up at the last minute.

As he hung up his suit jacket, his mind wandered back to Andrea. She'd let her guard down tonight with his family, and he'd gotten a glimpse of the warm and witty woman that lay beneath the consummate professional. He couldn't deny their mutual attraction, but he was surprised to realize he truly liked her.

That was unexpected.

As was the look that had passed over her face when Emmy hugged her. It had not simply been surprise. It was deeper and more painful than that. She'd recovered quickly, but he knew he hadn't imagined it. What had happened in her past to cause that sort of reaction to a girl's innocent excitement?

The question dampened James's enthusiasm for his teasing. Regardless of what Andrea might believe, he wasn't after someone to take to bed. If that were his goal, he had more than a few willing participants in London.

No, he'd been down that road in his youth. Casual sex only satisfied the momentary need, leaving him emptier and more restless than he'd been before. Of course, his twenty-year-old self had spent plenty of time denying it, ignoring that in large part what he had actually felt was guilt. That was not how his God-fearing father and aunt had raised him. It had just taken time to see he was only hurting himself with his actions.

Whatever others might believe, he hadn't returned to his reckless ways after Cassie's departure. He simply wasn't inclined to deny himself the enjoyment of flirting with a beautiful woman. He'd thought Andrea was just the sort to enjoy the interaction—tough, capable, smart. And she undoubtedly was. He just hadn't counted on the flash of vulnerability he'd seen tonight, nor the niggling suspicion she wasn't quite what she portrayed herself to be.

Given all the other conflict in his life right now, it was a complication he didn't need.

Chapter Nine

Andrea slept only a few hours despite her exhaustion, and she awoke while the sky was still dark, her heart thudding a staccato rhythm against her ribs. It took her only a few seconds to remember she was on the Isle of Skye, but by then the damage had been done. She was already ticking off her mental to-do list. Sleep would not be returning anytime soon.

She swung her legs from beneath the heavy down comforter and danced across the cold floor to retrieve her laptop. She flicked on the light at the desk and booted up the computer, yawning while it cycled through its start-up sequence.

"Focus," she said aloud. "By this time tomorrow you'll be on your way back home and away from Skye forever."

With a few hours distance from her last encounter with James, she could look at the situation more objectively. Of course she was attracted to the man. What woman wouldn't find him appealing in some way? She had probably just spent too much time dating serious, solid businessmen in New York if a little banter and a smile could make her heart skip a beat. Heaven knew most of the others hadn't even made it to the expected second-date kiss. She didn't even bother to find a date for work functions anymore. She'd overheard the speculations about her personal preferences, but she wasn't about to change her life to prove she was interested in the opposite sex.

I like men. I just don't particularly trust them. James MacDonald was a perfect case in point.

"And that is enough time spent on that subject." She retrieved a folder from her bag and began to put together the materials for her meeting with Ian later that day. James wouldn't be impressed with marketing collateral, but Ian seemed like he'd expect it. Details on company history, their capabilities, and a sheet of recommendations from past and current clients went into the foil-embossed folio with a copy of her business card neatly inserted into the front slot.

Andrea was contemplating what else to include when a light knock came at the door. She padded across the room and cracked it open.

James stood there, smiling sheepishly. "I didn't wake you, did I? I saw the light."

"No, I was just getting ready for the meeting later." She opened the door wider, letting in a rush of cold air. Her tissue-thin T-shirt gave her little barrier against the chill, and she hugged her arms to herself. "What's up?"

"I want you to see something. Put on a coat and come outside?"

"Okay. Give me a minute." She shut the door, then pulled on her coat and buttoned it over her pajamas. She thrust her feet into her single pair of practical footwear—lightweight running shoes—and put her hand on the door before she thought better of it and dashed back to the bathroom to brush her teeth. She caught her reflection in the mirror and made a face at her sleep-tousled hair.

"Too bad," she muttered. "Anyone who comes to my door this early in the morning will have to take what they get."

Outside, mist hung in the air, and the overnight drizzle had left a film of moisture over everything. She inhaled the cold, instantly energized by the bite in her lungs and the chill on her skin. James waited several steps away, holding two steaming travel mugs.

She gratefully took the mug he held out and sipped the rich, strong coffee while she studied him over its rim. Unlike her, he looked ready to start the day, wearing a button-down chambray shirt and a pair of comfortably faded jeans. He had thrown a weathered barn coat on against the cold, but it was unzipped, despite the fact she was already freezing. It was unfair that he could manage to make such a casual outfit look so good. He was like some annoyingly perfect J.Crew model.

But that was a dangerous line of thought. "What did you want me to see?"

"Come with me." James gestured with his head toward the deck behind her cottage.

She followed him and then stopped abruptly at the edge of the deck. The dim morning light cast the rippling clouds in shades of white and gray and silver, reflecting them back on the glassy surface of the sound. Fragile shreds of mist hung suspended in the air. Rocky mountains rose sharply in front of them, setting off the slim white column of the old Ornsay lighthouse. For a moment, Andrea forgot how to breathe, the incredible beauty of the scenery striking her in the chest.

James watched her silently, and she thought she glimpsed a smile from the corner of her eye, but she couldn't tear her gaze away. The sun was rising rapidly now, the colors changing from silver-gray to gold and streaking pink through the clouds, and she stared in rapt amazement at the fast-shifting landscape.

"This is my favorite time of day on Skye," he said.

"I've never seen anything like it. You feel it right here." She touched her heart, then instantly felt embarrassed. She wasn't usually the type to wax eloquent over scenery, however much it might touch her.

James just nodded. "Living in London, sometimes I forget there are still places on earth that look like this. I never get tired of it, and it never stops being a surprise."

"It's harder to take it for granted when you're away." Andrea sank down onto a wood lounge chair and cupped the travel mug, letting the warmth thaw her hands while she breathed in the morning quiet.

"Indeed. I confess I've considered moving back to Skye more than once, but I always wonder if I would appreciate it as much if I lived here."

"I'm not sure I could ever get tired of this view."

He studied her, and the scrutiny heated her cheeks. "I thought I'd show you the hotel after breakfast and then drive you to Broadford to meet Ian. Does that suit?"

"It does."

"I'm going to head up to the house about seven. Join me?"

She smiled. "I wouldn't miss it."

"Good. I'll see you in a bit, then." He disappeared around the cottage and left her alone to enjoy the sunrise.

Chapter Ten

Emmy flung herself at Andrea the minute she and James stepped through the front door. The little girl still wore her pink pajamas, and her dark hair had pulled loose from its ponytail in messy tendrils. "You came! Did you decide what you were going to teach me?"

James laughed. "Why don't you wait until after breakfast for the piano, Em."

"Then you can play dolls with me, Andrea!"

Andrea shot James a helpless look as she let Emmy drag her toward the coffee table.

"I'll be in the kitchen if you need me," he said, laughter in his voice.

Emmy pulled Andrea to the floor beside the table where her extensive collection of tiny dolls lay scattered across the surface. She really shouldn't have worn the skirt suit. She eased off her shoes and placed them neatly at the side of the sofa, embarrassment twinging at the memory of James's observation at the airport. It took a couple of minutes to find a position that was both comfortable and modest, but she finally settled on her knees with her legs and bare feet tucked under her.

By the time James called them for breakfast, Andrea possessed an intimate knowledge of the strangely tiny plastic dolls and their equally tiny plastic wardrobes. She looked up and saw James smiling at them in the doorway.

"Up for a traditional Scottish breakfast?"

"What do you think, Emmy?" Andrea said. "Should we give it a shot?"

"Uncle Jamie's a good cook," the girl said seriously.

"All right then. Up you go." Andrea tried to brush out the wrinkles now pressed into her skirt as she straightened, then gave up. Her dry cleaner could deal with it when she got back. "Can I help with anything?"

"No, table's already set and tea's on the sideboard. Go ahead and have a seat."

Emmy ran ahead of Andrea into the adjacent dining room, where Serena already sat with Max in her lap, dressed for the day in jeans and a colorful Fair Isle sweater. Andrea went to the electric kettle on the sideboard and made herself a cup of tea.

"Sleep well?" Serena asked.

"Very well," Andrea lied. "How about you?"

"After last night? Seriously thinking about hiring an au pair."

Andrea laughed. "Do you want a cup of tea?"

"If you don't mind, please. White, two sugars."

"Coming up." Andrea poured tea into another mug, made up the cup with milk and sugar, and placed it on the table. Serena gave her a grateful smile and quickly slid it out of the baby's reach.

Andrea seated herself next to Serena. "Ian's not joining us?"

"After last night, he'll make himself scarce. Besides, he's probably out on the water somewhere. Old rowing mate of his lives in Dunvegan now."

Andrea nodded and sipped her tea, relieved they wouldn't be subjected to a repeat of last night's tension. Somehow she felt like she'd gotten wedged in the middle of the simmering resentment between the two brothers, even if it had nothing to do with her.

"Good morning, Andrea." Muriel entered the room, the picture of a 1950s housewife in a shirtwaist dress and elegantly backswept hair. "Sleep well?"

"Better than Serena, I hear."

"I told you. A wee nip of Scotch, and the bairn will sleep soundly all night."

Serena gave her aunt an exasperated look. "That's grounds for visitation by child protection, Auntie."

"We did it when you were young, and you turned out just fine."

"Serena did." James entered with several plates balanced on his forearms. "I'm beginning to understand where you went wrong with me."

"Wheesht, Jamie." Muriel waved a hand in his direction. "It had nothing to do with the Scotch. Your father just dropped you on your head a few times too many."

James grinned and set the plates before them. Andrea looked down at hers in dismay. There was scarcely an inch of uncovered territory: fried eggs, a rasher of bacon, sausage, sautéed tomatoes and mushrooms, baked beans, and several slices of toast.

"Is this breakfast for the whole island?" She usually considered herself lucky if she had time for a cup of coffee and a protein bar before she rushed to the office.

"Busy day," James said. "You should eat up."

"We'd have to be running a marathon to justify this."

"Don't tempt him," Serena said. "He's always trying to get me up at sunrise to jog with him. The only thing my brother takes seriously besides his cooking is his exercise."

Andrea could believe it. James's button-down shirt fit closely enough to see the ripple of muscle beneath when he moved, and if she were completely honest, she'd already noticed the snug fit of his faded jeans. Given his propensity for cooking rich food, it took more than an occasional jog to maintain that kind of shape. Her gaze followed him as he left the room before she realized what she was doing.

"I'm afraid I'm on his side on that one," she said. "I run every morning when I'm home. I don't live far from Central Park. It's a nice way to start the day."

James returned with the rest of the plates and settled into the chair beside her. "I saw you brought your trainers. There are some spectacular views of Sleat you can't see from the main roads."

"I don't see when I'll have time for a run. My flight leaves at eleven tomorrow. I imagine we'll have to leave pretty early."

"That's a shame," James said. "I'd love to be able to show you the island before you go. Maybe after you're done with Ian I'll take you on a driving tour."

It was tempting. Skye's scenery tugged at her heart. But she'd already allowed herself to get too distracted by her client and his family. It was time to get back to work. "I need to wrap up everything this afternoon. I should have a preliminary proposal done by this evening."

"If that's what you prefer."

Was that disappointment in his voice? No, she must have misinterpreted it. He was now tickling Emmy, making the little girl squirm and giggle in her seat. Andrea repressed her smile.

"Enough, Jamie, let her eat her breakfast." Muriel shook her head. "Wee bairns, both of them."

Andrea dug into her meal with enthusiasm and once again insisted on clearing the table when they were finished. She scrubbed out the frying pans and placed the plates in the dishwasher while James put away the remnants of breakfast and wiped down the counters.

They were halfway to the front door when Emmy skidded to a stop in front of Andrea. Her face scrunched into a frown. "Are you leaving? You promised to teach me something."

Guilt crashed over her. "I forgot. I'm sorry. We have work to do, Emmy."

"Are you coming back?"

"Supper, if you like," James said. "We should be done in plenty of time."

She looked down at the little girl. "If you're good for your mom and great aunt today, I'll teach you how to play my favorite duet on the piano after dinner, okay?"

"You promise?" Emmy asked suspiciously.

"I promise." A pang bit into Andrea's midsection again, a combination of longing and something deeper, more painful. She swallowed hard and squeezed the girl's shoulder. "I'll see you tonight."

She stepped out onto the porch and forced down the feeling. She'd had enough practice that it was as natural as breathing. Almost.

Evidently she didn't hide her reaction as well as she'd thought. James peered at her with concern as they walked down the front steps to the car. "Are you all right?"

"I'm fine," she said quickly. Too quickly. "Let's go. I have a lot of work ahead of me."

He didn't push her as they drove back to the hotel, but she knew he was mulling her strange reaction. She'd never been terribly comfortable around children, even her niece and nephews, but Emmy ... when she looked at Emmy, she couldn't help but think about what might have been. But those thoughts served no one. They certainly changed nothing.

James parked in front of the hotel. "Wait here. I'm going to get us a couple of torches."

Andrea climbed out and surveyed the exterior of the hotel. The main house, the original part, was just a stone box that had been expanded outward over the decades. A timbered conservatory addition off one side gave it a slightly unbalanced look, as did the new framing off the rear. She took out her phone and snapped several pictures of the exterior.

"Here we are." James returned and handed her a flashlight, and she followed him to the door. He had to wiggle the key in the lock and thrust his shoulder against the door to unstick it from the frame.

"Moisture," he said. "The door likes to swell in the damp. Mind your step."

Despite its many windows, the interior of the hotel was dark and cool. Andrea flipped on the flashlight and swept it over their surroundings. Most of the plasterboard had been pulled from the framing, revealing plumbing and wiring on the interior walls and ceilings, and exposing the original stone on the exterior.

"Traditional croft-house construction," she said. "But with a second-story addition, correct?"

"Correct. The original structure dates from about 1820, and then the upper story was added in 1945. My great-great-grandmother was born here."

"Really? So the property has been in your family for a long time."

James nodded. "It was turned into a hotel shortly after the addition. My grandfather ran it until his death, and then our father took it over. Aunt Muriel oversaw it when he died two years ago."

"What happened then?"

"A storm took the roof off, did so much damage she had to close it. The hotel's assets wouldn't begin to cover the repairs, but Ian and I had the funds to put into the restoration. The roof and the foundation have already been addressed. The electrician will start the wiring next week, and then we'll be on to the cosmetics of it."

Andrea carefully picked her way through the bits of debris still clinging to the floor, taking in the proportions of the foyer. To the left lay a large room framed for double doors. To the right was an open living area. Stairs headed straight up in front of them, then took a sharp left turn to the second floor. "What are your plans for the layout?"

"The area to the right will be a lounge for guests. To the left will be the dining room. There's just enough room for nine or ten tables, which is more than enough. The hotel guests normally trickle down in the mornings, and dinner will be by reservation only."

Andrea ducked through the opening and walked into the sweeping space. "I'd expose the original stone," she said immediately, gesturing to the exterior walls. "And this fireplace ... you're keeping it, right?"

"I'd thought to. The contractor's trying to convince me it's not worth the cost to rebuild the chimney."

"It would be worth every penny," Andrea said. "I can just imagine this room in the winter, with a fire going and the snow coming down outside. I think you need some more windows on the west side of the building to catch the sunset, though. I know it's not traditional to the croft-house style, but you'll be glad for it when winter comes and it gets dark early."

"That's a good idea," James said, surprise in his tone. "How is it you know so much about this?"

"My undergraduate degree is in architecture. Most of my clients are in the UK, so I've studied traditional British construction in depth."

James led her up the creaky wood staircase to the first floor where the hotel's guest rooms were located, including an addition currently being framed over the kitchen on the back of the house. He pointed out the sites of the water damage and gave her an overview of the current plans for each room. Andrea scribbled notes in her pocket notepad and took photos of both the rooms and the views from the windows.

She paused in front of a window that looked out onto the sound, over the roof of the cottages. Mist still hung over the mountains in the background, but morning light glimmered on the water. It was a view worthy of a postcard. These front rooms would never be empty.

"It's going to be lovely. I can feel it. Some places have a real sense of history. A solidity. I see why you're so enthusiastic about the project."

"And here I pegged you for a marble-and-glass, big-city-hotel type of girl."

Andrea laughed and trailed a finger down the solid wood casement. "I love these old croft houses. Just don't tell anyone. It would completely destroy my image." She turned away from the window and saw James was watching her with an oddly searching expression. "What?"

"You're not at all what I expected, Andrea Sullivan." He cleared his throat as if he'd said too much and rushed on. "It was my father's dream to renovate this place. He always talked about updating it and having me open a restaurant here. I regret we didn't get a chance to do it before he died."

"I think he would be pleased with the direction it's going," Andrea said. "Some people would be tempted to renovate all the original character out of the place, but I like what you're doing here. Modern amenities don't have to mean losing what makes it special."

"Do you want to see the blueprints?" James asked. "They're back in my cottage."

Andrea hesitated.

"I'm just showing you blueprints. I promise, I've nothing untoward in mind." That mischievous twinkle appeared in his eyes. "At least not right this minute."

He was teasing her again, having tread dangerously close to a personal topic. "Very funny. Let's see the drawings."

Andrea led the way from the room and back down the stairs, her shoes rapping hollowly on the plywood subfloor. James locked the front door behind them, and she struggled across the gravel lot in her heels to his cottage.

As soon as they stepped inside, James asked, "Tea?"

"Sure." Andrea rubbed her arms through her jacket for a second. She'd forgotten about the cold in her enthusiasm over the hotel, but goose bumps still pricked her skin. "I understand why the British are so big on tea now. It's always cold."

James filled the electric teakettle that sat on the counter of the kitchenette and flicked the switch on the side.

"Let me get the prints for you." He moved to his desk, identical to the one in Andrea's room but outfitted with a printer and a laptop computer, and retrieved several rolls of paper from the galvanized steel bucket beside it. He spread them across the kitchen table.

"This is the exterior elevation, including the addition." He pointed out the extension that jutted off the back and curved around the side. "The facade is going to have to be adjusted to match the original stone, but I've already found a stonemason who assures me it can be done."

"Good." Andrea nodded her approval. She turned a page and braced her hands against the table as she bent over to survey the next sheet of blueprints. "You're putting showers in the en suite baths?"

"Small ones. I wanted to stick to the original footprint of the rooms, but Americans especially expect showers."

"True, but if you can only have one, you should choose the bath. An old-fashioned claw-foot tub goes a long way to establishing ambience." She carefully folded back the page and moved on.

In the back, past the floor plans and multi-view drawings, Andrea found the more detailed material takeoffs. She frowned as her eye landed on the dimensions for the beams in the main dining room. She tapped her finger against the drawing. "Double-check these dimensions. I don't think this is going to be adequate for the span."

"You really are quite surprising."

Andrea glanced up at James, unsure from his tone whether he was teasing, but he regarded her with undisguised admiration.

"I've been in this business for a while. You tend to pick things up."

"Tell me, then. What am I missing?"

She glanced back at the blueprints and considered. "A bar."

"A bar?"

Andrea pulled out a chair and sat, crossing her legs and tugging her skirt down automatically. "You yourself said there's nothing within walking distance, and the roads on Skye aren't great in winter. You could always serve cocktails in the reception room, but I really think you'd be better off with an attached bar." She flipped back to the exterior elevation drawings. "You already have this extension here being framed out. It wouldn't be much more trouble to extend it on the other side, maybe with a breezeway to the new kitchen so you could serve food at the bar as well. Do you have some paper?"

James retrieved a pencil and pad of grid paper from the desk and set them down in front of her. She quickly sketched a small rendering of the hotel, adding on a matching extension in rough strokes.

"It wouldn't be better to have a freestanding building?"

"This is more cost-effective, and it will take less to heat. Plus it shouldn't require separate permits. I think you'll find the bar will help offset your lower winter occupancy rates. Sleat residents will be more likely to come here rather than Broadford or Armadale to socialize, especially if you have good, inexpensive food."

James nodded thoughtfully. "I'll send the drawings over to Ian and see what he thinks."

"I can mention it today, if you like."

"Maybe I should come along and discuss it with him myself."

"I hardly think that's a good idea after last night." Andrea wondered if she was imagining the possessiveness in James's tone. She wasn't sure whether to be amused, pleased, or irritated. Maybe all three. "Don't worry. I'll let you know what we discuss. I'll take this with me." Andrea tore the drawing off the pad and set it aside, then began to roll up the stacks of drawings, group by group.

The teakettle chose that moment to begin spewing steam. James flipped the switch to warm and pulled out two mugs. "One sugar or two?"

"Two, please. Should I put these back?"

"If you don't mind. What do you think? Too early for biscuits?"

Andrea returned the drawings to the galvanized tub and tucked the pad and pencil back into the desk drawer. "It's never too early for biscuits."

"You're my kind of woman." He retrieved a package of cookies from the cupboard, placed a few on a plate, and set them on the table before her. He finished making up their tea and took the chair next to her. "What now?"

"I'd like to see your business and marketing plans, if you have them handy."

"I don't. Besides, I meant what do *we* do now? It's only half past ten. You're not supposed to meet Ian until one. I think hospitality demands I give you a tour of Sleat."

"I should probably get started on my proposal."

"You should, but you won't."

She took a sip of her tea, trying to hide her smile behind the cup. "Why won't I?"

"Because you can't resist the chance to spend a few hours with me seeing the sights. I assure you, I am an excellent guide."

Two or three hours in the car with him, doing something strictly recreational? He might have behaved himself this morning, but she didn't expect that to last long. Now that he knew which buttons to push, he wouldn't hesitate to do it. Over and over.

The thought reminded her of his comment in the bar about her clothing. The attraction was not one-sided. She just had absolutely no intention of giving into it. He, on the other hand …

No, he wasn't the kind of man to force the issue. She knew that much with certainty. This was all just some game, a battle of the sexes, and he wanted to make her break first. Which, of course, she wouldn't do. If she kept refusing to be alone with him, he'd just keep pushing the issue.

"All right," she said finally. "On one condition."

"What's that?"

"You have to deliver me to the meeting with Ian on time. Not a minute late."

"If you insist."

"Good. Let's go, then." Andrea stood and straightened her skirt. "I'll get my bag."

James beat her to the door with his long-legged stride and opened it for her, deliberately crowding her so they stood face-to-face, only inches apart.

"Thank you." She met his gaze levelly, even though her heartbeat was already accelerating. She lowered her eyes and moved quickly past him.

No two ways about it. This was a very bad idea.

Chapter Eleven

The woman was a complete mystery.

One minute, she'd give as good as she got with that sharp tongue and equally sharp mind. The next she'd withdraw behind a shell of cold professionalism. It was like seeing two different people, and James was never sure which one would surface.

Then there was the Andrea who would sit on the floor with Emmy or improvise on the piano with such a joyous expression it made his heart flip. Why was she so determined to hide that part of herself?

James cursed himself for a fool. For a short moment, he'd thought he and Andrea had been building some sort of rapport, then he had to ruin it by pushing matters too far. Now, fifteen minutes into their drive down the Sleat peninsula, she still hadn't said a word. She just sat stiffly in the seat, hands folded in her lap, staring into the distance. He'd wager she wasn't seeing a bit of the glorious scenery flying by the window.

Why do you even care?

He didn't. Or, he hadn't, until he saw the look on her face as she watched the sunrise, as if years of worries had fallen from her shoulders. If he hadn't witnessed the wistfulness in her expression as she talked about the restoration, he would have written it off to his imagination. But he knew that feeling well. It was too easy to let the demands of life suffocate him and drown out God's still, small voice, until the days became just an endless list. Something inside him recognized she needed a breath as much as he did.

He left her to her musings as he took the two-lane road through a forested section of Sleat and followed the River Ord until it emptied out near the shore. When they reached an overlook where Ord Bay and Loch Eishort met, he pulled off onto the side of the road.

"Why are we stopping?"

"Because it's worth a moment to appreciate. Come."

Andrea climbed out of the car, and James circled to meet her on the other side. Immediately she pulled out her mobile phone and began to snap pictures of the view.

"Beautiful," she said. "These will definitely help creative when they formulate their marketing plan."

James gently pried her phone from her fingers and dropped it into the front pocket of his shirt. "I'm going to hold onto this for you."

Andrea stared at him. "Give me my phone back."

"It's mine for now. You can have it back for your meeting."

"How dare you!" Anger flashed in those gorgeous eyes, a sign she was going to launch into a tirade on his ungentlemanly behavior. Before she could try, he gripped her shoulders and turned her to face the view again. She went still, muscles tensed beneath his fingers.

"Relax," he murmured into her ear. "Breathe. When you view it on a screen, you can't really see."

She threw a puzzled look over her shoulder, for a moment bringing her face close to his. If he just shifted forward a degree, he could capture her mouth with his own. She must have read the thought in his expression, because alarm flashed over her face. He quickly straightened and gave a little nod toward the scenery.

What was he thinking?

He took a deep breath and looked out at the loch, settling his own tumultuous thoughts. Rocks jutted from the choppy water, a stark brown contrast against the deep blue. Long shore grasses waved in the stiff sea wind, edging the sweep of sand in the distance. Just at the limits of their sight, boxy white cottages nestled in spring-green hills. He breathed in the salt air, listening to the soft lap of waves and the distant calls of seabirds. Beside him, Andrea closed her eyes, breathing deeply while the wind ruffled her hair, a slight smile stretching her lips.

She was beautiful. He couldn't pry his eyes away from her. When was the last time a woman had pulled him this strongly?

Dangerous thoughts. He shoved his hands into his pockets and leaned back against the car, forcing his gaze away from her. It was one thing to flirt and tease, to steal a kiss. The sudden squeeze in his chest was quite another. He recognized that feeling. It meant nothing good.

When she finally opened her eyes, he had his thoughts mostly under control.

"You're right," she murmured. "It's amazing. Sort of desolate and yet … peaceful."

He said nothing, but when she turned to him, he held out her phone.

"Keep it," she said. "For now."

He smiled. Maybe he was getting through to her after all. "On to our next stop, then?"

James stayed quiet in the car, not wanting to jar her from her peaceful frame of mind. She took in the landscape with a new light in her eye, smiling when he pointed out patches of wildflowers on the hillside or laughing at the spring lambs frolicking in the meadows. He didn't question why it was so important she see his home through his eyes. She needed a few minutes away from her life as much as he did from his own.

His enjoyment dwindled as the time edged toward one o'clock, since he knew he would shortly hand her over to Ian. He put on the canned enthusiasm of a tour guide and said, "And that's the end of our guided tour today. We should head back to Broadford. I did promise to deliver you on time."

She nodded. He sensed her struggling for words, but in the end, she only said, "Thank you."

Her husky tone did things to his gut he didn't particularly appreciate. "For getting you there on time?"

"No, for this. For making me really see."

It couldn't be an easy admission for her. He barely kept himself from reaching for her hand, instead forcing his attention onto the road. "You're welcome."

The drive back to Broadford passed too quickly, even in companionable silence. He pulled into the hotel's car park, noting Ian's car in front of the tan stucco building with its dormered, shingled roof.

"How should I contact you when I'm finished?" Andrea asked, reaching for her bag, the professional once again in place.

James drew her mobile phone out of his jacket pocket and handed it to her. "I programmed my number in. Just call me when you're finished. I have to go to market and pick up some things for dinner."

Annoyance flashed across her face. "You could have asked."

"I didn't think you'd mind." Actually, he'd known it would probably irritate her, but he hadn't been able to resist. He rather liked the way she looked angry. And she was far easier to deal with irritated than when she looked at him with that searching, vulnerable expression.

Coward.

"Fine. I'll call you when I'm done." Andrea tucked the phone into her bag and slid out of the car without saying good-bye.

He watched her disappear into the front doors of the hotel and then dropped his head onto the steering wheel, banging it a few times for good measure. *Idiot.* Annoy her, then send her to lunch with his good-looking, personable brother. Brilliant planning.

He jerked the gearstick into reverse and backed out of the parking space, then pulled onto Broadford's main road. It shouldn't matter to him what she did or what she thought. He and Ian would sign the contract, and she would be on her way back to New York. Maybe she'd check in with him by phone once a month to make sure he was happy with the progress on the hotel, but other than that, he'd have no further contact with the beautiful American consultant.

But when he drove straight past the co-op grocery, he was forced to admit that whatever feelings she brought out, he wasn't ready for it to be over.

Chapter Twelve

Only a few tables in the hotel restaurant were filled, and Andrea immediately spotted Ian at one near the window. She put on a warm smile and made her way toward him.

He rose as she approached. Whatever business he'd had this morning, on the water or otherwise, his beautifully tailored navy suit and maroon tie gave no hint of it now. Seeing Ian look so proper and professional in his business clothing made her realize James wore his own with a sense of irony.

"Andrea."

"Ian." Andrea gave him a polite nod. "Thank you for meeting me."

"Please, join me." He held out his hand to the chair opposite his, and Andrea took a seat. "Shall we order first?"

Andrea took a quick glance at the menu. The server, a lovely young woman with a bright smile and a long brown ponytail, appeared a few moments later, and Andrea ordered the seafood linguine and a sparkling water. Ian made his own selection and handed their menus to the woman before folding his hands on the table.

"I feel I should apologize for yesterday. I certainly didn't know you would be with James or I wouldn't have surprised him."

Very reserved. Very British. It continually threw her to hear the London-accented voice from a man who so strongly resembled James. "There's no need to apologize. I understand it must be difficult to do business with family at times."

He bowed his head. "You are quite gracious. So tell me, Andrea, what do you think about the hotel?"

"It has great potential." She retrieved the folder from her bag and pushed it across the table to Ian. "I've put together some details on our company and our capabilities. You can look it over at your leisure. I had been under the impression you were interested in a turnkey consultancy package, but I think you would be fine if we just looked at the marketing side."

Ian flipped the folder open, but she could tell he wasn't really seeing the contents. "To be frank, Andrea, I didn't know exactly what we needed. Jamie has not been forthcoming with details on the progress of the hotel."

Understanding dawned. "You wanted an outsider to assess it."

He gave a single nod. "Things have been … strained … between Jamie and me. It's not that I distrust my brother, but it's hard to know if he's passing on all the details. I'm sorry. I really don't mean to air family issues to a stranger."

"You need my professional opinion to know whether he's being truthful. I understand." She did understand, though it unsettled her to be talking about James behind his back. He was her client, after all. He owned the majority share in the property, even if he wasn't willing to sign off on anything without Ian's approval.

"I can assure you," she said, "James has matters well in hand. I've looked over the blueprints, and while there are a few items I think should be checked with a structural engineer, they look sound. He looks to have accounted for the wiring and plumbing for the upgrades. The house is being modernized to offer all the conveniences a contemporary traveler would expect, but it keeps to the traditional footprint. I can assure you, in a property of this age, it's a smart move."

"That's a relief," Ian said. "Thank you."

"The one thing I have recommended is that you add a bar." She retrieved her sketch and handed it to him. "This is one idea of what it might look like." She quickly outlined her reasoning as she had to James, and Ian nodded thoughtfully.

"I like the idea. It makes sense." He set the drawing down. "I'll discuss it with Jamie. At least I'll attempt to." A flicker of pain crossed his face. Obviously the falling-out bothered Ian far more than it did James, or maybe James was just more practiced at hiding it.

"One thing we might be able to assist with is project management. If communication is a problem, it could help to have someone neutral manage the flow of information for you."

"Like a construction counselor?" Ian said with a hint of a smile.

"Something like that, yes." Andrea smiled back. "It might help, considering neither of you are on site for more than, what, a week a month?"

"This is the first time I've been back in over a year," Ian admitted.

So there was some truth to James's accusation that it took a wake to get Ian to Scotland. No wonder he had seemed so shocked to see his brother standing in their aunt's living room.

Andrea hesitated, wondering how to best approach the topic. The last thing she wanted was to get in the middle of a sibling dispute, at least more than she already had. "If I may ... I don't think you need to worry about how your brother is managing the hotel construction. I really don't know him, but he seems to respect your opinion too much to do anything you'd find objectionable."

"Oh, I know that." Ian sighed. "He'd never purposely do anything to harm family, speaking terms or not. That's not what I'm concerned about. He's just been so erratic the last couple of years."

Unease stirred in the pit of her stomach. She didn't want to know any more, but she couldn't help herself. "How so?"

"I really shouldn't burden you with this. It's just ... this is not the Jamie I remember."

"Why do you say that?" Her heart beat a little too fast now, and she hoped she didn't seem too interested in the answer.

"First, our father died. He took it hard. Jamie was far closer to him than I was. Not long afterward, Jamie broke off his engagement."

Andrea sat very still, shocked by the words. "Oh."

His eyebrows drew together in a frown. "You didn't know?"

"About your father?"

"No, about his fiancée."

Andrea shook her head. "No. I don't keep up with celebrity gossip."

"You do know he was engaged to Cassandra Sinclair?"

"The actress?"

Ian nodded solemnly. "They were supposed to be married two years ago this June, but all of a sudden, he broke it off. He hasn't been the same since."

This was territory definitely not meant to be covered with a business colleague, but Ian seemed to need to talk about it as much as she wanted to know. "Why do you say that?"

"We were in the middle of negotiating space for a restaurant in Inverness. Then he just changed his mind. Said it wasn't what he was meant to do right now. Next thing I know, he's talking about renovating the hotel, opening a dining room. I guess it was something he and Dad had talked about years ago, but they hadn't gotten around to the details yet."

"That's understandable. I'm sure he feels the need to reconnect with your father after losing him that way."

"Right." Ian nodded, then leaned forward. "Just be careful. My brother is charming. Flirtatious. He tends to lead women on."

Andrea couldn't repress her disbelieving laugh. "You're warning me off from getting involved with James?"

"I know. It's cliché of me." Ian shifted uncomfortably. "You seem like a nice woman, and I know you're very professional. You probably deal with this sort of thing all the time."

"More than you'd think," Andrea said. "You don't have to be concerned. I'm here to finish this proposal, and then I'm on my way back to New York. I'll be handling the project from there, coordinating with our team in London. Believe me, I've dealt with men much more insistent than your brother."

But not nearly as appealing.

Ian wasn't telling her anything she hadn't thought on her own. Yet the warning still annoyed her. She remembered how James had made her stand and take in the landscape, free from distractions, as if it were important to him that she slow down long enough to truly experience his home. He had been trying to share something with her. That didn't match the cavalier picture Ian painted of him. It didn't even match the image he projected himself.

"I've offended you," Ian said quickly. "I apologize. I didn't mean to imply you couldn't handle yourself."

"No, I'm not offended. I appreciate your concern." The server returned with their sparkling water, and she nodded her thanks as the woman poured. She took a long drink, then asked, "Would it be out of line to ask how you fit into James's business? He introduced you as his COO."

Ian seemed relieved at the change of subject. "It's not out of line at all. I was a solicitor for six years. When Jamie incorporated the business, he asked me if I would act as general counsel. As the company grew, it made sense for me to take a more active role. You can probably tell Jamie is more of an ideas man than the detail type."

Andrea had thought James coordinated the details of his business rather well, but she just nodded. "So you've been involved from the beginning? Since the Hart and the Hound opened?"

"Yes. After that became such a success, he wrote his first cookbook. Then the other restaurants in London, the television program … It wasn't long before it was a full-time job. I left my law firm and came to work for Jamie's company."

"That must be difficult, working for your younger brother."

Ian sipped his own water and studied her with an amused expression disconcertingly like his brother's. "Are you probing my psyche now, Andrea?"

She cleared her throat, caught. "I'm just trying to understand the situation with you two. You have to admit, most men would have parted ways when things got … complicated."

"Complicated. You could say that." Ian folded his hands on the table and looked her directly in the eye. "I can assure you the situation with Jamie and me will not affect the success of this venture."

Andrea nodded, understanding what Ian would not say aloud. Their family issues were none of her business, and his tone said in no uncertain terms the topic was closed.

Ian was too polite to allow Andrea to wait alone for James after lunch, so they drank coffee on one of the leather sofas in the hotel's common area, carefully keeping to inconsequential topics. She managed to tease out a little of his history, enough to learn Ian possessed an MBA from Judge Business School at Cambridge, and he had given up an impressive competitive rowing career to pursue his law degree. Any family should be proud to have such an accomplished son. Yet she got the distinct impression James's gregarious nature and public acclaim outshone the accomplishments of his reserved older brother.

It was a situation ripe for conflict, but it didn't explain the reason behind their falling-out, especially when James seemed to be the one holding the grudge.

Ian rose with Andrea when the ugly green wagon pulled into the parking lot. He shook her hand firmly. "I appreciate you meeting with me. Jamie and I will review your proposal as soon as you can have it to us."

"I should be finished tonight. Should I email it?"

"I'd appreciate it. I'll look it over this evening."

"Good. Thank you again, Ian."

Andrea strode toward the front entrance, releasing her breath in a quiet whoosh. She was past her biggest hurdle now. Ian seemed pleased with her capabilities, and assuming the price was right, there should be no reason she couldn't close this deal by the time she left for the airport tomorrow. She just needed to get through one more evening with the charming and insistent younger brother without doing anything stupid.

"How did it go?" James asked brightly as she approached. He opened the car door for her as usual.

She waited until he climbed into the driver's seat before answering. "Very well. He liked the idea of the bar. I told him I'd have the proposal done this evening for you two to look at."

"So I take it more sightseeing is out of the question?"

"Unfortunately." She had to keep things professional from here on out, and more time alone with him would make that difficult. "It will take me all afternoon to put together my recommendations. And I did promise Emmy a duet tonight, so I should get started."

"Fair enough. Back to the hotel we go, then."

James backed out of the parking lot and turned onto the main road. "What time did you say your flight was tomorrow?"

"Eleven. What time should we be there?"

"Half past nine will be fine. We should leave about six."

Andrea nodded uncomfortably. Something had changed in the last two hours, but she was hard-pressed to say what. For someone who was always completely at ease, James was suddenly acting awkward with her.

It's for the best. Maybe he realizes he crossed a line. Maybe he realizes it's pointless to pursue me when I'm leaving tomorrow.

Since when was he pursuing her? So far he had flirted, but he hadn't made any effort to push it further than that. She should be pleased. So why did the thought bring on a pang of disappointment?

James said little on the drive back to the hotel. When they got out of the car to go their separate directions, he simply said, "I have to head up to the house later to start supper. Shall I come get you when I go?"

"Please." She smiled uncertainly, hesitated, then headed for her cottage, crunching unsteadily through the gravel lot.

She intended to buckle down as soon as they returned, but instead she wandered through her cottage, straightening the duvet on the bed, pushing in the kitchen chair, buttoning the placket of her gray suit where it hung in the wardrobe.

"Stop procrastinating." She forced herself to sit in front of her computer, but that only earned her several long minutes staring at the blank screen. "Just finish it already. Then you can leave and stop worrying about all this nonsense."

Except she wasn't so sure she wanted to leave.

She groaned and massaged the tense muscles in her shoulders. That was ridiculous. She had traveled all over the world, and never once had she been reluctant to go home. Her beautifully furnished apartment waited for her, and this time she had almost a full week until she had to leave on another trip. There would be jogging in Central Park and lazy evenings with old movies and huge bowls of popcorn. It wasn't Tahiti, of course, but it was still downtime.

Andrea forced her mind back to the screen. Fortunately this proposal was an easy one. The needs of the MacDonald brothers were straightforward: project management, a full marketing plan, ongoing metrics. At one time, she would have been the one writing up the marketing plan, but this proposal needed just enough detail to convey the value her company could lend to the project. Then Andrea would pass it on to the various teams who would be involved in the actual implementation, and she would follow up on a weekly basis to make sure the timeline was being met and the client was still pleased with their work.

She pressed her fingertips to her temples and forced herself to organize her thoughts. Then she started typing.

She managed to keep her mind on her work this time, and she didn't notice the changing color of the light from bright white to dusky orange until she had to flick on the desk lamp.

"Good," she said at last. She read the document over with a satisfied nod. It was based on her boilerplate proposal, but she included enough specific details to make it relevant to the project. Ian would be impressed. She didn't think James would care about the presentation as long as it hit the highlights.

The knock at the door startled her from her thoughts, and she glanced at the clock. Six already? She saved her file and rushed to the door, where James waited. "Give me just a minute to email this to you."

She attached the file to the message and quickly typed in both Ian's and James's email addresses. The cursor hovered over the "send" button for a moment before she forced herself to press it. Then she closed her laptop with a decisive click.

Project complete, she thought as she grabbed her purse from her bed. Once the MacDonald brothers had inked their signatures on the bottom, she could head back to New York, away from the ridiculous feelings James and his island stirred up inside her.

Chapter Thirteen

Emmy claimed Andrea as soon as she walked in the door, just as she had done that morning. The dolls had been put away, but an enormous tub of crayons and a drawing pad the size of the coffee table had taken their place. "Come draw with me, Andrea!"

"Emmy, Andrea doesn't want to sit on the floor with you in her nice clothes again." Serena sat on the sofa in front of the television while Max gummed a teething ring on the rug between her feet.

"I don't mind." Andrea's suit was already wrinkled anyway. "I have nieces and nephews. I spend most of my time on the floor at my sister Becky's house."

"Here, use this one." Emmy thrust a red crayon into Andrea's hand and shoved a piece of paper at her. "I'm drawing mermaids, but you can draw whatever you want."

"That's very kind of you," Andrea said wryly.

Serena laughed. "You're a good sport. Jamie usually tries to divert her to paper airplanes or something less girly."

"I heard that," James called from the kitchen. Serena grinned in his direction.

Andrea doodled on the paper. "So you live in Inverness, Serena?"

"Yes. Jamie's so busy, I try to visit Skye when I know he'll have some free time."

Andrea felt a pang of guilt for intruding on what should have been a family week together. "How long will you stay?"

"Just through the weekend. Emmy has to be back for the start of summer term on Monday."

"And what do you do?"

"This." Max began to whimper, and Serena hoisted him into her lap before it could turn into a full-blown wail. "Eventually I may go back to work, but right now it's more important to be available for Max and Emmy. As much as I swore I'd never be a trust-fund cliché."

Trust fund? Andrea blinked a couple of times, and Serena clapped a hand over her mouth, reddening.

"Oh, forgive me. That was completely tasteless. It's just become a joke among the three of us. Mum's family is absurdly wealthy, and they're baffled as to why we'd want to make our own way in the world."

Serena jiggled Max on her knee with a rueful smile. "Let's face it. Mum gave us trust funds. Dad gave us stubborn Scottish pride. Until Edward died, you can guess which won out."

"I can understand wanting to make your own way in the world." Andrea hadn't asked anything from anyone, even in the days she'd shared a two-hundred-square-foot Manhattan apartment with two other girls, surviving on packaged ramen noodles. Still, it cast James's comments in an entirely different light. Was that how he'd pegged her so easily as a small-town girl? She'd thought his assessment of her was meant to be complimentary, but now she wasn't so sure.

"What about you, Andrea? Do you enjoy what you do?"

Andrea paused, surprised. People usually commented on the glamorous hotels and exotic locales. Few ever asked her what she thought about the job itself.

"For the most part," she said finally. "I love walking into a property for the first time. No matter how run-down or depressing it looks, it holds such potential. It's the best feeling to come back months or years later and see what it's become. I just don't enjoy waking up in the middle of the night and not knowing where I am, or walking into an airport and not being able to remember where I'm going next."

"That would drive me mad," Serena said. "I enjoy visiting Jamie and Ian, but I'm always eager to get back home."

Emmy relented and handed over a blue crayon, so Andrea began to outline her scribbled flowers. Only then did she notice the delicious smell wafting from the kitchen. "What is he making?"

"No idea, but it hardly matters," Serena said. "Everything he makes is stellar. Lots of people can cook, but Jamie's something special."

"I'm beginning to see that," Andrea said slowly.

Serena gave her a knowing look. "I imagine you are."

Andrea looked away before she could blush at the implication. Were her feelings that obvious? And here she thought she had done such a good job of hiding them, at least from the rest of James's family.

Emmy abandoned the crayons and paper, and Andrea took it as a sign that she was allowed up off the floor. She settled herself on the sofa next to Serena and turned her attention to the television program. After a few moments of complete bafflement, she decided she'd made the right decision by not owning a TV and wandered into the kitchen.

James stirred something in a large skillet on the range, a frilly pink apron wrapped around his waist.

Andrea stifled a smile. "Pink's your color."

He threw her a grin over his shoulder. "There's a plain one around here somewhere, but I suspect Serena of hiding it to make me look like a fool."

Andrea sidled over to the stove, glad his usual good mood had returned. "What's this?"

"Pork medallions in Montmorency cherry sauce. I improvised." He scooped some sauce from the pan with a spoon and held it out to her for a taste.

The flavor of cherries, at once sweet and sour, burst on her tongue, balanced with other rich and tangy flavors. Balsamic vinegar, maybe, and a touch of wine. "If that's what you call improvisation, you should give up planning completely."

"Not too tart for you?"

"Nope, it's perfect. Can I do something?"

He sent her a curious glance. "You really don't like to be idle, do you?"

"Guilty as charged. What do you need?"

"There's a bottle of Sémillion chilling in the refrigerator if you'd like to pour. This is almost ready."

Andrea retrieved the wine from the refrigerator and took the corkscrew from the drawer where she had seen him stash it the night before.

"I've been thinking," James said. "You should stay."

"What?" Andrea turned and almost bumped into him where he stood only inches behind her. She backed up until she was pressed into the cabinets. "Stay where?"

"Stay here on Skye for the week." He leaned forward and spoke softly into her ear. "I promise you will have a good time."

Despite herself, she shivered at his proximity. She braced her hands on the counter behind her. "I just came here to give you my professional expertise, Mr. MacDonald."

He laughed softly at her retreat to formality and backed off a step. "I know you did. Tell me something, though. If you leave here tomorrow, can you still go to Tahiti?"

"No," she said. "I had to cancel my reservations."

"And is there hope of rescheduling anytime soon?"

If only she could. She'd gone to so much trouble to ensure her vacation, only to have it called off at a moment's notice. Now she was booked solid for the next three months. "Probably not."

"What's your office number in New York?" James picked up the cordless phone on the kitchen counter.

Andrea blinked in confusion, but she gave it to him, and he dialed quickly. "James MacDonald for Michael Halloran."

He waited silently for the transfer. "Mr. Halloran, good morning. No, not at all. Ms. Sullivan is everything I expected." The smile he gave her made her flush to her toes. "In fact, she's been so insightful, I'm wondering if I can borrow her for a few more days. I'd like to get her professional opinion on some other matters. Friday at least." He nodded and winked at her. "No, I'm sure it will be a most productive week." He passed the phone to her. "He'd like to speak with you."

Andrea took the phone, wanting to scowl at him, but her heart was beating too fast for her to do anything other than concentrate on steadying her voice. "Hello, Michael."

"How's it going, Andrea? Can you close this one?"

"Of course. It's just … a little more complex than I expected." She frowned when James laughed silently beside her, his eyes dancing. "How long will it take you to wrap it up?"

"Until Friday, I think. I'll be back in the office on Monday."

"Close this one, Andrea. You know what's at stake for you."

"Of course. I will. Talk to you soon."

Andrea hung up and handed the phone back pointedly. "I don't know what you expect that to accomplish."

"I just bought you the rest of the week out of the office. I know it's not a tropical vacation involving sun and white-sand beaches, but you have to admit, I am a very good tour guide."

"Do I have any choice?" she asked. "You've practically ensured I can't leave without losing my job."

He actually looked surprised. "Of course you have a choice. We're going to hire your firm regardless. That was never in question."

"Then why do you want me to stay?"

He leaned close again. "Because I want you to fall in love."

"Excuse me?" she squeaked.

He straightened, holding the stack of plates he'd been reaching for behind her. "With Scotland. You're halfway there already; you just need a little push. Could you take the wine glasses to the table?"

Andrea gathered the glasses silently and carried them to the dining room, her jaw clenched. He was toying with her. The larger part of her—the part that had clawed her way to this position through hard work and without relying on her feminine wiles—resented it to the bone.

It was the part of her that didn't, the part that thrilled to the promise in his voice, that worried her.

Chapter Fourteen

James smiled to himself as he began plating their supper. First a drizzle of his balsamic reduction, followed by a mound of wild rice, then an artful swirl of pork medallions beneath the cherry sauce. Andrea bustled around the kitchen, trying to be casual, but he could feel both nervousness and resentment boil off her like steam from a kettle. She might pretend he had forced her into staying, but she had agreed to it of her own free will. Or at least she hadn't refused.

If he were to be honest, his own pulse wasn't feeling entirely steady at the moment, though he didn't know if it was his fear she would say no or the almost irresistible desire to kiss her every time she was within arm's reach. He might have intended to lure her out from behind her stolid professionalism, but standing that close had sent his imagination into overdrive. She was not the only one ensnared by the force of attraction between them.

For the first time since he conceived the idea this afternoon, he wondered if he was making a mistake.

He finished plating the meal, including a smaller portion for Emmy, with his mind only half on his work. So she had agreed, more or less. Now he just had to make sure she didn't regret her decision.

He went to lift the plates and remembered the apron. He snatched it off and tossed it on the countertop, stifling a groan. Had he actually just tried to play seductive while wearing pink ruffles? He was lucky she hadn't laughed him out of the room.

Andrea barely looked up when he set the plate in front of her, though she murmured polite thanks. When they were all seated, Muriel bowed her head and thanked the Lord for the food, the gathering, and their guest.

"It's a shame you're leaving tomorrow," Muriel said. "You've scarcely gotten the chance to see Skye."

"Actually, James has convinced me I'd be remiss in my research if I didn't stay a little longer." Andrea's eyes met his, the challenge in them clear.

"Did he now?" Muriel said calmly. "Well, you couldn't ask for a better guide. He's jogged or hiked almost every inch of Skye at some point or another. But you won't go far in your fancy clothes."

"I thought we might go to Fort William tomorrow," James said to Andrea. "Buy you some suitable things."

"Can I go?" Emmy asked. She looked confused at the laughter that rang out around the table in reply.

"I think they want to do grown-up stuff," Serena said in a stage whisper.

James smiled as two spots of pink rose to Andrea's cheeks. "You'll like Fort William," he said. "If we're lucky, we might see some porpoise in the loch."

"Really?" Andrea said. "I've never seen a porpoise before."

"Even in Tahiti?"

"This would have been my first time," she admitted. "The closest I usually get to water is the Hudson River. I thought I should expand my horizons a bit."

"I feel even worse, now, that we ruined your trip," James said. "We'll have to make this week special."

Her eyebrows lifted, and she studied him like she didn't quite believe he was serious. Then she smiled—a true smile, not the polished, rehearsed one. It knocked the breath from him.

"Did you decide what we're going to play?" Emmy asked suddenly.

Bless her for her timing. Everyone's attention turned back to the little girl, giving James a moment to compose his thoughts and force air back into his lungs.

"I think we should keep our song a secret, don't you?" Andrea said to Emmy. "So everyone will be surprised?"

"Good idea." Emmy nodded seriously.

Serena and Muriel volunteered to clear the table at the end of the meal, and Andrea followed Emmy to the piano. James leaned on the door frame and watched them perch on the bench, side by side.

"I'm going to teach you the melody, okay?" Andrea demonstrated a simple tune and then watched as Emmy played it several times. "Good. Now I'll bring in the harmony. We'll practice a little so we can show off when they all come back."

By the time Serena and Muriel returned from the kitchen, they had worked out the details enough to make a respectable duet. James led them in a loud round of applause, and Emmy grinned broadly as she bounced up off the bench.

"You're a natural," Andrea said. "Keep with it. You'll be playing the Royal Albert Hall before you know it."

"Thanks, Andrea," Emmy said and threw her arms around her neck.

Expressions shifted over Andrea's face—surprise, dismay, that fleeting pain he'd already noticed—before she could manage to return the embrace. "You're welcome. Keep practicing, all right?"

"Will you play something for us?" James asked.

"I couldn't possibly—"

"Oh, please do!" Serena exclaimed. "It's been ages since anyone but Auntie has played."

"There's always been music in the house," James finished for her. "Our father taught pipes and fiddle. Unfortunately none of us inherited his talent."

"I'm sure that's not true," Andrea said. "Anyone can play, given enough practice."

"Then you'll play for us?" James said. "Trust me, if you miss a note or two, we won't know the difference."

Andrea looked reluctant, but he could feel the draw the piano had for her. "I suppose. I'll play something you all might know."

Andrea took a deep breath and laid her hands lightly on the keys. James nodded silently when he recognized the piece from the first notes, Debussy's "Claire de Lune." It was a long step from his usual rock or jazz, but this was one of the few classical pieces he knew and loved. He had always thought it a simple piece, but as Andrea moved from the quiet chords of the initial measures into rolling, sweeping arpeggios, he realized how wrong he'd been, just as he realized how far short she'd sold her ability.

The delicacy of her playing was like nothing he'd ever heard, turning even the slightly tinny sound of the old piano into something ethereal and beautiful. He caught his sister's gaze across the room and saw his surprise echoed in her face. This was not the playing of a casual musician, but a gifted, deeply dedicated pianist. A slight smile came to Andrea's lips and her eyes closed halfway, an expression of peace and wholeness he had seen once before as she looked out onto the waters of Skye. It looked as though she interpreted every note with her body, her hands gliding gracefully over the keys. He'd never noticed how much the music felt like the ebb and flow of the tide, the notes floating and rolling like waves, until he saw her sway with the rhythm of the melody.

Her playing spoke louder than anything she could have said. This meant something to her, and she had chosen to share it with them.

The last notes faded into silence, and his family remained quiet, as reluctant as he to fracture the spell. Muriel broke it first, wiping dampness from her eyes with the back of her hand. "That was beautiful, my dear. You are one talented young lady."

Andrea opened her eyes in shock, and the peaceful expression faded into dismay, as if she had forgotten their presence. She rose from the bench abruptly. Her voice trembled when she whispered, "I need a glass of water. Will you excuse me?"

James exchanged a confused glance with his family as she strode unsteadily from the room. He followed her into the kitchen, where she was filling a glass from the tap. She lifted it to her lips with a shaking hand.

"Are you all right?" James asked quietly, stopping a safe distance away.

She looked up, startled again by his presence, and forced a smile. "Of course."

"This wasn't just something you picked up, was it?"

A smile flickered over her face. "Not quite."

"Do you want to tell me about it?"

"No, not really." She took a long drink of her water and set the glass down on the countertop with a clink. "I'm tired. Do you think we could go back now?"

The tremor in her voice told him she was barely holding onto her composure. He should just retrieve her coat and escort her out, let her deal with whatever memories lay connected with her astounding talent. He was never one to do the smart thing, though.

Instead he closed the space and turned her to face him. She jerked in surprise at his touch, but she didn't try to pull away as his fingers smoothed her collarbones, and then brushed soothingly down her shoulders. Her eyes drifted closed as his fingers gently kneaded the knots in her shoulders, and she let out a long sigh.

"Better?"

"Better," she whispered, swaying toward him. It would be so easy to close the gap between them, take her fully in his arms, see where things went from there. Before he could turn the thought into action, her eyes snapped open, and she stiffened beneath his hands.

James stepped back. "Do you still want to go?"

"If you don't mind."

"I'll get your coat." James left her in the kitchen and ducked back into the living room, where Serena and Muriel waited with Emmy, their expressions concerned.

He shook his head at their unspoken question. He didn't under-stand what was behind her reaction any better than they did. "I'm going to take her back down to the cottages. There's a bowl of fruit in the refrigerator for dessert."

"Thanks, Jamie," Serena said.

James kissed his sister and Emmy, but when he came to Muriel, his aunt gripped the back of his neck hard and whispered in his ear, "She's fragile, that one. Handle her with care, Jamie."

He wanted to say he wasn't handling her in any fashion, but he couldn't bring himself to voice the flippant words. He just nodded, retrieved Andrea's coat from where it was draped over the arm of the sofa, and returned to the kitchen to help her put it on.

On the way out, Andrea smiled brightly and thanked Muriel for her hospitality, but for once, James could see cracks in her hard, pol-ished shell. They crunched back to the Subaru in silence, enveloped by the misty night air. Once they were safely ensconced in the car and headed back down the drive, she said in a small voice, "I'm sorry. I didn't think it would affect me that way."

"You're entitled to have feelings," he said, though it really wasn't what he wanted to say. How did such a talented pianist find herself working as a hospitality consultant? How did a woman who obvi-ously felt things deeply manage to live such a staid, ordinary life? He sensed she couldn't, or wouldn't, address the questions, so he changed the subject instead. "I thought we could leave for Fort William right after breakfast tomorrow. Make a day of it. There's plenty to see."

"That sounds great. What time should I be ready to go up to the house?"

"Seven, if that suits?"

"Seven is fine."

Their headlights splashed against the whitewashed stone of the hotel as he pulled into the lot. He parked and killed the engine and lights, plunging them into darkness. He opened her door wordlessly and escorted her to the cottage, where he hesitated. He could see the emotions tumbling around behind her eyes when she turned to face him, but he couldn't pinpoint whether the source was panic or something else.

"I know you want to ask," she said.

He reached out and tucked a stray piece of hair behind her ear. The frigid strands released the subtle scent of her perfume into the air, drawing him closer. He trailed his fingers down the side of her face and felt her sudden sharp intake of breath. When his eyes drifted to her lips, parted in surprise, all he wanted to do was find out if they were as soft as they looked, if she tasted as sweet as she always smelled.

He couldn't do it. She was vulnerable tonight, and he wouldn't take advantage of that. If she kissed him, it should be because she wanted to, not because she didn't have the presence of mind to refuse.

He dropped his hand. "You'll tell me when you're ready. Good night, Andrea."

"Good night." She slipped into the room and closed the door behind her. The deadbolt slid home on the other side with a heavy clunk.

He stared at the bright red door for the space of a heartbeat and headed for his own cottage before he could change his mind.

She wasn't what he needed right now. Cassandra had been that dangerous combination of fragility and strength as well. She'd taught him that heartache came in the form of beautiful women whose vulnerability roused his protective instincts.

But the comparison was hardly fair to Andrea. Cassandra had fooled him into believing her innocence and openness were real, when it turned out to be a role she played when it suited her. Their engagement had been a boost to her career: a publicity ploy, a diversion while she secretly carried on with her then-married costar.

Andrea, on the other hand, asked for no help. Wanted no help. She hid her thoughts deep and masked her vulnerability well. She'd made her opinion of his reputation clear, and yet tonight she'd actually shown him a measure of trust.

He couldn't break that trust. The last thing he wanted to do was turn what was supposed to be a relaxing week into an experience she'd regret. How in the world did he manage to get himself into these situations? He'd meant to have a little innocent fun, but he hadn't counted on a concert pianist who almost fell apart when she performed.

He toed off his shoes and sank into the chair in front of the television, flicking it on with the remote. He reached for the weathered, leather-bound Bible on the table beside him and set it in his lap, but he didn't open it. He knew the inside well, its pages worn, dog-eared, and marked by a kaleidoscope of colored Biro pens. Duncan MacDonald may never have set foot inside a church other than the day he married James's mother, but he lived by the words in this book. Just holding it brought back an ache two years had done nothing to abate.

His dad should be here right now. He would know what to do. If James had taken his father's last advice, he might have avoided the whole mess with Cassandra in the first place.

The elder MacDonald would have liked Andrea, though. Her musical talent alone would have endeared her to the man who'd taught cèilidh pipe and fiddle to children on the island for almost thirty years. Besides, his father had as much of a weakness for beautiful women as James did.

"I wish you were here," he said aloud, smoothing the cover of the Bible. "You'd know exactly how I should proceed."

But he already knew what to do. His father's answer had usually been one of two things: "Wait on the Lord," or "Treat others as you wish to be treated."

James wasn't all that skilled at waiting, but he did know how Andrea wanted to be treated. She was in desperate need of rest, but not solitude. Something in her craved a connection or she wouldn't have submitted to his touch so easily. She'd allowed him a brief glimpse at the wounds behind her capable exterior, and the last thing he wanted to do was give her a reason to retreat behind the shell.

Chapter Fifteen

Andrea stepped out of her shoes and tossed her coat onto the nearest chair, thoroughly unsettled. It had been a night of terrible decisions. First she had agreed to stay in Skye with James for the rest of the week, for no other reason than he had asked her to. Then she'd played the piano for him and his family, even though she'd known the feelings it would stir up. She certainly hadn't rebuffed his touch like she should have. Either time. As it was, the memory of his hands on her shoulders—first comforting, then unsettling—sent a current of electricity straight down her spine. Had she given him the slightest indication she would have welcomed it, he would have kissed her good night.

She was fairly certain she wouldn't have resisted.

"You're losing it, Andrea," she murmured. She unzipped her skirt and stepped out of it, trading the businesslike wool for the comforting flannel of her pajamas. What was she thinking? She was fine on her own. She didn't need a man. Didn't want a man. Especially not one who moved through the female population like a tornado, leaving devastation in his wake.

Andrea sighed and reached for her cell phone before she remembered there was no signal at the hotel. She picked up the room phone and dialed her sister's number. She didn't wait for Becky to talk after she picked up.

"How much of an idiot am I really?"

"Uh, hello to you too, Andy. What did I miss?"

"I'm changing my return flight to Saturday."

Silence stretched for several seconds. When Becky spoke, Andrea could hear the smile in her voice. "That's interesting."

"It's stupid is what it is. I can't afford to spend the week sightseeing in Scotland when I should be home working." Andrea dropped onto the bed and drew her legs up beneath her.

"You already planned to go to Tahiti. I don't see the problem. Unless of course the scenery you're staying for isn't of the landscape variety."

Andrea smoothed her hair back fitfully. "He's … I don't know …"

"Gorgeous?" Becky suggested. "Talented? Charming? Gorgeous?"

"You said *gorgeous* twice."

"Well, it bears repeating, considering who we're talking about."

"You're finding this way too amusing."

Becky laughed. "Of course I am. I never thought there would be a guy who could get under your skin. Really. It's been a long time coming."

"He's not under my skin. It's just …"

"Yeah, that was convincing. Did he kiss you?"

Andrea threw herself back against the pillows. "No! Of course not … Not yet." She had to pry the last part out.

"Well, get on with it, then. You've only got three full days left. I wouldn't waste them if I were you. Call me when you get around to it. I want details. I bet he's a fantastic kisser."

"You're hopeless." Andrea pressed her fingertips to her temples. "Thanks for being absolutely no help."

Becky paused for another long moment. "Andy, I know you've spent the last eight years pushing everyone away. But not every man is like Logan. What's the worst that could happen if you let someone in just a little bit?"

"You know what could happen," Andrea said darkly. "You were there. Besides, a man who lives three thousand miles away on a different continent is hardly relationship material."

"You never know what God has in mind for your life. Maybe there was a reason you got sent to Scotland at the last minute."

"I gave up on the 'God's plan' thing years ago, Becks. If there was a purpose in that whole sordid mess with Logan, I can't imagine what it might be."

"It made you who you are today. A successful, focused, talented woman with a lot to offer. I wish you would remember there's more to you than your career."

Unexpectedly, tears pricked Andrea's eyes. She wiped them away before they could take up permanent residence and swallowed down the lump in her throat. "I love you, Becks."

"I love you too. Just try, sweetie. If you think he's trustworthy, let him in a little. If it makes you feel better, it's only three days. It's like … relationship training wheels. If everything goes south, you've got a plane ticket home on Saturday."

"You're completely right, of course." Andrea sighed. "Thanks."

"Anytime. Now go have some fun."

Andrea hung up the phone. Her sister was right. It was silly to get all worked up over this. After all, James had done nothing but flirt and promise her a better time than she'd have back in her office in New York. That couldn't be too difficult, could it? She was in a beautiful place with a handsome man who cooked spectacular meals. If she couldn't see that as a dream vacation, she possessed very little imagination.

Unfortunately she had no shortage of that trait tonight. When she finally settled into bed and closed her eyes, all she could think about was his fingers on her cheek and what might have happened had he not, at the last minute, turned away.

Andrea awoke the next morning with a flutter in her stomach. For a moment, she lay ensconced in the fluffy duvet, trying to place the feeling.

Anticipation.

How long had it been since she had awakened feeling anything other than dread about the day before her? It had been years, maybe decades, since she hadn't had to struggle against the heavy weight of anxiety just to get out of bed.

She dressed in the most casual outfit she could assemble from her business wardrobe, though the lipstick-red Jimmy Choos had to make a comeback. She used a light hand on the makeup and let her hair dry into natural waves in the absence of a hair dryer.

James knocked promptly at seven. She opened the door, and her heart tripped. In jeans, a fitted black turtleneck, and a black leather jacket, he epitomized the words *effortlessly handsome*. Okay, maybe not effortless. The cut of the jacket definitely suggested a certain London designer's spring line. She had to admit, the man knew how to dress.

"What's wrong?" he asked, glancing down at himself. "Did I get toothpaste on myself or something?"

"No," she said slowly. "I was just thinking how nice you look."

He actually looked embarrassed by the compliment. "So do you. Except those shoes aren't made for walking."

"I know, but all my trousers are hemmed for heels. I could hardly wear running shoes. Besides, how can I turn down the justification to shop?"

"Women." He threw the word back with a twinkle in his eye as they walked toward the car.

"Oh, don't think I don't recognize that designer jacket you're wearing. You don't know the meaning of the words *off the rack*."

James laughed and held the door open as she climbed into the car. "I don't suppose the fact the designer's a friend of mine makes it any better?"

"No, actually, that's even worse."

"Just don't tell my family, then. I'd never live it down."

Their arrival at Muriel's house was a repeat of the day before. Emmy claimed Andrea immediately, this time to mold play dough, while Serena gulped down an enormous mug of coffee and fed Max cereal at the low table. James immediately disappeared into the kitchen.

When Andrea didn't smell bacon, she assumed she would be saved from another massive breakfast. That notion fled when he called them to the table to a platter of eggs Benedict, complete with the richest, creamiest sauce she'd ever tasted.

"Sinful," Andrea said. "The road to hell is definitely paved with hollandaise."

Serena laughed. "Now you see the real reason we visit Skye. It's good I don't live here, though. I'd weigh twenty stone by Christmas."

After breakfast, Andrea attempted to clear the plates, but Serena waved her off. "No, you two get going. It's almost two hours to Fort William."

James detached his car keys from his key ring and set them on the sideboard. "I'm going to leave the keys to the Subaru in case you need it. Don't hold dinner for us."

Andrea frowned at James as he led her out the front door and around to the garage. The door rolled up to reveal a silver Audi sports sedan. She crossed her arms over her chest and looked pointedly between James and the sleek luxury car.

He shrugged. "I never said I only owned one car. I promise you, it's much more comfortable than the Subaru."

Andrea let herself smile as she slid into the front passenger seat, where she was immediately enveloped by the masculine scent of leather and his cologne. When James climbed in beside her, she said, "All this big talk, and yet you consciously try *not* to impress a woman."

"Maybe I don't want a woman who needs to be impressed by an expensive car."

"So the Green Monster is a test?"

"I like that. The Green Monster." James backed out of the garage and turned the car down the pitted drive. "It's not a test, though you would have passed. You don't seem hung up on material things, despite the absurdly expensive shoes."

"Like I told you before, I'm just a small-town girl at heart, regardless of my shoe collection."

"Andrea, my dear, you aren't *just* anything."

For once, he wasn't teasing. He actually sounded reproachful. She shook off a flutter of nervousness and quickly changed the subject. "Was moving to London a huge shock after growing up on Skye?"

"I'd gone to school in Edinburgh, and we visited our mother in London every summer. But, yes, it was still a shock."

"Why did you stay so long there?"

"Time passes and you barely notice. Before I knew it, it had been ten years. Opening the restaurants in Scotland was almost an excuse to come back home."

"Nice that you have that luxury," Andrea said wryly. "Most people can't just decide to expand their business because they're homesick."

"My success is a blessing. It was unexpected. I suppose my kind of cooking connected with the things people loved: traditions, home, family. I still get letters telling me my recipes remind me of their grandmothers' cooking. Only better, of course."

"As long as you're humble about it."

He laughed. "I do my best."

Andrea had met all sorts of men in her business travels. Some truly were humble, appreciative of their success. Most thought wealth and status gave them the right to do whatever they wanted. She'd had to extricate herself from the grasp of entitled, inebriated clients more than once, walking the tightrope between keeping a professional distance and maintaining their good graces.

It was exactly what she had been doing in London with James.

But he didn't deserve the comparison. Those men wouldn't bring her to a family dinner or give her an escape when she had a panic attack. They wouldn't offer to take her sightseeing and shopping without expectations in return.

At least, she didn't think he had those expectations. If he did, he wouldn't have held back from kissing her even though he'd clearly wanted to. He might have a reputation as a ladies' man, but he had done nothing but flirt. So far.

Raindrops spattered down on the windshield, and James squinted at the sky. "I may not have picked the best day for high street shopping. Of course, we like to say in Scotland: 'If you don't like the weather, wait five minutes.'"

"So I've noticed. I don't mind a little rain, though."

"Is that so? What happened to Scotland being wet and miserable?"

"I said cold, not wet. And maybe it's not quite so miserable."

James slanted her an amused expression. "We'll hope it passes quickly, then. I don't want you to miss the chance to see the loch and the views of Ben Nevis. If it were later in the year, there would be some incredible hikes we could take."

"So you really are an outdoorsman," she said. "Aren't you full of surprises?"

"No more than you."

He was referring to her playing the night before, but he was sticking to his word that he would let her tell him when she was ready. She chewed her lip, wondering how much she could safely reveal without treading on subjects she didn't share with anyone.

"I double-majored in architecture and music at NYU." She waited for the inevitable barrage of questions, her stomach tight.

"That explains it. Doesn't NYU have one of the best music schools in the country?"

She relaxed at his delicate treatment of the topic. "Yes, it's known for music performance."

"It's a shame you don't play more. I can't even whistle in tune, but I grew up with a musician in the house. I recognize talent when I see it, and there's no doubt you're something special."

Heat rushed to her face, and she willed it away in embarrassment. What was it about this man that kept her constantly off guard? She had blushed more in his presence these past days than she had in the last ten years.

"Thank you," she managed finally.

"You're welcome. Now you might as well get to it."

"Pardon?"

"You've got a captive audience for at least another hour. You know you're going to feel guilty all day if you don't get some work done. So go ahead. Give me your pitch." He was smiling, but he didn't seem to be joking.

"All right. You sure?"

"Of course. Convince me I'd be crazy to pass up this opportunity." He shot her that wicked grin again.

It came almost as a relief. This James was far easier to handle than the sensitive one who treaded lightly around topics she wasn't sure she wanted to discuss. She launched into an overview of the proposal she had emailed the night before, pausing only to answer James's occasional questions.

"You've been paying attention."

"I know it's hard to believe I can be serious, but I do mean to make this hotel a success. It's been closed for over a year, and the longer we wait, the harder it will be to retain our regular guests. We've had families book their holidays here every summer for years. Once they find another spot, they may not come back."

Andrea murmured her agreement. "You've got matters well in hand. If your contractor is good, you should be booking for Christmas."

"I think so too. Fancy a Christmas in Scotland? Skye is lovely under snow."

"Becky would kill me. It's the only time I'm ever guaranteed to see her and the kids. That's assuming I don't get called out of town at the last minute."

"Don't tell me you'd actually let them send you on a business trip on Christmas."

"If it's a big enough deal, I don't have much of a choice."

"You always have a choice."

Andrea turned her head so he couldn't see her face. Maybe she did have a choice, but it had become increasingly difficult to spend time with her sister's happy family. They loved her, of course, welcomed her, but she didn't belong there. Small-town girl or not, she didn't fit into Becky's cozy life any better than she melded with the domestic scene at the house in Isleornsay.

"So what about marketing?" James asked.

Andrea turned back toward him and abandoned her melancholy thoughts, grateful for the change of subject. If only he didn't read her so easily. She quickly outlined her thoughts on marketing for the hotel, which she would convey to the London team once she had a signed contract in hand.

Armed only with the knowledge that Fort William was the Highlands' biggest town, Andrea was unprepared for the charming village that spread from the edge of Loch Linnhe. A jumble of buildings lined the street, some of which looked like they dated back to the eighteenth-century fortress, while others were built in Tudor or Georgian styles. Ahead on the motorway, a brown welcome sign proclaimed in Gaelic, *Fàilte do'n Ghearasdan*, with its English translation—"Welcome to Fort William"—below it. James slowed as they entered the town, then turned onto a small intersecting street where he found a parking spot along the curb.

The morning's weather had transitioned from threatening to just plain dreary, and a damp wind blew off the loch, throwing Andrea's hair into her eyes as she stepped onto the street. She buttoned up her wool coat and thrust her hands into her pockets to keep them warm.

"The coldest winter I've ever spent was a summer in Scotland," she muttered.

"I always thought it was San Francisco."

"Mark Twain must never have come to the Highlands."

James laughed. "Come, clever girl. And mind your step in those shoes."

Fort William's High Street was narrow and bordered by slender, crowded buildings on either side, following the original layout of the road from the town's days as a military installation. Stone pavers lined the sidewalks, and cobblestones set in a fan pattern undulated down the center of the street. She wobbled precariously on the uneven surface until James guided her to the sidewalk with his hand on the small of her back. She peered into store windows with interest as they passed: one sold woolen goods of all types, from tartan blankets to brightly woven kilts; another a vast assortment of Highland whiskeys.

"I'd be more than happy to stay here while you shop," James said.

"Don't pretend you don't enjoy this, clotheshorse." She grabbed him by the elbow and pulled him away from the window. "You know what you're planning for the week. You need to help me."

He moved away from the display with pretend reluctance, but as she went to release his arm, he put his hand over hers and squeezed it to his body. After a moment of hesitation, she left it there. It had been ages since she'd walked arm in arm with a man. It felt nice.

No, it felt more than nice. The warmth seeping from his body through his coat made her stomach flutter with a delicious nervousness she hadn't felt in years.

James paused before the door of a small boutique with an attractively dressed window. "This might suit, don't you think?"

Grateful for the escape from her thoughts, she let go of his arm and ducked into the store. It sported displays of simple, outdoorsy clothing, and she soon had her arms heaped with garments on the way to the changing room. A few quick changes to assure her of her size, and she was back at the counter paying for three pairs of jeans, several simply cut blouses, a quilted gray coat, and a pair of sporty leather shoes that would suit walking or hiking. She retreated to the dressing room to change into several pieces of her new wardrobe.

When she emerged again, James smiled warmly. "Perfect."

He took one of the paper shopping bags from her hand and held the boutique's door open for her. Once they stepped back onto the sidewalk, Andrea realized how tall he actually was. In the heels, she had almost been able to look him in the eye, but now she had to tilt her head up to meet his gaze. The feeling of vulnerability took her off guard.

James kept up a constant stream of talk, pointing out landmarks and drawing her attention to shop displays or restaurants he frequented. He could be a comfortable companion when he turned off his ego long enough to be serious.

But that wasn't quite right either. He was comfortable with his fame and his money, but if Muriel was to be believed, the teasing, playful nature seemed to have grown out of his childhood love of pranks. Maybe Andrea really had done him a disservice with her snap judgment. He would probably act much the same if he were living paycheck to paycheck, working as a short-order cook.

"I'm getting hungry," she said suddenly. "How is that even possible after your breakfast?"

"Fresh air and exercise. I know just the place. Let's cross."

His choice for lunch was a wood-clad pub, wedged between a brick Georgian and a building with a pseudo-Tudor facade. Gold letters on the bright red sign above the window proclaimed The Blooming Fuchsia.

She opened the door before he could reach it and stepped into the warm, crowded interior.

Polished wooden booths with padded backrests lined the inside walls, and smaller tables with cane-backed chairs clustered in the center of the room. A gleaming mahogany bar with brass accents stretched the length of the opposite wall. The hearty aroma of pub food mingled with the earthy, hoppy fragrance of beer. It was well past lunchtime, but patrons still packed almost every available seat, and voices hummed together beneath the low ceiling.

"Some of the best food in the Highlands," James said in her ear, his hand resting briefly on her back. "Let's snag that table in the corner before someone beats us to it."

They slid into a small booth and took menus from the rack on the wall. Andrea scanned hers quickly, and then snapped it closed. "I'll trust your judgment."

"Are you sure?"

"Absolutely. It's your tour of the Highlands. I'll leave myself in your capable hands."

He grinned a little too broadly, and she suppressed the childish urge to kick him beneath the table. The waitress approached just in time to save him a knot on his shin.

"A flight of the local ales on tap," James said immediately. "Steak pie for the lady, bangers and mash for me."

"I've had steak and Guinness pie." She'd expected something less ordinary, given James's enthusiasm about the place.

"Not like this you haven't. It's the love child of bœuf bourguignon and a Cornish pasty. You'll think you've died and gone to heaven."

She settled back in the seat and looked around the pub. It was more traditional than James's, now that she had something to compare it to: more clubby, less sophisticated. Maybe she hadn't given the Hart and the Hound a fair shake after all. He'd managed to achieve the feel of the traditional corner pub while making it upscale enough for the trendy Notting Hill location.

"You never stop, do you?" James said.

"Stop what?"

"Working. Don't try to deny it. You get this look on your face when you're analyzing your surroundings. Like you're trying to sum it all up in a neat paragraph."

It was exactly what she had been doing. He really did read her too easily. "I was just thinking I owed you an apology for calling your pub middle of the road."

"I'm not easily insulted," he said. "I'm just wondering how I might get you to relax for an hour."

"I know how to relax. This is still a business trip, remember?"

"Even you are allowed a lunch break now and then. Look, here comes your ale."

Andrea stared doubtfully at the tray the waitress sat before them, six small glasses set in a little wooden rack. "I'm not going to drink all those."

"Of course not. It's just meant to let you sample the different ones from the region." He removed the lightest-colored ale first and held it up. "It's a bit like tasting wine. This one is what's known as a Light 60. First consider what it smells like. Some have notes of chocolate, others citrus or coffee. And then taste." He slid the glass across the table to her.

Doubtfully, she sniffed the ale. "I smell … honey?" He nodded encouragingly. She took a sip, then made a face. "Burnt honey. This one is all yours."

He smiled, took the glass back, and then passed her another. "Next."

She sampled the rest of the glasses as James prompted her with questions. His eyes sparkled as he watched her, his arms folded on the tabletop.

"You take this all very seriously, don't you?"

"Ale is to British food as wine is to French," he said. "The concept of ale pairing is just as sophisticated. The flavor of one enhances the other."

Andrea leaned back in the booth, warmed by his enthusiasm. No wonder he was so successful on camera. He loved sharing his knowledge and his skills. People could spot a phony, but she was beginning to believe James MacDonald was the real deal. What a shock to discover it wasn't just marketing after all. Had she become so jaded she could no longer take someone at face value?

"That's a serious look. What are you thinking?"

She realized she had been staring at him. She struggled for something plausible to say—anything but the truth—then exhaled in relief when the server approached. "Look, here's our food."

"Now who's changing the subject?" he teased, but he didn't press as the woman set their plates before them.

Andrea's first bite of the steak pie was everything he had promised. "This is absolutely phenomenal. Even better than your pasta, if such a thing were possible."

"Try this." He pushed his plate toward her. "The bangers are made fresh on site. This is venison, I believe."

She delicately cut off a small piece of the sausage and tasted it. "It's good. But the pie is truly died-and-gone-to-heaven perfection." She devoured the rest of the pie, aware of James's amusement at her enthusiasm, but she didn't care. Ladylike went out the window with food this good.

"Do you want to meet the owner?" he asked, signaling the waitress when they were finished. "She's a friend of mine."

"Sure. I'd love to tell her how wonderful this was."

The waitress approached, and James asked, "Is Erica in today? We'd like to give her our compliments."

The server disappeared through a door behind the bar. A few minutes later a petite blonde emerged, dressed in a black chef's jacket, hair pulled back into a French braid. Her face lit up when she saw them.

"James! I don't believe it! What are you doing here?"

James slid out of the booth, and the woman threw her arms around his neck. He squeezed her warmly and released her. "I'm showing a friend around Fort William today. Erica, this is Andrea Sullivan. Andrea, my colleague, Erica Baird."

Erica held out her hand, and Andrea shook it firmly. "Welcome to the Blooming Fuchsia," she said in a precise English accent. "How are you finding Fort William so far?"

"Charming," Andrea said. "Is this your place?"

Erica swept the room with a proud gaze. "It is. I hope you enjoyed the food."

"Absolutely. The steak pie is amazing."

"It figures. You didn't tell her, James?" Erica laughed and rolled her eyes at him. "It's his recipe. He gave it to me as a gift when I opened the place."

"Only the filling recipe is mine. You've done something special with the crust." Then James said to Andrea, "If it weren't for Erica, I wouldn't have made it through the pastry segment of my advanced certificate. I'm complete rubbish at baking. I owed her one."

"You went to culinary school together, then?" The pang she felt at the revelation surprised her. Surely it wasn't jealousy. She didn't have any right to feel that. Still, the easy familiarity between them hinted at a long and close acquaintance. She just couldn't tell how close.

"In London, yes. James was the one who told me this place was up for sale a few years ago. I said he was daft for suggesting I move to Scotland. But here I am. The place tends to get under your skin, whether you want it to or not."

"I'm beginning to notice that."

Erica gave an emphatic nod. "Well, then, I won't hold you from your plans. Thanks for stopping by, James. Andrea, it was lovely to meet you. Enjoy your trip."

"She seems nice," Andrea said when the chef had retreated to the kitchen. "Old friend?"

James raised his eyebrows. "Do I detect a hint of jealousy there?"

Andrea gave him a supercilious look and took a drink from the nearest glass to save herself a reply. Unfortunately it was the burnt-honey ale she'd rejected earlier, and she narrowly kept a look of disgust off her face. "Your past is your business."

James didn't seem to believe her. His eyes traveled to the glass, and his lips twitched. "In any case, we never dated. She's like a sister to me. She's done a great job with the place."

"Yes, she has." Andrea tried not to feel pleased with the fact he felt compelled to reassure her. She had no right to feel possessive. It wasn't as if this were a date.

As they left the restaurant, though, and James again tucked her hand between his arm and his body, that was exactly what it felt like.

Chapter Sixteen

They stepped outside into a bright spill of sunshine through the gap in the clouds. Patches of blue winked through the gray ceiling, even though it merely gave the illusion of warmth. The damp, cold air immediately chilled Andrea through the quilted fabric of her new coat.

"Where to now?" James asked.

"I think you promised me a view of the loch."

"Then to the loch we go." He turned her down an intersecting street, and the wind that had been blocked by the buildings hit them full force. She shivered as the cold air funneled down the neck of her coat.

They stepped onto the wood pier, and their feet thudded dully against the decking. Only a few pedestrians ventured here on a Wednesday afternoon, either going to the seafood restaurant that dominated the pier or heading for the passenger ferry. James picked a spot at the railing that overlooked the loch and gave a sweeping view of the city behind.

"The ferry goes across to Camusnagaul," he explained. "You'd get a better view from the tour boats, but if we watch closely, we still might get a glimpse of the porpoises and otters that live in the loch."

Andrea closed her eyes and lifted her face to the sky, breathing in the loch's briny scent. The sunshine barely staved off the chill. "The pace is so much slower here."

"I found it maddening when I first came back from London," he admitted. "Especially the sheep."

Her eyebrows lifted. "That's the second time you've mentioned sheep."

"They're a menace on Skye. All over Scotland, actually. Sometimes a flock of them just decides to wander across the road and you have no choice but to wait for them to pass. Forget hurrying them along either. They just stare at you." He narrowed his eyes. "They lay in wait for motorists and then fling themselves into the road."

Andrea laughed at the picture he painted, imagining the animals huddled together in a field, plotting their revenge on passing motorists. "I never thought sheep could move fast enough to fling themselves anywhere." A gust of wind caught her full in the face, and a shiver shook her whole body. "Is April always like this?"

"No. Sometimes it's actually cold."

"Tahiti definitely wins this round." She rubbed her arms for warmth and scrunched down deeper into the collar of her coat.

"This might help." James reached down into one of her bags and withdrew a bundle swathed in tissue paper. He tore off the wrapping to reveal a woolen scarf, gray and lilac tartan shot through with silver threads. He folded it in half, then draped it gently around her neck and tugged the ends through the loop.

Andrea's heart thumped against her ribs, the feeling curiously similar to panic. "You shouldn't have. I couldn't possibly—"

"Shh. You've been freezing all day. Consider it a souvenir of Scotland, and just say thank you." He tugged down the zipper of her coat, tucked the scarf's fringed ends inside, then zipped her back up. Somehow he managed to make the gesture both casual and intimate. She struggled to respond, but the words stuck in her dry mouth.

"You don't like it? I thought since you said your favorite color was purple, and you were wearing a gray suit …"

He'd actually put some thought into the gift, and that made it even more unsettling. She looked up and saw the uncertainty on his face. It may have been the first time she'd ever seen him in less-than-complete control of a situation.

"It's lovely," she said finally. "And very thoughtful. Thank you."

He met her eyes and smiled. Even now, it managed to dissolve her composure. "Your hair is caught. Here, let me."

He slid his fingers beneath the edge of the scarf and freed her hair. His hand against her skin made her thoughts surface sluggishly, muddling all the reasons she should back away. When he bent his head toward hers, she stopped thinking and succumbed to the force that pulled them together, as strong and irresistible as gravity.

Their lips met, just the lightest touch, but it was enough to send a zing of electricity across every nerve ending. Her hand rose to rest lightly on his chest as she moved into him, but before the kiss could go any further, a shrill ring penetrated her hazy thoughts.

Andrea jerked back a step and scrambled in her purse for her cell, then stared at it dumbly when she realized it wasn't ringing. James held up his own phone.

"I'm sorry. I have to take this." He gave her an apologetic smile and moved away a few paces. "James."

Andrea let out a long, shaky breath. What had she been thinking? How could she have possibly allowed him to kiss her? No, she had been a willing participant. She had taken complete leave of her senses if she was actually contemplating getting involved with a client.

It wasn't exactly involvement if she was leaving on Saturday, though.

And that just made it worse. After the situation in London, her behavior would be under intense scrutiny. Getting involved with James on a personal level would make the incident with her last client look like a lovers' quarrel, not a legitimate case of sexual harassment. If there were any question about her behavior, she would become a liability to Morrison instead of an asset. It could end her career. At the very least, it could end her bid for the vice president position.

Yet the mere recollection of that brief touch turned her limbs to jelly and made her breath catch in her chest. It wasn't a promising sign for the state of her self-control.

James's alarmed tone startled her from her own thoughts.

"Are they all right?" He swore softly beneath his breath and then shot her another apologetic look. "Okay. Put his mum and sister up somewhere under a false name and call in Jonathan to consult. He'll have some ideas on what to do. In the meantime I'll ring Ian and see if he has any contacts who might help."

James ended the call and raked his free hand through his hair.

"What's wrong? What's happened?"

He met her eyes, the worry plain on his face. "One of my students was shot."

"What?" Andrea gasped.

"I have a cooking program for at-risk youth. Kyle's one of my most promising students. Good lad, but his older brother got him involved in a gang years ago. Now the brother's in prison, and Kyle's out of the life, but they've been threatening him. I guess they finally made good on it."

Andrea just stared, processing. "Is he all right?"

"He's in intensive care with three gunshot wounds to the chest. It's a miracle he's even alive."

"And they called you?"

"Who else is going to help them?" James asked with a twinge of bitterness. "I've tried to get involved before, but Kyle wouldn't hear of it. He was afraid they would retaliate against his family. We're beyond that now, I think."

"Who's Jonathan, then?"

"Security."

"As in, your bodyguard?"

A smile played at the corners of James's mouth at her shocked tone, even though his eyes remained worried. "Private security consultant. He's a good bloke, useful to have around. I use him when I travel to Asia and India."

Andrea gulped. It was an aspect of James's life she'd never considered, though she should have. She knew a few executives who carried kidnap and ransom insurance, and her brief glimpse of the Secret Service years ago had alerted her to the kind of threats people in the public eye faced. Still, it was an uneasy reminder of how abnormal his life actually was.

But that wasn't the topic at hand. "How does Ian fit in?"

"He has some contacts at the Met." At her blank look, he explained, "Metropolitan Police. Do you mind?"

"Of course not."

James pulled his phone back out and dialed. She listened as he explained the situation and asked Ian to make a call. Apparently his brother had a contact who was fairly highly placed in the police department. She shook her head. She'd never get over how they managed to work together despite their animosity.

James hung up and returned the phone to his coat. "Sorry about that. Shall we go?"

He offered his elbow. After a moment's hesitation, she slipped her hand into the crook of his arm again. She'd hardly expected him to take such a personal interest in his students. When she read about his program, she'd assumed he had set up the funding for it, not that he was involved in the lives of the kids themselves.

"What?"

"Nothing. I think it's nice you want to help."

"They're good lads, all of them." He shrugged. "I can't help thinking if I hadn't grown up with money and parents who took an interest, I might have ended up like them. I had a second chance. And a third and a fourth. Some of them have never had a single one."

Andrea mulled the statement over while they walked back to the car. For once, he didn't try to talk or joke, and she could feel the tension in his arm beneath her hand. His mind was clearly on the situation with his young student.

"If you need to go back to London, don't let me stop you. That's more important."

"What?" He seemed startled by the suggestion. "No. It's better I stay here."

"Why?"

"I'm not exactly low profile."

"Obviously you care about the boy. You don't think he'd want to see you? Or are you worried about how it would reflect on your program?"

He fixed her with a reproving look. "If Ian and I aren't around to answer questions about his involvement in the program, it will blow over in the news. It's better if Kyle and his family disappear for a while. Jonathan's good at that sort of thing."

Shame washed over her. Once again she had automatically attributed to him the most selfish motive. "I'm sorry. I didn't think of that."

"It's fine." He squeezed her hand against his side. "It's a tough situation. I feel bad for Kyle. He's trying to do right, but it's not so easy to escape your past mistakes."

If anyone understood the truth of that statement, it was Andrea. Yet here she was, tempted to repeat them. She was unspeakably foolish for even contemplating any sort of personal acquaintance with him.

The thought sat like a weight in the pit of her stomach. She followed him numbly down the side street where they had parked. He put her packages in the trunk, and she climbed into the passenger seat.

She didn't look at him. "We should talk about what just happened."

"What did just happen?"

Blast the man. He was going to make her say it. "We kissed."

"I don't know what the American definition is, but that was not a kiss. Almost a kiss? Barely a kiss—"

"Fine. Enough. I've got it." Andrea forgot her determination not to meet his eye and glanced at him. His serious expression was gone, and now he looked thoroughly entertained by the conversation. "We almost kissed, then. It can't happen again. You're my client."

"What does that have to do with anything?"

"Do you know how hard it is to be a woman in this business? I work twice as hard as my male colleagues, and they still say I'm only successful because I use my looks to get ahead. Do you think there haven't been rumors I've slept with clients?"

Her voice trembled, and she reined in her emotions before angry tears could follow. She never cried. She wasn't going to start now.

"Is that what this is about?" He reached out and gently turned her face toward him. Despite her determination to keep their relationship strictly professional, his touch still sent a tingle through her.

"Andrea, I promise you, I never meant to imply I expected anything but your professional expertise in return for signing this contract."

"Then why are you so determined to make me stay?"

He dropped his hand from her cheek and instead gripped the steering wheel in front of him. "A few years ago I was like you. Consumed with work. Obsessed with building the business. My father and I had been talking about renovating the hotel for years, opening a dining room there. I was too busy to leave London.

"And then it was too late. He died of cancer. I didn't even know he was ill. He didn't want to burden me." His throat worked, and his knuckles whitened on the steering wheel.

"So that's why Skye. For him."

He nodded. "It's easy to say you'll make time for what's important tomorrow. But we're only guaranteed this particular moment. Life's too short to rush through it." He started the car and pulled away from the curb without looking at her.

Andrea fingered the edge of the scarf, conflicted to the core. Her sensible side told her to maintain her distance. She had worked too hard for too long to make this life for herself, to leave her past behind. She couldn't let some random stranger shake up everything for which she had worked.

Yet the smaller and no less insistent part of her said James was not random; this was not just another man who wanted her simply as a way to pass the time. That three days was not too short to feel the stirrings of an emotion she had buried long ago. She had promised herself she would never again leave herself vulnerable to the kind of pain she had experienced with Logan.

Neither of them spoke as he rejoined the road leading out of Fort William. Andrea stared blindly out the window, twisting the scarf's fringe around her fingers.

James cleared his throat. "It's a couple hours back to Skye. We could stop at Eilean Donan on the way. And then I thought we might have supper in Portree."

"Whatever you think."

"Would it help if I promised not to kiss you?"

Andrea jerked her gaze to his face. "Yes."

"Okay. I promise. But that means you're going to have to kiss me." He was deliberately provoking her now. "I won't."

"You realize I'm going to take that as a challenge, don't you?"

"You take—"

"Yes, I believe you've already told me that once."

She scowled at him. "Have I told you you're insufferable?"

He chuckled, unperturbed by her tone, and she struggled to hold on to her irritation. It was too hard to maintain her distance when she acknowledged the connection she was beginning to feel with him. Yes, he could be egotistical and annoying. He was far too aware of the effect he had on women. But he also cared about people. His students, his family. It was difficult not to want to step inside that affectionate circle as if she belonged there.

It was far safer to think of him as the cocky restaurateur who used his looks and fame to get what he wanted.

She turned the conversation away from thoughts of him and kissing and the unwanted feelings those topics conjured up. "I want to know what you did to get kicked out of three schools before the age of eighteen."

"That's going to cost you. You remember the rules."

Him and his games. "Don't I have the right to refuse to answer?"

"I'll give you one pass. My first school didn't suit me because of its … rigidity. I wandered about where I shouldn't and got up to all sorts of trouble."

"That's not specific enough," she said. "I want details."

He grinned. "I skipped lecture, broke into the headmistress's rooms to steal her unmentionables, then put them on the statue in the courtyard. In full view of the school."

Andrea repressed a smile. "How about the next?"

"That one involved a sheep in the girls' lavatory. That's all I'm willing to say on the subject."

"You and sheep. What about the third?"

"The third I actually didn't get chucked out of. The headmaster strongly encouraged me to take my exams early. I passed, and all of Scotland's boarding schools breathed a collective sigh of relief."

That hardly surprised her. Intelligence and a distinct disregard for authority made a particularly bad combination.

"Okay, your turn." Andrea braced herself for the most embarrassing question he could devise.

"Why did you really spend every day after school at the movie theater?"

That stopped her cold. "I don't know if I want to answer that."

"You don't have to. But it means you have to answer anything else I ask you."

"And you won't hesitate to take full advantage. Fine, then. My mom died of an aneurism when I was twelve, and my father couldn't cope. He started spending all his time at work. Becky was already away at college, so my aunt stayed with me after school. She wasn't like Muriel, though. I went to the movies to escape her."

"No one ever knew?"

"I said I was playing piano in the school orchestra. It didn't last long, because eventually my dad wanted to see me perform. Now I want to know, what's the worst decision you've ever made?"

"Getting involved with Cassandra."

His frankness surprised her. "Right. The actress. How long were you two together?"

"Four years. Engaged for two. You really don't know anything about it?"

"Only what Ian told me."

James's expression darkened. "What exactly did Ian say?"

"Just that you split up around the time your father died. I hadn't heard anything about it."

"You're the only one, then. Half the world watched the breakup of our relationship like a spectator sport. We were tabloid fodder for half a year. Have you ever been in love?"

"Is that rhetorical? Or is that your question?"

"Both."

She could refuse to answer, but she found she didn't want to. "Yes. His name was Logan. I was twenty-two when we met."

"What happened?"

She gave him a wry smile, even though the effort cost her. "I married him. So we have something in common after all. We both have people in our past we regret."

"I wouldn't necessarily say I regret it."

She frowned. "I don't understand. You said it was your worst decision."

"God has a way of working these things for the best," James said. "I didn't end up marrying her, but she pushed me to take chances in my career I might not have otherwise considered. I don't waste time wishing I could change things."

"If I'd known what was going to happen, I would have run the other way." She wouldn't have fallen for a pretty face and prettier lies. She wouldn't have lost her friends, her community, her entire future.

"I wouldn't be in the place I am now if it hadn't been for my past. Would you?"

"You sound like my sister, Becky."

"Becky must be very intelligent, then."

Andrea cracked a smile. "She is. Just never tell her that. I'm subjected to enough big-sister wisdom as it is."

The silence that followed was more comfortable, and Andrea stared out the window at the passing landscape until James said, "Decision time. Stop at the castle or go back to the island?"

Andrea hesitated. She'd already been lulled by the easy tenor of the day. The sensible thing would be to go back to Skye, but a little bubble of rebellion welled up inside her. What was the point in staying the week in Scotland if she refused to see the sights?

"Castle."

"Now that you're no longer wearing stilts, there are some nice easy walks you might like. Or we can just pretend we're in a *Highlander* film."

If it had been his intention to make her laugh, he succeeded. "That's right. I'd forgotten they shot that movie there. I suppose you'd fit the part. Do you have a kilt?"

"Of course I do. What kind of question is that to ask of a MacDonald? Last time I wore it was Serena's wedding."

"I think I'd like to see that."

"Oh?" He waggled his eyebrows at her comically. "I suppose that's only fair since I've already gotten an eyeful of your legs. Mine aren't nearly as spectacular."

Andrea bit off a surprised laugh and felt the pink retake its place in her cheeks.

James made the turnoff for Eilean Donan and followed a short drive down toward the water, then found a space in the parking lot. Andrea's eyes were already locked on the breathtaking castle before them. A long stone bridge stretched from the shore to the island where the main keep stood. It looked just like Andrea had always thought a castle should, with crenellated walls and square towers. Twisted, shrubby trees and long grasses clung to the side of the island. Right now, the tide was low, but she could imagine what it would look like completely surrounded by water, only accessible by the long bridge.

James opened the door for her, but he didn't move out of her way when she stepped out.

"It's cold." He rearranged the scarf at her throat for warmth, then slid his hand down her arm and took her hand. He looked into her eyes for a long moment, as if asking whether she would allow the gesture. Then he winked, and it felt more like a dare.

Just when she felt like she'd gotten her footing with him, he caught her off guard again. She fumbled for words. "Are we going to stand here all day?"

"No, ma'am."

She had to admit she didn't mind the feel of her hand in his as they walked toward the ticket office, him matching his long stride to her shorter one.

"This place was named after an Irish saint from the sixth century, even though there wasn't a castle here until the thirteenth," he said. "*Eilean* means *island* in Gaelic."

"Do you speak Gaelic?"

"A little. My aunt spoke it around us when we were young. I only remember a few phrases. Most are not fit for polite company."

"Say something," she said.

"Hmm. *An toir thu dhomh pòg?*"

"What does that mean?" From his expression, she was willing to bet she didn't want to know.

"Just something we like to teach the tourists. Let's buy our tickets."

She followed him into the small ticket pavilion and wandered through the racks of souvenirs while he paid for their admission. On the way out, he took her hand again and led her toward the graceful bridge. Her spirits rose as they stepped onto the long stone walkway. Wind buffeted them on the exposed path, and she let herself move a little closer to him for warmth as they peered off the side at the tidewaters.

"I love old places," she said. "They have weight to them. Sometimes New York feels so transitory. Even London with all its history doesn't have the same feel as Scotland."

"The cities are too busy." He shifted so he blocked some of the wind for her. "The quiet is deep here."

She glanced up at him, surprised by how well he understood her thoughts. "That's exactly what it is. Deep quiet." For a man who surrounded himself with the trappings of a city life, he was remarkably comfortable with the quiet.

They crossed into the castle courtyard where they explored the nooks and bends of the old structure. James held her firm, even up the long flights of stairs, only releasing her hand when they had to move single file to avoid other visitors. She couldn't help the little lurch in her chest every time he reclaimed it, nor could she convince herself to pull away.

"What do you think?" James asked. "It's a little cold for walking, and we might get rained on. Do you want to chance it?"

"Shouldn't we be heading back anyway? You said something about dinner in Portree."

"Portree it is, then." They started back across the bridge, and he squeezed her hand. "Admit it. You're enjoying yourself."

"I am."

"But you're not ready to give Scotland your complete approval."

She shot him a mischievous smile. "It might be growing on me. It still isn't Tahiti, though."

"Now that's definitely a challenge. I hope you know what you're getting yourself into. I don't back down from challenges."

Inwardly, that was exactly what worried her.

Chapter Seventeen

The light was dimming into a dusky twilight when they crossed over the Skye Bridge. James glanced at Andrea to ask if she was ready for supper and saw her eyes were closed, her chest rising and falling in deep, even breaths.

"I'll try not to be insulted that I put you to sleep, love," he said with a smile.

She was softening toward him. He hadn't been sure she would allow him to even hold her hand, but she'd gripped it tight while they walked. For a time, her serious expression had lightened to one of pure delight. And yet their single not-quite-kiss had sent her scrambling back behind her excuse of professionalism.

Was it all due to Logan? What could the man have done to her that it colored everything in her life? Cassandra had been no prize, for certain, but James had moved on. Andrea, on the other hand, had walled up an entire part of her past to avoid the pain and simply built on top of it.

James sighed and ran his fingers through his hair. This was madness. Why her? Why now? He'd sworn he'd never fall into this trap again. If he were going to have another relationship, it would be with someone quiet and demure, the type of woman who was willing to let him take the initiative in a relationship. The kind who wouldn't balk if he wanted to buy her gifts, or see strings attached to every gesture. Not an obstinate businesswoman who challenged him on every point.

And what had made him start thinking about a relationship anyway? He wasn't looking for one. He'd been completely satisfied with his life, the casual acquaintance of pretty women …

Ones who hang on your every word. Ones who are far more interested in your status and wealth than you as a person. And you've been happy to exploit the fact.

The thought made him shift uncomfortably in his seat. He'd never thought of himself as shallow. Just … pragmatic.

Or did that make him heartless?

Andrea had been surprised to find he actually took an interest in Kyle. She'd obviously thought the program was founded out of guilt or obligation, not out of a genuine desire to help these teens. And why would she think otherwise? If he'd spent half as much time fund-raising for the program as he spent in the spotlight, he probably could have already expanded beyond London. It wasn't as if that city had cornered the market on troubled youth with dim prospects.

The thoughts chafed like a badly tailored suit. No wonder Andrea was so reluctant to take things beyond the professional.

The truth is never comfortable, is it?

He exhaled heavily and flexed his hands around the steering wheel. Melancholy served no one. He'd promised to show Andrea a good time in Scotland, and that was what he was going to do.

He navigated toward his favorite seafood restaurant, perched in a row of similar buildings above Portree's quay. Andrea would enjoy the views and the food. Her staunch determination not to lose her heart to his country was weakening by the hour. He saw it in the delighted smile that crossed her face now and again, the spring in her step when they explored something new. Andrea had Scotland in her blood already, even if she couldn't yet admit it.

He parked on the street outside the restaurant and sat silently for a minute, watching her sleep. She looked younger and more vulnerable, long eyelashes fanned prettily atop those high cheekbones, her full bowed lips drawn up in the beginnings of a smile. If she dreamed, it was a good dream.

He brushed hair back from her face, allowing his fingers to linger against her cheek. For one mad moment, he imagined waking her with a kiss, but he'd promised he wouldn't do anything of the sort. Instead he rubbed her arm lightly. She stirred, but she didn't wake.

"Andrea," he whispered. "We've arrived."

Andrea's eyes fluttered open. She smiled at him before she was fully conscious. Then her expression shifted to a frown, and she sat up straight. "I'm sorry. I didn't realize I'd dozed off."

"You've had a long week. We can go back to the hotel if you'd prefer."

"No, of course not. Give me a minute to wake up." She stretched with the sinuous movements of a cat and combed her fingers through her windblown hair. "How bad do I look?"

"You always look beautiful." The words spilled out before he could consider them, and he rushed on. "Don't worry, this isn't an elegant restaurant, but the food is wonderful."

"I always trust you when it comes to food."

"You can trust me on more than that, Andrea." He got out of the car before he could see her reaction.

Chapter Eighteen

Port Righ Seafood could in no way be confused with a fancy restaurant, but when they stepped inside, Andrea was charmed all the
same. Wood paneling, old photos, Windsor-style tables and chairs:
all contributed to the homey, old-fashioned feel. It reminded her of
the seafood restaurants that dotted New England's harbors, drawing
tourists with promises of ocean-fresh chowders.

The hostess, a perky brunette dressed head to toe in black, lit up
when they entered. "Jamie MacDonald! I didn't know you were back!"

"Just for the week. Gail, this is Andrea. Andrea, Gail."

Andrea maintained her smile as the girl gave her a thorough
once-over. She knew the small-town routine well enough. James was
a hometown celebrity, and Andrea, being an outsider, was a threat.
Gail's gaze clearly held a challenge. She sighed and followed the
woman to a window table that overlooked the harbor. Would they
always be subjected to that sort of treatment?

Oh my. When had she started assuming a relationship between
them?

She took the chair James held for her and opened her menu, but
her eyes just skimmed it blindly. She pushed it away, unread.

"Surprise me."

"Feeling adventurous?"

"Always. Just pick a good wine to go with it."

She stared out the window as James perused the menu, but he didn't get very far. First the restaurant's owner came from the back to shake his hand. Then one of the waitresses appeared and crushed him in an embarrassingly showy hug.

"Just a quiet dinner?" Andrea said.

"Sorry." He grimaced. "Even the people I don't know know me."

She struggled to squeeze words from her tight throat. "The life of a celebrity."

"Life in a small town," he corrected. "Either I went to school with them, or my dad taught music to them. Sometimes I think he knew every last person on Skye."

The waitress—a different one—approached to take their order, and James quickly rattled off a list of dishes without looking at the menu. When she left, James extended his hand across the table, palm up. Andrea reluctantly put her hand in his, feeling the prickle of questioning gazes on her back.

"So tell me. What do you want to do tomorrow?"

Andrea forced herself to relax and breathe, though the combination of imagined scrutiny and the movement of his thumb against the back of her hand made it nearly impossible. "I thought you promised me a sunrise jog."

"Are you sure that's how you want to spend your holiday? Wouldn't you rather sleep late?"

"I don't sleep in," she said. "It's a waste of perfectly productive hours."

"So a jog first. Then a tour of the island?"

"I'd love to see more than just Sleat—"

"Jamie! What a surprise!"

James jerked his head toward the speaker, who was still at least ten feet away, drawing every eye in the restaurant. The woman was petite but curvy, with short blonde hair and a sprinkling of freckles across her nose. Most people would call her cute, but Andrea thought no woman could more properly be called a cat. She could practically see the claws.

James put on a smile, but it was a canned expression. Andrea knew what genuine warmth from him felt like, and this was downright frigid. "Hello, Bree."

Bree flashed what she probably meant to be a coy smile. "Jamie, I can't believe you didn't let me know you were coming to town. I would have made sure I cleared my calendar." Her glance barely touched Andrea before it landed back on James.

"Sorry, Bree. I'm only here for a week, and I've been busy." He favored Andrea with a warm smile.

Bree apparently decided she couldn't ignore Andrea any longer and thrust out a hand. "I'm Bree. Jamie and I are old friends."

I bet you are. She shook the woman's hand. "Andrea."

"American?" Her eyebrows flew up, and she shifted her attention to James. "Naughty lad. You have been busy."

Andrea suppressed the urge to smack the woman. She knew Bree's type all too well, and not for a moment did she believe the woman still had any sort of relationship with James.

When no one responded to the hint, Bree changed tacks. "Are you going to hear Davy's band on Friday? You know they're playing in Inverness."

James glanced at Andrea. "What do you want to do, love? Fancy driving to the city for some music? They're fantastic."

"You know I'm up for anything." Andrea gave him a look that hinted at far more intimacy than they currently enjoyed.

James's smile broadened. He turned to Bree and said, "Maybe we'll see you there, then."

Bree's smile faltered. "Good to see you, Jamie. Nice to meet you, Andrea."

The woman swished back across the restaurant, drawing as much attention in her departure as she had in her arrival.

James gave Andrea a wicked grin. "Nicely done."

"Thank you. Old girlfriend?"

"Town gossip, more like."

"So we've just become the latest topic of conversation?"

His hand went out to her again, meant to be reassuring. "Does it bother you that much?"

Andrea didn't answer, keeping her fingers laced tightly together in her lap. Anything she said would be a half-truth.

"You don't want anyone to think we're together."

She jerked her eyes to his face. He was the most ridiculously confident man she had ever met. Surely he didn't need her reassurance. "It has nothing to do with you. I'm just not comfortable with everyone looking at me."

"Sweetheart, you can't help it. Every eye goes to you the minute you walk into a room."

Heat rose to her face again. Why couldn't she manage to control that around him? "That's not what I mean."

"Is that why you don't perform anymore?"

"Yes." She'd told him practically nothing, but it was more than anyone in her life beside Becky knew.

"We don't have to go to the concert. There will be a lot of people from Skye, a lot who know me. Davy's another hometown success story."

"Do I have to decide now?"

"You can decide whenever you like, as long as you give us three hours to get there."

Their appetizers arrived, and talk shifted to the safer topic of food. By the time their entrees arrived, she had almost forgotten they were under scrutiny. Once again, James had chosen well: locally caught scallops, shrimp, and sea bass. He wasn't just taking his tour guide duties seriously. He was equally determined to prove her wrong about the food.

They finished the meal with strong coffee and a pair of rustic fruit tarts, gazing down on the harbor while the sunset turned the cloudy sky pastel shades. Boats bobbed peacefully in the harbor, from the graceful sailboats to the rugged, weathered fishing boats.

"You have officially done the impossible," she said softly, letting out a contented sigh. "I think I love Skye."

"I had every confidence in you."

"Don't you mean every confidence in yourself?"

"I'm just the driver. You're the one who needed to relax long enough to see what's in front of you."

There went the humor again. Everything he said had a double meaning. "I'm not relaxed enough to kiss you, if that's what you're implying."

"Then I still have some work to do." James signaled their server for the check. "Tell me the truth, though. This is the longest you've gone without thinking about work."

She hid her smile in her coffee cup. "It is. Just don't let it go to your head."

"Oh, I can't. Not when I've got you to remind me of my faults."

Andrea laughed. He was the most annoyingly likeable man she'd ever met. "If I didn't know better, I'd think you like the abuse."

"Only from you, love." He paid the check in cash and laid the folder on the table for the server. "Shall we go?"

"Where are we going?" she asked as James helped her on with her coat.

"It's been a long day. I thought we might go back to the hotel."

"That's probably a good idea. I did fall asleep in your car."

She ignored the eyes on them as they left, though it took supreme force of will to keep her face expressionless. Only when she was safely ensconced in the cocoon-like interior of his car did she manage to breathe easily. She had walked the gauntlet and lived through it.

That implied the day had been a trial, though, and other than her discomfort in the restaurant, it had been the most carefree day she'd experienced in years. "Today was lovely. Thank you."

"You're welcome."

He laid his hand, palm up, on the console, and she put her hand in his. "It's been a long time since I've held hands with someone. It's nice."

"I can live with nice."

Andrea watched his face in the dim light and looked down to their clasped hands. "You know, I'm beginning to think you're a fraud."

"How so?" Once again he sounded amused, but he squeezed her hand tighter.

"You talk a good game, but you're content to hold hands with me all day."

"Only because you won't let me do more than that."

There went the easy, flippant answer. "Why do you do that? Why are you so determined to let everyone think the worst of you?"

He shot her a quick glance before he returned his attention to the road. "How do you know it's not true?"

"Is it? Do you really just go from one woman to the next?"

"I date a lot, yes."

"Do you sleep with them all?"

He choked on a cough. "My, you're direct."

She could hardly believe her own boldness. It was one thing to banter. It was entirely another to grill him about his romantic history. But she had to know the truth. If this were all just a ploy to get her into bed, she'd put an end to it this minute. "Should I take that as a yes or a no?"

He took a long time to answer, or maybe it just felt that way because she was holding her breath. "I'm no saint, Andrea, but I do have boundaries."

She exhaled slowly, unwilling to acknowledge how much the answer relieved her. Not that he had answered the question directly, but the implication was clear. "Why, then?"

"It was easier."

"Than what?"

For a moment, she thought he wasn't going to reply. "Than letting everyone see how I really felt after Cassandra and I split."

"Wait. Ian said you called off the engagement."

"She'd been having an affair with her costar." His hand tightened around hers again.

"Does Ian know that? Because—"

James shook his head sharply. "No. And I don't want him to."

She frowned, baffled. "Why would you let everyone believe you dumped her if she was the one who was wrong?"

"For one thing, it would have hurt her career. She makes her living playing ingenues."

"I'd say she brought that on herself," Andrea muttered.

"For another, the truth made me feel like a pathetic dolt who couldn't guess his fiancée was cheating on him." His smile was closer to a grimace than true amusement. "As it was, I couldn't go anyplace without cameras in my face. You can't imagine what that's like."

Andrea gritted her teeth against the rush of memories. She could still see the flashbulbs when she closed her eyes, remember the shouted questions, the jostling of reporters and photographers around her. She squeezed her eyes shut, her breath catching in her throat. She tried to untangle her hand from James's, but he held her firm.

"What's wrong?"

"Nothing. I'm fine."

"No, you're not." A note of concern crept into his voice. "Did I say something wrong?"

"Of course not. I'm fine."

"You said that before, and it was a lie both times." His touch had been gentle before, but now it was like iron, unyielding, holding her hand fast.

She hadn't noticed the twilight fading to full night, but now the headlights swept the parking lot of the hotel as he pulled up in front of the cottages. He killed the engine and lights and let the silence lapse. When she didn't say anything else, he dropped her hand with a sigh and opened his door.

Andrea climbed out and shivered in the cold while he retrieved her packages from the trunk, relieved he wasn't going to press the issue further. He followed her silently to her door, then unlocked it with his key and placed her bags inside. Before she could step through, he pulled the door closed, trapping her between his body and the wooden slab. She jerked to a halt before she could slam into it and spun around.

"What are you doing?" she blurted.

He put one hand on her waist and braced the other by her head. Even though he only held her loosely, she felt the shock through her body as surely as if he'd crushed her to him. He bent his head and murmured in her ear, "Something is bothering you. I'm considering the best way to make you forget it."

His warm breath raised chills along her skin, even though his hand still barely touched her waist. A shudder of longing ran through her. "You promised."

"I did. Unless you want to change your mind."

"You're still my client."

"I think we've gone far beyond a business relationship, don't you? Kiss me."

"No." The word didn't sound convincing, especially considering her breathing had gone alarmingly uneven.

He threaded his fingers through her hair, drawing her closer. She could do nothing but stare up at him, her voice caught in her throat, her heart hammering in anticipation. His gaze caressed her face and lingered on her lips, building the ache inside her to an almost unbearable level.

Then he smiled and stepped back, releasing her so quickly she almost stumbled. "I always keep my promises, Andrea." He strode back toward the car, but halfway there he turned back. "Jogging in the morning?"

"What?" Andrea struggled to regain her composure, blinking while her mind shifted gears. "Oh, right, jogging. Yes, I'll be ready."

He gave her that dazzling grin and pulled the car door open. "I'll be up at the house for a while if you need me. Number's on your desk. Sleep well."

Not likely. She sagged against the door for support while the car reversed out of the parking spot and turned back up the drive. With her knees this weak, she couldn't even take comfort in the fact she hadn't allowed him to kiss her. For a moment, she'd been so sure …

She let out a groan. He'd played her again. He'd never meant to kiss her, but he had accomplished exactly what he intended. She no longer remembered her misgivings from the car.

Unfortunately there was another whole set in their place.

Chapter Nineteen

James scrubbed a hand through his hair as he drove up the dark road toward the family house. He'd intended to tease—or maybe shock—Andrea from her sudden panic. He had just overestimated his own self-control when it came to her, or maybe he'd underestimated the sheer force of the attraction that crackled between them. His words about keeping his promises had been as much a reminder for him as for her.

The more he learned about her, the harder it was to stick to the surface-level flirtation he had intended. She was like no other woman he'd met: sharp, driven, successful. He'd genuinely enjoyed every moment he'd spent in her company. Every once in a while, he got a sense of how wicked her sense of humor could be if she'd just let it loose.

He smiled again at how she'd handled Bree. Some women would have instantly gone on the defensive, but Andrea had just watched her like one would view a child with a tendency to exaggerate. Her sultry tone and private look had shut down the nosy woman altogether. He admired a woman who kept her composure.

He'd shattered that composure tonight, no doubt about it. It wasn't just professional considerations that kept her from acting on her feelings, though. Each detail she revealed hinted at some terrible hurt in her past, and they all had to be wrapped up together. He'd be willing to bet Logan had been some sort of celebrity, someone in the public eye. Did he have something to do with the end of her promising performance career? Was he the reason she harbored a phobia about public scrutiny?

James realized he'd been idling in his aunt's driveway for several minutes and shut the car off. He shouldn't have come here. Serena would take one look at his face and know exactly what he was thinking. At least Ian's car was missing, or he would have turned around straightaway. His sister's teasing was one thing. His brother's disapproval was quite another.

James let himself into the house. Light flickered from the television, illuminating the living room in staccato bursts. Serena lay curled up beneath a blanket on the sofa, watching some Scottish drama.

"Emmy and Max in bed?" he asked, shrugging out of his jacket.

"Just." Serena leaned over and clicked on the lamp. "Did you have a good time?"

A smile crept onto his face. "It was nice."

"I know that look." Serena was smiling too. "I'd say it means you got a good-night kiss."

"No, I promised her I wouldn't kiss her."

"Why on earth would you do that?"

"I'm wondering the same thing myself." He sank down on the sofa and propped his feet on the coffee table. "I just don't want her to feel forced. I want her to make a conscious decision, not just get wrapped up in the moment." Though he wasn't above helping that decision along a bit.

"My brother is growing a conscience?"

"Don't say that. You make me sound like some awful lothario."

"No, I know you're not. But Jamie ... you break hearts without meaning to. You always have. You stick around until things get too serious, and then you're gone, on to the next one. Look at Bree. You dated, what, ten years ago? She's still carrying a flame for you, if you didn't know."

"Oh, I'm aware of that. We ran into her tonight at the restaurant."

Serena grimaced. "How'd Andrea take it?"

"She was brilliant. Shut Bree down without ever losing her smile."

"I can see why you like her, then," Serena said with a chuckle. "I've been wanting to take Bree down a peg for years."

"Andrea's different," James said slowly. "She's strong and independent, polished ... and yet completely fragile. I'm afraid if I move too fast, she'll shatter."

"Doesn't seem to me like you have a lot of time. Saturday's coming quickly." Serena twisted the blanket pensively. "Could you love her, do you think?"

"It's a bit early to be throwing that word around, isn't it?"

"Not necessarily. Could you? Given time?"

"You mean the time we don't have?" He arched an eyebrow, but his sister knew his diversionary tactics too well to be fooled. "Maybe."

Serena gave him a reproachful look, and he held up his hands.

"What do you want me to say? I'm not pledging my undying devotion to a woman I've known for three days. But could I see this turning into something more? Yeah. I could."

Serena was silent for a long stretch, and he sensed he wouldn't like what she was going to say next.

"What does she believe in, Jamie? Do you even know?"

"She wears a cross. She doesn't flinch when I mention spiritual things, but she's not all that comfortable with discussing it. I think she's had some bad experiences."

Serena patted his shoulder, the picture of the older and wiser sister, even though she only had two years on him. "Find out before you lose any more of your heart to this woman. You of all people know what happens when a relationship isn't based on compatible values." She rose from the sofa and tossed him her blanket. "There's some shortbread in the kitchen if you want it."

"I do. Your shortbread is the best."

"It's the only chance I ever get to show you up in the kitchen. I seize it when I can. 'Night, Jamie."

James turned off the television and stared at the blank screen. His sister was right. He had been avoiding this question, but he couldn't ignore it any longer. He needed to be sure he wanted to pursue this, because Andrea tightened her grip on him with each passing day.

He only lingered long enough to grab two of Serena's biscuits. Then he traded the Audi for the Subaru and drove back to the hotel. His heart plummeted when he saw Ian's vintage roadster parked out front of his cottage. Perfect timing. He pulled in beside it, turned off the ignition, and yanked the keys out more roughly than necessary.

Ian popped open his door and unfolded himself from the low-slung sports car. He looked as polished as always, even in trousers and a polo shirt, his wavy hair cropped into submission. Always professional. Always in control.

James didn't look at him as he flipped through his key ring. "What do you want?"

Ian held up a large envelope. "Delivering Andrea's contract for you to sign. Can I come in?"

"I don't see why. I'll take it now." James held out his hand, but Ian made no move to hand it over. "Fine. Suit yourself."

James left the door open, not looking to see if Ian followed. He tossed his jacket onto the bed and placed his keys and wallet in their usual place on the nightstand. The door clicked closed, the only indication his brother had followed.

"Where's Andrea?"

"I would assume she's in her cottage where I left her." James crossed his arms over his chest and stared at his brother. "Why the sudden interest?"

Ian placed the envelope on the table and pulled out a chair for himself. "No need to get defensive. I was just asking."

"I can't imagine why I would get defensive. You talked to her about me? What happened to keeping business and personal lives separate?"

"She deserved to know." Ian looked at him, his expression almost sorrowful. "She's a nice woman. I thought she should be on her guard."

Anger and humiliation tumbled around in his head. His brother thought so little of him that he thought he needed to warn Andrea? No wonder she had seemed so surprised when he admitted his reputation was mostly undeserved.

Then he sighed. Ian would never change. There wasn't any point in trying. "I guess she didn't listen. She decided to stay the week."

"Serena told me."

"So that's the reason for this visit? Come to give me some brotherly advice? I think I can manage well enough on my own."

Ian toyed with the edge of the envelope. "You know, you might think of someone other than yourself for once. Your behavior doesn't just reflect on you, it reflects on all of us. Your family, the company, the charity."

"What would you know about my behavior? When have you ever actually asked me anything? You'd rather accuse than learn the truth."

"Fine, I'll ask. Have you slept with her?"

He meant Andrea. The question made James feel nauseous. "Get out."

Ian rose and placed the envelope on the table, its bottom lined up neatly with the table's edge. "She's too good for you, Jamie. If you had any sort of conscience, you'd let her go."

The words struck him squarely in the chest, and his reply spilled from his mouth before he had time to think about it. "Like you let Grace go?"

Ian blanched, a sure sign James's aim had been true. "We're not talking about Grace."

"No, but we should be. That's what this is about, isn't it? The woman you loved left you, and now you can't stand to see me happy. Maybe you're content pining over someone who's never coming back, but I'm moving on with my life."

Ian's throat worked convulsively, and a muscle in his jaw pulsed. He pushed his chair back under the table, his movements measured, controlled. He spoke to the floor. "I have never once intentionally hurt you, Jamie."

Ian strode to the door and let himself out, clicking it shut quietly behind him.

James stared at the exit until he heard the rumble of the engine and saw headlights arc across his windows. Then he sank into the chair Ian had just vacated, regret squeezing the air from his lungs.

Ian was right. Misguided as he might be, he really believed he was doing James a favor. But James had purposely gone for the jugular, struck the place he knew was most tender. No matter how angry Ian made him, he didn't deserve that.

James slumped back in the chair and stared at the ceiling. Was that how everyone saw him? Cruel? Lecherous? Untrustworthy? He saw the photos in the tabloids and the society pages, of course. Most reported the names of his companions with an air of amusement, almost as if it were a game to guess who he'd been seen with this week. The women didn't mind. They were all struggling actresses or singers or dancers, glad for the publicity, even more appreciative of a nice evening out with a man who kept his hands to himself. He flirted, he teased, occasionally he kissed, but it went no further than that.

Oh, he knew what people assumed. They would assume those things without his help. After all, why wouldn't a man take the opportunities seemingly presented to him?

Was that how Andrea saw him too?

James closed his eyes. It had only taken the merest mention of her to send fury boiling up. It was one thing for people to speak ill of him. It was another for them to make assumptions about her.

Like they made assumptions about the long string of women he had dated in London.

He groaned. He'd been a selfish git. How had it never occurred to him to think how his reputation reflected on them? No wonder Ian was so angry with him. It hardly mattered that he was doing nothing wrong if everyone thought otherwise. He'd been so focused on avoiding the speculation over his split with Cassandra, he'd never really considered how the alternative looked.

Or maybe he had, but until he met Andrea, he just hadn't cared.

She wasn't like those girls, making her living on stage, accustomed to gossip. She was a businesswoman who desperately wanted to stay out of the public eye. She'd already told him she thought he was a self-indulgent playboy. She would be crazy to give him a chance.

He could say he didn't care what she thought, but now he recognized it as a blatant lie.

Chapter Twenty

Andrea slept restlessly, tossing beneath the fluffy down duvet until the sky outside began to lighten. Sleep had eluded her for a long while the night before. She should have been pleased James had taken his promise not to kiss her seriously, but instead she'd spent the evening frustrated by the fact he was a man of his word. When sleep finally came, it was plagued by troubling dreams of James and Logan and the blinding pop of flashbulbs.

She threw off the covers and climbed out of bed. She dug out her jogging clothes and slipped them on, then pushed the table back to clear a spot large enough to stretch. She didn't have a sticky mat, so bare hands and feet on the wooden floor would have to do for traction.

"Focus," she told herself aloud, as she bent double and exhaled her worries out in one long breath.

Andrea had already worked her way through thirty minutes of sun salutations and moved onto a series of arm stands by the time James knocked on her door. She struggled to hold her balance in crow pose for a few more seconds, her legs off the ground, knees braced against the back of her arms, while he rapped on the door.

"Wakey, wakey, eggs and bakey!"

A startled laugh popped from her mouth, and she collapsed into a graceless heap on the floor. She clambered to her feet and yanked open the door. "I thought you'd never get here."

"Pardon me for thinking you might want to sleep a bit longer." James made a face, but his eyes still twinkled. He seemed perpetually amused by her. She wasn't sure if that was a good thing.

"I told you I don't sleep in." She lifted her hair from where it already stuck damply to her neck. "I like to loosen up with some yoga before I jog."

She opened the door wide to admit him and went off in search of her running shoes. She perched on the arm of a chair while she pulled them on, surreptitiously watching him as he paced her kitchenette. She had opted to cover every last bit of skin in microfiber running pants and a lightweight shell, but he wore a pair of loose athletic shorts and a snug, long-sleeved T-shirt that showed off his muscular build to fine advantage.

"Aren't you going to freeze?" She nodded toward his outfit while she pulled on a fleece ear warmer.

"I'm used to it." He gestured to the door. "After you."

She let him set the pace, a brisk walk up the gravel drive, then followed him into a jog once they hit the cracked pavement. The morning sky had already started to shift from its mottled gray, and now pink and orange streaked the lightly clouded sky. Birds sang in the brush and one occasionally swooped down toward the water. The quiet filled her, broken only by the soft scuff of rubber soles on the pavement and the faint sound of their breathing.

She noticed he was holding back to accommodate her shorter stride, so she pushed the pace a little faster.

"Competitive, are we?"

"It has nothing to do with competition." Her voice sounded a little breathless now. "I'm still working off last night's dinner."

"Trust me, I understand. I have to jog now and then too."

"Jogging a few miles every day doesn't give you that body."

He raised his eyebrows, looking far too pleased by the compliment. "Thanks for noticing."

Warmth flooded her cheeks, and she prayed it could be passed off as exertion. She shouldn't have been so frank with her admiration. "You're welcome. Now either speed up, or stop checking out my butt. You're making me uncomfortable."

"I am doing nothing of the sort," he protested, but he chuckled and let the distance lapse between them before he caught up. "Left onto that little trail up ahead. You see it?"

"I see it." She turned off the pavement onto a hard-packed dirt path, little clouds of dust puffing up behind her. A thick carpet of grass dotted with spring wildflowers spread over the low hillside, craggy rocks jutting up through the earth. The grade was gradual, but still steep, and Andrea's breath came more heavily as they wound their way up toward the top of the hill. She slowed to a walk, and then clambered up a fall of loose rock. When she reached the top, a smile broke over her face.

The entire Sound of Sleat spread out in front of them, a wide expanse of blue. Gentle waves lapped at the rocky beach below, creating lacy ripples of white froth against the dark sand. Across, she could see the mountainous edge of the Scottish mainland. The sun had finally risen, and now the sky was a brilliant blue, dotted with fluffy white clouds. Had she ever seen anything so breathtaking?

At that moment, she no longer cared that she was missing out on Tahiti's white sand beaches.

James watched her for a while, then said, "Come, sit and rest for a minute."

She dragged her gaze away and climbed onto the boulder next to him. The stirring in her chest when she looked out on the landscape was an altogether unfamiliar yearning. Somehow it felt as dangerous as her attraction to the man who sat beside her, as if letting the peace of Skye seep into her would only set her up for disappointment.

"My father used to say that God created Skye during the first six days so he'd have someplace to come rest on the seventh," James said.

"That's blasphemous."

"I'm sure the minister thought so, but my father's relationship with the church was as uneasy as mine. Still, he had the strongest faith of any person I've ever known. I didn't always appreciate that, but I do now."

Andrea glanced at him. This wasn't the way she'd imagined the conversation turning. She had been raised in the church, but too much had happened to believe there was some divine plan at work. "You're the last person I expected to start talking about God."

"It's not exactly something I publicize. I'd never have gotten any-place in this business if I made a point of it. It's not like America. Ian was always afraid he'd lose his job at the law firm if anyone learned he was a Christian."

"It's not that different back home, at least not in New York. Saying you're a Christian is like saying you're from Pluto. Everyone thinks you must be crazy."

"Is that what happened to you? Too much outside pressure?" His tone was gentle, genuinely curious.

"No, I just ..." Andrea swallowed and looked across to the mountains on the mainland. She avoided the topic when she could, even though Becky still pushed. Her sister was one of the few people who knew the reason behind Andrea's crisis of faith. She might be the only one still holding out hope she would come back around. "Christians like to talk about love and forgiveness, but they're no better than anyone else. They'd sooner judge you than accept you. I'd rather be a heathen than a hypocrite."

"If you believe that, why do you still wear this?" James reached over and touched the cross dangling from the gold chain around her neck.

"It was my mom's."

"A woman of faith?"

"You could say that. She taught Sunday school the whole time we were growing up. Took us to church even though my dad wouldn't go. She hadn't had the easiest life by the time we came along, but she never gave up. She thanked God even for the bad things in her life. I don't know, maybe I'm just hoping there are others out there like her. Maybe someone will come along and prove me wrong."

"It reminds you to persevere."

The words startled her. "Yes. It reminds me to keep moving, to get through another day."

"Life isn't just supposed to be about getting through another day," James said softly. "I used to think if I could only just finish the next project or accomplish the next task, then I could slow down and enjoy myself. Not that I didn't love what I was doing, I just wasn't ..."

"Present?"

He nodded, his gaze distant, lost over the water. "Now I think, if this was my last day on earth, was it a worthwhile way to spend it?"

Andrea hugged her knees to her chest and rested her chin on them, viewing him sideways. "And is it?"

"I wouldn't be here if I didn't think it was. Maybe I should ask you that question."

"I think so." She had to tear the admission free, but once she did, a weight lifted from her. The way James watched her, his expression warm and open, made all her resolutions shudder. It was a completely different sensation than the heat that sizzled between them the night before, but it was no less powerful.

"I'm glad." He held out a hand to her. "If you're rested, we can go down the opposite side and circle around."

She gripped his hand and hopped off the boulder. This time he took the lead down the other side of the hill, setting a comfortable pace. Her heart beat a little faster than the exercise warranted. What had just happened on that hill? Every day it seemed James opened up to her a bit more, revealed some of the thoughts he hid behind his flippant attitude. Was it just a way to hold everyone at arm's length? And what did it mean that he was willing to give her glimpses of his serious side?

By the time they reached the hotel, Andrea felt pleasantly exhausted, even though her legs were rubbery and her chest tight. The cement jogging paths of an urban park hadn't quite prepared her for James's cross-country route, but it had been worth it for the view across the sound. So far, he had an unerring aim to her heart when it came to showing her Skye's beauty.

She paced a circle in the gravel lot, cooling down, while he ducked inside his cottage. He returned a minute later with two water bottles and tossed her one. She caught it in midair, twisted off the cap, and gulped down half the contents.

"I won't be able to eat for a while, but I should still go make Serena and Muriel breakfast. You hungry?"

"No. I'm finally in the negative after last night's dessert. I'd settle for a piece of fruit or something."

"Go ahead and have a seat on the deck. I'll see what I have."

She walked around to the deck behind James's cottage and plopped in a chair. Seabirds soared over the brilliant blue water, diving and calling to one another in the bright morning sunshine. She sipped her water and wondered what it would be like to have this view in her backyard every day. She'd probably never get anything done. She'd already been up for two hours, and work hadn't even crossed her mind.

James reappeared with a banana for each of them and seated himself in the chair beside her. "What would you like to do today?"

"I don't know. What can't I miss? I have less than three full days left." The idea of sightseeing around Skye lifted her heart in anticipation.

"We could drive the loop around the island. Trotternish is spectacular. It's really up to you how much walking you want to do after that jog."

"You don't actually think you wore me out with that little walk, do you?"

"I beg your pardon, then. How about I pack a hamper, and we'll see where the day takes us."

"Fair enough." She leaned her head back against the chair, enveloped in post-workout lassitude. "For once, I actually feel like I'm on vacation. Do you know I went to Hawaii last year, and I ended up writing a PowerPoint presentation on the beach?"

"You didn't."

"I did. I rather need the forced rest." She chuckled at the memory. "What time should I be ready to go up to the house?"

"Whenever you like. I'll make our lunch now and then we can go." He pushed himself to his feet. "Just come over when you're finished."

She tipped her water bottle to him. "Thanks for the run."

He grinned. "Thanks for the view."

"Very funny." She wrinkled her nose at him, but she watched him walk away before sinking back against her deck chair. She should probably check in with the office this morning, but she didn't want to lie to Michael about her plans for the day. She also didn't want to spoil the morning's relaxed mood. The idea of spending the entire day with James, sightseeing and enjoying herself without a thought to business, sounded far more appealing than she had ever thought possible.

She pushed herself up from the chair and crunched back across the gravel to her cottage. She toed off her running shoes and walked to the bathroom. The claw-foot tub had old-fashioned separate hot- and cold-water taps, and it took a minute to figure out the right proportion of hot to cold water in the bottom of the tub. It was a mark of this morning's light mood that she found it more charming than irritating.

The room phone rang shrilly. James or Becky? She hurried back across the room and picked it up.

"Andrea, how's it going?"

She blinked. "Michael? What are you doing calling me at this hour? It's two a.m. in New York."

"Something like that. I wanted a progress report from my best closer."

Andrea sat down on the edge of the bed, frowning. "It's going fine. I've closed half-million dollar deals and never heard from you. Why are you checking up on me now?"

She could hear his hesitation on the other end of the line. "You have to admit, your last appointment didn't go so well."

A sick feeling crept into her stomach. "I hope you're not suggesting I did the wrong thing in defending myself against a client who was harassing me."

"Of course not, Andrea," he said hurriedly. "You just might have handled things more delicately."

"More delicately? I think the fact he was able to walk out of the elevator on his own power showed my level of restraint."

"No one is begrudging you your right to take care of yourself." Michael had on his conciliatory, anti-lawsuit voice. "If anything, I'm just calling to make sure you're comfortable with the situation. MacDonald has a bit of a reputation when it comes to women."

"So I hear," Andrea said dryly. "James has been a perfect gentleman." Today, at least.

"First-name basis, huh? I hope that means you're getting close to a signed contract."

"I'll get it signed, Michael. I'm not the highest producing account manager in Morrison's history for no reason. So I know you won't have a problem with the fact I'm going sightseeing around

Skye today. If that bothers you, you can take it out of my vacation time. I've got plenty."

"Whoa, I have no problem with you taking some time for yourself, Andrea. Just making sure you're on track here."

"Got it. I'll call you on my way to the airport Saturday. When I have a signed contract in hand."

"Good girl. I'll be waiting."

Andrea slammed the handset into the cradle and stomped back to the bathroom to turn off the taps before the bathtub overflowed. As if his most accomplished account executive needed babysitting. Apparently all it took was one cretin who didn't understand the word *no* to erase the memory of the hundreds of sales she'd made for Morrison. She flexed her hand, pleased to find it didn't hurt anymore. Hopefully the creep's sore jaw had persisted longer than her bruised knuckles.

She stripped off her workout clothes and stepped into the over-filled bathtub, where she forced herself to let the hot water soak away her irritation. Leave it to Michael to destroy her one peaceful morning with business.

If she only had one more day on earth, would she really want to spend it thinking about Michael and the next big deal?

She braced her bare toes against the porcelain lip of the tub. A week ago she would have said yes. Being here in Skye with James would have felt like a waste of time, a distraction. But a distraction from what? From her career? From her goal of becoming vice president? She wanted it no less now than she had before, but it was a means to an end. What was supposed to be waiting for her across the finish line? Peace? Happiness? Time to enjoy her life?

For the first time, she wondered if the unencumbered existence she had built for herself, free from attachments or obligations, was as appealing as she'd always thought it to be. What point was there in success when there was no one to share it with?

She wasn't going to answer those questions in ten minutes in a tub of warm water. For once, though, she knew very clearly what she wanted from the day. She wanted to bask in the beauty of her surroundings. She wanted to breathe in clean salt air and feel the sun on her face. She wanted to walk hand in hand with James, have his arms around her, feel his lips on hers.

Acknowledging those desires set her heart fluttering like a trapped bird. She forced the panicked feeling down and made her breathing even out again, even though she felt like she stood on a precipice. She couldn't see the bottom, didn't know if jumping would earn her a soft landing or dash her against the rocks. Could she summon the courage to leap?

Chapter Twenty-One

James washed quickly, his mind occupied with the conversation he'd had with Andrea atop the hill. The more he learned about her, the more he saw how much the secret in her past had affected every aspect of her life. It seemed like she had turned her back on the person she had once been: her music, her faith, even her family. His heart ached at every new glimpse of pain. He had known plenty of personal tragedy in his life, but he always had his beliefs to fall back on, even in the times he didn't live by them.

Andrea hadn't given up, though. She was seeking, waiting for something to prove her wrong. Something to make her believe again.

He just hoped he hadn't missed his chance. Instead of being an example of a man of faith, he had just reinforced her skewed image of him by letting her believe the lies and speculation for so long. Truthfully, he hadn't done much to show her otherwise.

He hated when Ian was right. Not that James would ever admit it to him.

He pulled on jeans and an Oxford shirt and toweled his wet hair dry before he sat down at the desk to call Bridget. Fortunately it sounded as if it had been a quiet week at the office with both him and Ian in Skye.

"How's Kyle?" he asked.

"Out of ICU, though they're still watching him closely. Jonathan set his family up in a flat in Islington for now. He figured it would be less conspicuous than a hotel."

"Good. Let me know if anything changes?"

"Of course. Has Ian heard anything from his friend at the Met?"

James had forgotten to ask amidst the drama of the previous night. "I'll find out when I see him later. I'll be out for the rest of the day, but I'll check in tomorrow."

"Don't tell me you're actually taking some time off."

"Why would I need to take time off? Every day's a holiday with you, Bridget."

She snorted. "I've known you too long for those lines to work. Just tell me this—is she pretty?"

"Gorgeous. But don't tell anyone. It'll ruin my work-centered image."

"Good-*bye*, James."

He hung up the phone, grinning. At least he didn't need to be concerned with what his assistant thought of him. He'd taken her daughter to a network party years ago. Of all people, Bridget knew what kind of man he really was.

Blast Ian. He would be continually second-guessing himself now. It was so much easier when he didn't give it a thought.

He made two minor adjustments to his May calendar, and then started making lunch in the cottage's tiny kitchen. While Andrea met with Ian, James had picked up the makings of what he hoped would be an impressive picnic. He was just packing the last items into the hamper when Andrea rapped on the door. She wore next-to-no makeup, her hair curling wildly in the damp sea air, but he found her effortless beauty even more appealing than her polished business exterior image.

"Right on time," he said. "I just finished."

She sniffed. "I smell fish."

"After last night, I assumed you liked it."

"I do. Besides, even if I didn't, it would probably still be wonderful." She trailed off. "Why are you staring at me like that?"

"Am I?" He smiled carelessly to disguise the fact he had indeed been staring and wondering why in the world he'd ever agreed not to kiss her. "Let me get my coat and the hamper, and we'll head up to the house. I'll try to make it quick. I have someplace amazing to show you."

"You're going to torture me with that statement and not tell me where we're going?"

"Of course I am. But believe me, it's worth the wait."

"It better be after that buildup." She winked at him and turned on her heel toward the door.

Had Andrea actually just winked at him? A slow smile spread over his face. He picked up the hamper and followed her out. Whatever the reason for her suddenly light mood, he wouldn't complain.

Even the sight of Ian's car parked in Muriel's driveway couldn't dampen his spirits, though he prayed his brother's naturally reserved nature would prevent a scene in front of Andrea. He needed to talk to him about Kyle, and that would be difficult if he was tempted to take a swing at him.

The aroma of baking met them when they entered the front door. "Hello?"

"Andrea!" Emmy squealed and darted into the reception room, once more nearly bowling her over.

James chuckled and shut the front door. Once, he'd been Emmy's favorite visitor, but Andrea had clearly usurped that status. "What smells so good, Em? Your mum baking again?"

"I made muffins." Serena poked her head out of the dining room. "Join us while they're still warm."

"C'mon, Andrea!" Emmy grabbed Andrea's hand and half-led, half-dragged her toward the dining room. James shook his head. They'd be lucky to make it to his intended picnic spot before night-fall, especially if Emmy managed to convince Andrea to play the piano before they left.

The whole family gathered at the table around a basket of blue-berry muffins and a large platter of sliced fruit. Ian rose immediately, and James stiffened until he realized he was just being polite. That was Ian. Old-fashioned to the core.

"May I speak with you outside for a moment?" James asked.

Ian nodded and tossed his napkin onto the table, his expression giving away nothing. He followed James out to the front steps.

"I talked to Bridget this morning. Kyle is out of ICU. Have you heard anything from the Met?"

Ian relaxed perceptibly. Apparently he was as tense over the situation as James. "I got a call this morning. They know who did it. They're sitting on his grandmother's flat. My friend will call me when they pick him up."

"Good." That was something, at least. "Jon's got the family settled in Islington for now."

"That's good to know. Thanks for the update." Ian turned toward the door and paused with his hand on the door. "James …"

James didn't know what Ian saw in his expression, but whatever it was made him change his mind. He shook his head and headed back inside.

Andrea was sitting at the dining table with Muriel and Serena, eating a muffin and drinking tea. Serena and Andrea erupted into laughter, which they quickly squelched when the men reentered the room.

"What's so funny?" James asked suspiciously, looking between the two.

"Nothing at all." Andrea tried for an innocent expression and failed miserably. "Since your services aren't required here this morning, does that mean we can go?"

"It does. Let's get our coats."

Andrea tried to pry their destination out of James all the way to Portree, but James refused to give her more than meager hints. Instead he took her hand and told her stories about summers spent on Skye while on holiday from boarding school. For once, she didn't flinch every time he recaptured her hand after shifting, and she twined her fingers with his in an unexpected show of familiarity.

He had no idea what had changed to make her so affectionate, but he wasn't going to complain. Her hand felt good in his, soft but not delicate. Small women made him feel like he was going to accidentally crush them. Cassie had been positively petite, but Andrea's hand was strong and solid, a pianist's hand.

"Where are we, exactly?" Andrea frowned out the window at the changing landscape. The road was single-track, just wide enough for one car, with small lay-bys every so often to accommodate oncoming traffic.

"Outside of Uig. Just wait. You'll see."

The road wound downward into a little glen. Andrea rolled down the window for a better view of the landscape. Even though James preferred the east coast's mournful, craggy features, this part of Skye possessed an enchanting air. A carpet of bright green grass covered the rolling hills, as if velvet had been draped over the landscape, creating odd conical peaks and valleys. Little patches of trees were beginning to leaf out with their spring foliage, and short, scrubby bushes huddled together on the hillsides. In the distance, white horned sheep clustered in the meadow while their spring lambs frolicked nearby.

"This is Fairy Glen," James said, giving her hand a squeeze.

He pulled off onto the grass and parked. This early in the season, there were no other cars, so they would have the scenery to themselves. Andrea climbed out and turned in a slow circle to take in the panorama. He watched her over the roof. Something about her expression reminded him of himself when he had first come back to the island after years of absence. Even heartbroken over the death of his father and the split from his fiancée, the landscape had roused something inside he had kept buried for years.

His dad would have said the land recognized its own. There had been MacDonalds on Skye for over a thousand years, even before the castles and keeps that now lay ruined around the island. Whatever it was, the pace and the pressures of his life in London had dissipated like the morning mist was burned off by the sun. If he could have seen his own face, he thought he might have looked like Andrea right now.

He retrieved the picnic hamper from the car's boot and circled to her side. "Your castle awaits, my lady."

"Castle?"

He pointed to a dark shape jutting above the hills in the distance. "Castle Ewen. It's not precisely a castle, it's just a rock formation, but it has the best view of the valley."

Andrea pulled on her jacket, and they headed down the road toward the tower. James reached for her hand, and she laced her fingers with his again, as if she had been expecting it. Soon they left the road in favor of the bracken ridge, the foliage muffling their footfalls. A few insects buzzed in the meadow, and birds called occasionally in the trees. Sheep bleated in the distance.

James stole glances at Andrea as they walked, impressed by the fact that she didn't feel the need to fill every moment of silence with idle chatter. She seemed content to soak up the stillness, to take in every detail of the landscape. Overhead, a raptor circled, soaring on outstretched wings.

He tugged her to a stop and pointed. "Look. A golden eagle. You can tell by the wings."

She turned her face to the sky, watching its path against the scattering of fluffy clouds. "It's incredible."

"It's rare," he said. "They nest on the island, but they're hard to find. I've never even seen one."

She met his eyes and smiled. "Maybe this place really does hold some magic."

She looked so appealing, her hair windblown and her eyes spar-kling, it was all he could do not to kiss her right there. Instead he just smiled back and agreed. "Maybe."

They tramped through the grass for almost an hour, winding through the small valleys and passing grassy, cone-shaped hillocks. Andrea made little exclamations of delight as she spotted rabbits in the brush or clusters of wildflowers just beginning to emerge from the green carpet. Finally they rejoined the path that circled around the tower. Up close, the rock formation stretched high into the sky, far taller than it had looked from the distance. Stubborn, hardy foliage clung to the rock sides, and a long narrow path led steeply up into the cleft of the formation.

"Our final destination," he said, pointing to the top.

The climb was short, but steep, and the path squeezed through a narrow opening in the rocks. James followed behind Andrea, ready to catch her if she slipped, but she scrambled up the slope with the ease of a practiced hiker. He emerged onto the flat, grassy top sec-onds behind her.

The view of the glen spread out around them. A small loch reflected back the sun and sky, a glimmering blue pocket in the broad expanse of green. James moved toward the edge, but Andrea remained firmly rooted in place.

"Come, Andrea, you should see the view from here."

Andrea crept forward slowly.

He threw her a quizzical look. "What's wrong? Are you afraid of heights?"

"Not afraid exactly. Just wary. I'm okay if there's a handrail or something, but standing this close to a sheer drop-off …"

"It's not that steep." When she still didn't move, he held out a hand. "I promise I won't let you fall."

Reluctantly she moved forward and grasped his hand. Not exactly far enough to be in any real danger but close enough to see the rocky sweep down to the base of the cliff.

"This makes me feel a little ill," she said, but at least she was smiling.

James set down the hamper. He stepped behind her and wrapped his arms around her securely, pulling her back against him. "Is that better?"

It wasn't quite how he'd imagined getting her into his arms, but he wasn't going to quibble over details. He breathed in her perfume and momentarily lost his train of thought. Her heart thrummed against him, but she relaxed slightly in his arms.

"This really is an inconvenient problem for sightseeing," she said.

"I'm finding it rather convenient myself."

She elbowed him hard in the ribs.

"Ach, woman! You're a lot stronger than you look, you know." He let go of her and rubbed his injured ribs ruefully.

Andrea gasped and pulled his arms around her again. "I didn't say you could let go. What if I'd fallen off the edge?"

"From six feet away? I hardly think it constitutes a risk."

She twisted around to look at him. "You are enjoying this."

"Immensely, and in more ways than one."

He thought that would earn him another elbow, but instead she laughed. The sound seeped into him like the warmth of the spring sun. She had laughed before, but rarely so freely or so openly. They stayed that way for another minute or two, taking in the spectacular view off the side, and then she said, "I think that's about all I can take. You promised a picnic?"

"All right, if you insist." He let go of her, though he still kept a steadying arm on her elbow until she was safely away from the edge. The flush had crept back into her cheeks, and she avoided his eyes as she looked for a likely spot for their picnic. Either she was embarrassed by her fear of heights, or she hadn't been quite as afraid as she claimed.

She tramped around the top of the tower as if carefully considering the location for their picnic, but from the slightly unsteady way she'd stepped away from him, he figured she was using the excuse to put distance between them. "How about here?"

"Fine by me." James pulled a tartan flannel blanket from the hamper and spread it out onto the grass. She knelt as he began to unpack their feast. Two stemless wine glasses came out first, followed by a tall glass bottle. He held it up. "Sparkling water. I didn't think wine was the best idea, given the climb."

Next came out two melamine plates and real cloth napkins, followed by several plastic containers. James popped the lids and pointed to each dish. "My take on tuna Niçoise sandwiches, new red potato salad, and fresh fruit. I was going to bring some sorbet, too, but I figured it would melt."

"This is the fanciest picnic I've ever had." She smiled and unfolded a napkin across her lap while he poured her a glass of water.

"Advantages of sightseeing with a chef." He arranged the items on her plate as carefully as he would have in a fine restaurant and set it on the blanket before her.

She took a bite of the sandwich, and her eyebrows flew up in approval. He'd hoped she would like it. This was one of his favorite recipes, even though it was remarkably simple: seared tuna, seasoned delicately with olive oil, vinegar, and Dijon mustard, then layered with hard-boiled eggs and spring greens on an artisan roll. Even a day old, the bread was fantastic, a perfect balance of soft custard-like crumb and flaky crust.

"You're an artist," she said. "Truly. This makes me think of spring and country air and ..." She broke off, blushing again.

Did she have any idea how appealing that shy little habit made her? Even more so because he had the feeling he was the only one who coaxed it out of her.

He smiled, an expression that seemed to have taken up permanent residence on his face around her. "You appreciate food more than any non-chef I've ever met."

She accepted the compliment with a pleased smile of her own, leaning back on her hands while the breeze rustled her hair. "You love this place. I can see it in your face when you bring me somewhere new. Why did it take you so long to come back?"

He'd asked himself the same thing. "The arrogance of youth perhaps? There's a certain prejudice against Scots in England. Not like there used to be of course, but it's still there. Once I succeeded in London ..."

"You didn't want to acknowledge your roots."

"Something like that." The smile faded. "When my dad died and I came back for the funeral, I realized what I had been missing. You bury the past, and maybe you lose a little of what made you who you are."

Tears glimmered along her lower lashes before she blinked them away. "That's what Becky says. But sometimes the past is better left buried. Just because circumstances shaped you doesn't mean you should dwell on them."

"But you have to face them before you can move on."

"It seems to me you and Ian have plenty of unfinished business."

James flinched as the comment struck home.

Andrea's eyes widened. "I'm sorry. I shouldn't have said that."

"No, you're right. Ian and I have always had a complicated relationship. When our parents split up, they let us—made us—choose where to live. Serena and I chose Skye with Dad. Ian chose London with Mother. After that, he assumed the man-of-the-house role, always wanted to give me advice. Eventually I stopped visiting. I got tired of hearing from Mother about how I should be more like Ian."

"Is that why you rebelled in school?"

He gave her a wry look. "No, that was just my own mischievous nature. The fact it infuriated Ian and Mother was just an unexpected benefit."

"You don't like being told what to do."

"Does anyone?"

"No, I suppose not. We all want to be in control of our lives."

"Sometimes we don't know what we need," James said softly, catching her eye. "Sometimes we have to have matters taken out of our hands."

"That sounds suspiciously like you're fishing for a compliment."

She was too quick. He grinned. "Only if you're handing them out."

She laughed. "It hasn't turned out too bad so far."

"That's the best you can do? I'm going to have to try a little harder, then. I have somewhere else in mind."

"Good. I, for one, would like to get off the top of this death trap." Andrea began to pack their plates and silverware into the hamper.

"Are you sure you wouldn't like one last look over the side?"

She narrowed her eyes. "Tempting as that sounds, I'm wise to your plan now."

"Next time I'll try to be less transparent."

He caught her smile before she turned her back on him to fold the picnic blanket. When she finished, James shoved it back into the hamper and then led the way down through the crevice.

He took Andrea's hand again when the path leveled out and emerged onto the green hills. They didn't linger in the meadows this time, taking a more direct path back to the car. He squinted at the sky, where the fluffy clouds over the mainland were giving way to a gray ceiling.

"Looks like rain," he said. "And the wind's beginning to pick up."

"Don't worry, I won't melt." She squeezed his hand. "If we only have today and tomorrow, I don't want to miss anything."

"Have I actually been successful?" he asked in mock astonishment. "Do I hear Andrea Sullivan wanting to enjoy a holiday? In Scotland?"

"Oh, shut up." She gave him a shove, and he ducked out of her way, laughing.

Since Andrea was determined to see Skye's points of interest, James turned the car north toward Uig, intending to take the long loop around and hit the most spectacular natural sights. Most of the roads this far onto the Trotternish peninsula were single-track, and more than once, James had to pull into a lay-by and wait for a vehicle to pass in the opposite direction. When they finally arrived at Duntulm, he found a parking spot in the gravel by the side of the road.

He and Andrea walked out to the promontory, where the ruins of the old MacDonald castle stood, their hands linked. Errant clouds slid in front of the sun, driven by the stiff sea breeze, alternately casting their surroundings in shadow and sunlight. The water made a moody blue contrast to the dark, rugged edge of Harris in the distance.

The idea James's ancestors had built this castle, lived and died here, always seemed somewhat surreal. His clan was the largest in the world, but somewhere in the tangled branches of his family tree, he knew he was descended from the MacDonalds of Sleat who had built the castles on the island. Maybe that was why his father had never wanted to leave. There was too much history, too much MacDonald blood spilled over this small expanse of Scotland.

The ground near the castle was marshy and uneven, bisected by several lines of wooden fences to keep holiday-goers from pitching off the heights to the rocky break below. The closer they got to the cliff where the ruins lay, the harder Andrea gripped his hand.

"You do realize I might pass out," she said. "I may have used up all my courage on the fairy tower."

"Then stop here and enjoy the view." He paused at a cluster of stones that had once been the castle's foundation and slipped an arm around her. She relaxed against him and looked out over the incredible vista, and he watched the uncertainty fade from her face in favor of quiet appreciation.

"Let's go into the ruins, shall we?" he asked.

She nodded, finding his hand again. They tramped around the dirt floor, surrounded by the crumbling walls of the old castle. He held her around the waist as they peered through the keyhole opening in the front wall that framed a view of the sea. He found himself watching her as much as the scenery, enjoying the look of pleasure on her face and the feel of her body pressed alongside his. He didn't dare draw attention to the fact in case she panicked and withdrew again, but she seemed content to rest in his arms. It was a small step, but at least it was one in the right direction.

Chapter Twenty-Two

The first fat drops of rain struck them as they climbed back out from the floor of the castle. Clouds blotted out the sun again, and frigid wind buffeted them outside the protective shelter of the stone walls.

"Race you back to the car?" James asked.

Andrea didn't think he meant it literally, but the skies apparently did, because they chose that moment to shed their full burden, loosing drops so large they stung when they struck her skin. She grinned at him and took off at a sprint up the marshy hillside.

Andrea dared a glance back and saw him following a few paces behind, laughing as he ran. She beat him to the car, but by the time he fumbled his keys from the pocket of his jeans, she was shivering and soaking wet. He quickly unlocked the doors, and they dove for the shelter of the wagon as if of one mind.

The doors slammed with a hollow thud. Rain drummed dully on the roof and splattered the windshield. Andrea shivered violently as water dripped from her sodden hair down her face.

James started the engine and flipped on the heater. "I'm so sorry."

Laughter bubbled up inside her. "Did you actually just apologize for the weather?"

He smiled sheepishly. "I suppose I did. Cold and miserable, remember?"

"And horrible food," she added. "I think we can agree that one isn't true."

"Good. I would hate to spoil your newfound fondness for my country. Wait here." He jumped out of the car into the downpour and popped the hatch in the back. By the time he got back into the driver's seat, he was even wetter than before.

"This should warm you up." He pulled the picnic blanket out from under his coat and draped it around her shoulders, then pushed her wet hair back from her face. His touch stirred a riot of sensations in her middle. He started to pull away, but she curled her fingers around his hand and held it against her cheek.

"I'm beginning to think you are a good man, James MacDonald."

He froze, his fingers twining with hers, but he didn't say anything.

"I've been thinking I should learn a few words of Gaelic while I'm here. What is it you said? *An toir thu dhomh pòg?*"

"Do you have any idea what that means?"

"Serena told me."

"And what did she tell you?" He seemed to be struggling against a smile.

Andrea leaned across the console and pressed her lips to the corner of his mouth. "Will you kiss me?"

"Close. More properly, it means, 'Will you give me a kiss?'"

She laughed, and it came out far shakier than she expected. "James, stop talking and just kiss me."

He smiled and brushed the back of his fingers against her cheek, then lowered his mouth to hers. The first touch sent a shiver down her spine that had nothing to do with the cold, and she sighed against his mouth. His fingers tightened on her shoulder, but his lips remained gentle, softly exploring, tasting. Somewhere in the recesses of her mind, she knew he was holding himself back.

His patience was torture. She gripped his jacket and pulled him closer. The urgency of his response stole her breath and made her head swim. He buried his hands in her hair, and Andrea surrendered to the moment, reveling in the taste of him, the restrained strength in his touch. When his lips traveled across her jaw and down to her throat, a whimper slipped from her mouth.

The sound must have brought him back to his senses, because he froze and lifted his head a fraction of an inch, his breath coming in bursts.

"You're killing me, Andrea," he whispered. He pressed another lingering kiss to her lips, then released her completely and fell back against his seat.

Her cheeks instantly heated. She had gotten wrapped up in the moment, driven by the need for closeness, connection. He probably thought … Well, she didn't want to know what he thought. "I didn't mean to … I'm sorry."

"I'm not sorry at all." He raised her hand to his lips so her fingers curved against his cheek and kissed her palm. The mere press of his lips in such an unexpected place sent a thrill of electricity through her body. From the little smile he gave her, he knew it too.

"We should go back to the hotel," he said. "You're soaked."

She looked down at her jacket, the light gray fabric now charcoal from the rain. "What's the hurry? We can't get any wetter, can we?"

"You only say that because it's positively steamy in here now." His mouth curved into the wicked smile that had gotten her into this situation in the first place. "Let's go change into dry clothes, and I'll make you a cup of chocolate."

"All right. You sold me with the chocolate."

James eased the car from the turnout, driving slowly in the steadily falling rain. The windshield wipers thudded against the windshield with every sweep, giving her something to focus on besides the man next to her. To say she hadn't wished for that moment since she met him would be a bald-faced lie. She just hadn't been willing to succumb to temptation when she thought she was just another conquest to him.

The rain dwindled to a spatter as they curved around the other side of the peninsula. James pointed out the Old Man of Storr, a particularly spectacular volcanic rock pinnacle, but they didn't linger long. Despite her earlier words, she was chilled to the bone, the cold even more biting in contrast to the flush of heat she felt anytime he touched her. She spent the drive back alternately shivering and trying to calm her racing pulse.

He opened her door and took her hand to help her out. "Go take a hot bath and change into some dry clothes. Then we'll go up to the house, and I'll make you the best cup of chocolate you've ever had."

"Up to the house?" she asked with a lift of her eyebrows. "What's wrong, James? Don't trust yourself alone with me?"

"Not remotely." He tugged her closer for another kiss, lingering long enough to weaken her knees and convince her of the wisdom of his decision.

"I see your point." She dragged herself away from him and dug for her keys in her purse. "I won't be too long."

"Take your time."

Andrea let herself into her cottage after two tries with the lock and shut the door firmly behind her. She leaned against it for support, cooling her cheeks with her chilled hands. If she could form a coherent thought, she would list all the reasons why this had been a terrible idea. Instead a stupid smile spread across her lips. She might be out of practice with this sort of thing, but as kisses went, those belonged in the record books. She just wished they hadn't been over so quickly.

She dropped her purse onto the bed and headed straight to the bathroom where she filled the tub for the second time that day. She hung her wet jacket and scarf on the hooks behind the door and perched on the edge of the tub to remove her shoes.

Did she dare believe she was more than just a temporary distraction to him? She believed him when he said his reputation was no longer deserved, and his actions today told her he was keeping a firm hold on his self-control. Which was good, considering her own felt awfully shaky.

That didn't bother her half as much as the realization that what she felt now went far beyond the physical.

She buried her face in her hands. How could she have let this happen? The issue of work concerns aside, they lived thousands of miles away from one another. His life was here in Britain, hers in America. A long-distance relationship could never work, even considering she flew to or through London every month.

Not that he had said anything about a relationship at all.

"Stop it." Her voice echoed in the tiled room. She had two choices: end this right now, or enjoy the last bit of time they had together, regardless of the consequences to her heart. The smarter option was obvious. It just didn't have a chance.

Chapter Twenty-Three

James fumbled with his keys and let himself into his cottage, pulling off his damp jacket as he entered. First order of business was a hot bath to stave off the chill. Then again, given what had just happened, he might be better off with a cold shower.

He let his breath out in one long, shaky exhalation. Just recalling Andrea's response to his kiss sent his pulse rate through the roof again. He'd suspected a passionate nature lay behind her cool, controlled exterior, but he'd really had no idea what he was asking.

This woman was going to make the next few days sheer torture.

"It's your punishment for being an idiot," he said aloud. "You deserve it."

Somehow, though, as tempting as those few short minutes in the car had been, they didn't shock him half as much as her willingness to relax with him, hold his hand, stand close to him. That sort of intimacy seemed to come far less easily than the sparks that flew when they kissed.

He crossed to the bathroom, littering wet shoes behind him as he went, his unresponsive fingers fumbling with the buttons of his shirt. The last time he had let a woman get under his skin, he had devoted himself to her and received only a tabloid-documented humiliation in return. He had been so blindly in love with Cassandra, he couldn't see her wholesome image was just a construct, and he was merely means to an end. Two years later he only now felt neutral enough to say her name aloud.

Why on earth would he want to put himself through that again?

And what made him think Andrea was interested in more than just a casual friendship? It wasn't as if they had planned or even wanted the chemistry between them. She'd been very clear about her goals in Scotland, and a relationship was not one of them.

No, Andrea might have let her guard down enough to share a few moments of closeness, but she was far from ready for true intimacy. His attempt at the fairy tower to get her to open up had rebounded on him. She'd struck out as if threatened, throwing his own conflict with Ian back at him. That wasn't the sign of someone ready to leave her hurts behind and take a chance on love.

Besides, why should he even want to show her not all men were like Logan? That she could overcome the hurts of her past? How could a mere four days with this woman erase all the lessons he thought he'd learned and make him want to dive back into the madness that broke his heart?

"Because you're not thinking rationally. Now that you've kissed her, you want more."

If only it were that simple.

James was ready to go long before Andrea, dressed in dry jeans and a woolen pullover, a muffler wound around his throat against the early evening cold. He dragged on his leather jacket and wandered onto the deck behind his cottage to wait.

The rain had passed, but low clouds still tangled the peaks of the mountains on the mainland and wreathed the top of the Ornsay lighthouse. Now that the wind had died down to a soft breeze, only isolated patches of ripples disturbed the glass-like surface of the sound. He breathed deeply in the stillness and willed away the twist in his chest at the thought of Friday's fast approach.

Andrea would be on her way back to New York on Saturday, and he'd spend the weekend in Skye with his family before flying to Glasgow as planned. He loved Isleornsay. So why did the prospect of Andrea's departure dim his enjoyment of it? Why did he feel so little pleasure in the idea of attending to the business he'd so painstakingly built over the last decade?

Lord, why am I suddenly questioning my life?

The involuntary prayer felt foreign in his mind. How long had it been since he'd prayed? Not the brief words of blessing before a meal or a word of thanks for a good outcome, but a real prayer? Opening his heart in stillness and listening to whatever God wanted to speak to him?

Long enough that he couldn't remember when.

James sank onto the deck chair, awash in shame. He could admit he'd never been particularly religious. Like his father, he'd rejected the liturgical church traditions. But he'd been raised to pray and read the Bible. Even when he'd not been living a Christian life, it was always somewhere in the back of his mind.

No. He remembered when he'd prayed last. When Cassandra had returned his engagement ring. The breakup of his relationship following so closely on the heels of Duncan MacDonald's passing had jarred everything he thought he knew about his life. When he hadn't received a satisfactory answer to his questions, he'd stopped asking.

James shoved his cold hands into his coat pockets. He'd told himself he'd healed from that heartbreak, but he'd really just become calloused. Here he thought he had the answers for Andrea, and he was just as lost in his own mess as she was.

I'm sorry, Lord. I'm an idiot. I thought I'd done so well on my own, but I forgot to ask what You want for me.

He pressed his clasped hands to his mouth. It felt presumptuous to ask what he wanted to ask. As long as he'd been busy and happy, he could do without God. Now that he was conflicted over his life, he was going to come crawling back?

"Did I take too long?"

James jerked his head up at Andrea's voice and stood quickly. She'd changed into dry clothes and donned her wool coat, but her hair was still damp. "No, I just got here." He held out a hand, and after a moment's hesitation, she came to him. He wrapped his arms around her and pulled her back against him as he'd done on the fairy tower.

Please. He didn't even know what he was asking, but he loosed the prayer all the same. He pressed his lips to her hair, breathing in her scent and enjoying how well she fit against him.

"If you can't find me tomorrow, I'm probably hiding out somewhere so I don't have to leave," she murmured.

"You won't hear any complaints from me." He rubbed her arms briskly. "It's cold, and I promised you something to warm you up."

"Is that so?" She turned to face him and raised her eyebrows.

"Chocolate, you vixen."

"Somehow I'm disappointed."

"Can't have that, can we?" He pulled her closer and proceeded to kiss her until the cold was the last thing on either of their minds.

A few hours with the family might be a very good thing. Now that James knew Andrea wouldn't object, he constantly wanted to pull her into his arms and kiss her breathless. Any more time alone with her would only serve to complicate matters.

He almost groaned when he saw his brother's car.

Andrea gave him a quizzical look, reminding him she knew nothing about their conversation or Ian's assertion that Andrea was too good for him. Bad enough that James wondered if it were true. She didn't need to know they were under scrutiny from his brother and business partner as well.

Still, his stomach churned with nervousness at what Ian might say when he saw the two of them together. Not just in one another's presence, but *together*. His brother was always a gentleman, and they had managed civility that morning, but he'd been rather vocal about James's pursuit of Andrea. James made a point of taking her hand on the walk up to the front door.

They entered to a flurry of coats, rain boots, and diaper bags in the living room. The activity ceased when they walked in, all eyes going to their clasped hands.

"What's going on?" he asked, forcing himself to sound casual. Ian's gaze landed heavily on him, but James didn't look in his brother's direction.

Serena tied Emmy's shoes with practiced hands, despite the little girl's squirming on the sofa. "Ian's taking us to dinner. Auntie's been telling us about this place in Dunvegan for ages, and we figured you already had plans. I hope you don't mind."

James had to wonder about the timing. Was this Muriel and Serena's attempt to give them some privacy, or were they trying to avoid a confrontation between him and Ian? He wouldn't put either scenario past them. Serena struggled to get Max's chubby arms into a coat and then heaved him onto her hip.

"Did you get the change of clothes, dear?" Muriel asked.

Serena stopped in mid-bustle. "Blast. Andrea, can you hold him for a minute?" She didn't wait for an answer before she thrust the baby into Andrea's arms and rushed off back down the hall.

Andrea's startled expression melted into one of dismay.

"Here," James said, extending his arms. "I'll take him."

"No, I'm okay." She shifted Max over to her other hip as the baby grabbed a handful of her hair.

"No, no," she said gently, disentangling herself from the baby's grip. "Don't pull."

She pretended to munch Max's hands, and the baby squealed with laughter. A smile crept onto James's face.

"Makes you think, doesn't it?" Serena appeared beside him and nudged him with her elbow.

"Oh, shut it."

She just laughed and gave him a devious grin. "Have a nice evening. Just not too nice. We'll be back soon."

James shook his head while Serena recovered Max from Andrea's arms. Ian's gaze bored holes into him. After a few false starts involving Emmy's missing bunny and a forgotten trainer cup, the five of them finally made it out the door. Ian nodded politely to Andrea as he passed, but he didn't give James a second look.

James let out a sigh of relief. Thank God Ian's manners won out over his desire to dress him down.

They stood in the silence left by the family's abrupt departure. So much for the safety of a crowded house.

Andrea broke first. "That was subtle."

"Not their strong suit, but they mean well. Shall we get the chocolate started?"

She followed him into the kitchen and slid onto the stool at the island while he collected the ingredients for their treat. When he pulled out a large bar of chocolate, her eyes widened. "When you say chocolate, you mean chocolate!"

James chuckled and retrieved a quart of milk from the refrigerator. "This is not exactly low calorie. But it is absolutely worth it."

She leaned forward to watch as he chopped the candy bar with a heavy-bladed knife. "I hope you don't have anything extravagant planned for supper."

"I thought maybe you'd like to learn how to cook something."

"I'm a New Yorker. I use my oven for storage."

He gaped at her. "Surely you're joking."

"Nope. Right now I have winter sweaters in it." She cast him a mischievous look. "That's why God invented chefs. So Manhattanites wouldn't starve."

"Oh, is that so?" He poured the milk into a small saucepan and set it on the stove to heat. "Observe well, Ms. Sullivan. Besides heating the milk gently, the real secret to this recipe is good quality chocolate."

"You know, one of these days, I'll have to actually watch your show. You're pretty good at this cooking thing."

James turned around and shot her an amused look. "Ms. Sullivan, are you flirting with me?"

She shrugged, but the look she gave him was positively sultry, enough to make his mouth go dry. He took a step toward her, but she shook her head and pointed toward the stove. "Watch your milk, Jamie. Don't want to get overheated."

He grinned. She was a firecracker, no doubt, high heels or not. Then he realized she'd called him by his nickname for the first time. It left a strangely warm glow in his chest. "Jamie, huh? Does that mean I get to pick a nickname for you?"

"Well, my sister calls me Andy."

"Hmm, Andy doesn't suit you. Maybe I'll call you Legs." He shot her a wicked glance. "After all, that's what I noticed first about you."

She narrowed her eyes at him. "In that case, do I get to call you Ego?"

He threw his head back and laughed. "Andy it is, then. Now stop distracting me. You still haven't told me what you want to make for dinner."

"Omelets."

"You have my extensive culinary knowledge at your disposal and you pick omelets?"

"I like them," she said defensively. "And I might actually have a hope of making a decent one. We both know I'm never making coq au vin."

"Omelets it is. But first, we drink chocolate." He added a few small pieces of the chocolate and whisked the now-steaming milk until the chocolate melted into a dark pool. Once all the chocolate was melted, he added a splash of vanilla and a pinch of cinnamon, then poured the rich drink into two large mugs.

"Your chocolate awaits, my lady." He set the cup in front of her and watched as she took her first sip.

Her eyes widened. "This is sinful. You're right. We say *hot chocolate* in America, but it's really just cocoa. It's not the same thing at all."

James slid onto the stool next to her. "Haven't I earned some sort of appreciation for my culinary prowess?"

She sipped from her mug, repressing her smile. "You're incorrigible."

"No. Just completely infatuated." He took the cup from her hand, set it on the counter, and kissed her lightly, tasting the chocolate on her lips. "On second thought, let's order takeaway so we have more time to do this."

She laughed and pulled away from him. "No way. You promised me omelets. Besides, what happened to self-control and all that?"

"Overrated." He moved in for another kiss, but she slipped off the stool and out of his reach.

"Come on. Dinner first. There will be plenty time for the rest later."

"Do you promise?"

She gave him a mysterious look over her shoulder and his last defense against her crumbled.

He was in such trouble.

Chapter Twenty-Four

In James's presence, Andrea felt like a fifteen-year-old girl with her first crush, giddy with anticipation. She might be setting herself up for a fall, but it was hard to care, especially after the look he had given her a minute ago.

She rummaged in the cabinet for a mixing bowl while James brought out not only eggs, but half the garden: tomatoes, onions, garlic, asparagus, and mushrooms. He dove back into the refrigerator for a block of Irish cheddar wrapped in wax paper.

"Okay, first lesson. Cracking the eggs." James took one out of the carton with a flourish, rapped it sharply on the edge of the bowl, and deposited the egg into it with a swift one-handed movement. "Your turn."

Andrea looked at him doubtfully, but she cracked her egg and dumped it into the bowl—along with half of the mangled shell.

"Maybe I should do the cracking."

She shot him a mock-scowl. "Are you saying I can't even crack an egg?"

"Well, the evidence doesn't lie."

"It's an egg."

He peered into the bowl. "Andrea, omelets are not supposed to be crunchy."

She laughed and gave him a bump with her hip. "Fine. You do the eggs. I'll wash my hands." She moved to the sink and scrubbed the raw white from her hands. Eyes narrowing, she thought better of the towel and flicked water across the kitchen. Droplets spattered James's face and shirt. She laughed.

"Very mature, Ms. Sullivan." He wiped his face with his forearm and pretended to frown at her. "Get over here, or you'll be relegated to eating carryout for the rest of your life."

She pretended to grumble on the way back to the island, but the warmth in his gaze as she approached made her heart do a giddy little skip. "What now?"

"Well, now we beat them like so"—he demonstrated—"with a little water instead of milk to make them fluffy. And then we chop the veggies. What do you like in yours?"

"Onions, tomatoes, and mushrooms."

"Start with the onion, then." He crooked a finger at her. "Come here."

Her eyebrows lifted, but she sidled around the island. He smoothly slipped behind her, pinning her between the counter and his body.

"How exactly does this make supper?"

"Wheesht, woman. Patience. First, the proper way to hold a knife." He waited until she picked up the chef's knife and adjusted her fingers on the handle, thumb and forefinger gripping the back end of the blade below the tang. He closed his hand over hers and placed an onion in front of her. "Now we slice off the root and stem end ..."

His breath tickled her ear, distracting her from her task. If she just turned her head a bit, her lips—

"Concentrate, you little minx," he murmured huskily. "I've not got a mind to make a trip to hospital tonight."

"Fine." She heaved a dramatic sigh as he guided her through the process of dicing an onion, his hands covering hers. "I would have learned to cook a long time ago if I had known it was a contact sport."

His laughter rumbled through his chest. "I only give special students this treatment."

"I would hope so." She stopped. "Wait. Who exactly have you been heating it up with in the kitchen?"

"Jealous?"

"No. Just … curious."

"Sure you are." He nudged her to get her attention back to the second half of the onion. "Only Cassie. And she wasn't all that interested in learning something so—"

"Practical?" Andrea hardly imagined Cassandra Sinclair doing anything as mundane as cooking. Not that she much wanted to imagine her doing anything with James.

"Domestic."

She felt the sudden tension in his body and stilled her knife hand as he pressed his face to her hair. She didn't dare to breathe.

"I didn't really leave her, you know. She left me."

"For the other guy?" Andrea murmured.

"When I found out about the affair, I told her she had to choose between him or me. She chose him." He squeezed her hand and then resumed chopping. "I guess I shouldn't be too surprised. It was Phil Kane."

Andrea blinked, stunned, while she scrambled for something to say. Philip Kane was perhaps the only star bigger than Cassandra Sinclair. He'd have to be in order for Andrea to know who he was. "Would you really have stayed with her?"

He inhaled deeply. "Had she been sorry … yes. I would have forgiven her."

Andrea blinked, stunned. She wouldn't have been so forgiving in that situation. She hadn't been that forgiving, as a matter of fact. "I don't understand that choice."

He shrugged. "I loved her. At least, I thought I did."

She set down the knife and turned to face him. "No, I meant her choosing him over you. It's a big step down, if you ask me. Phil Kane seems like an arrogant jerk."

He stayed silent for so long she wondered if she should have been less free with her thoughts. Then he slid one arm around her waist and pulled her gently to him, covering her mouth with his. She melted into him like the chocolate into the milk, surrendering completely to the kiss.

Cassandra Sinclair was a complete idiot.

The omelets were delicious, but only because James took over early in the process. Andrea proved to be as hopeless at flipping an omelet as she was at cracking an egg.

"Can I just forget the whole omelet thing and turn them into scrambled eggs instead? That, I might be able to manage."

James smiled at her across the table. "Or you can stick with me, and then you won't have to cook at all."

Andrea took a drink of water to wash down the egg stuck in her suddenly dry throat. He sounded like he was teasing, but something serious had crept into his expression since he talked about Cassie, and the look in his eyes made it hard to breathe. She shifted her gaze back to her food and said nothing.

James took the hint and changed the subject. "So, it's still early. What do you want to do tonight?"

"I don't know. I don't really feel like being in a crowd of people."

He grinned at her.

"Behave. That's not what I meant." She toyed with her fork, her pulse speeding a bit. "Would you like me to play for you?"

The grin faded into something softer. "I would love for you to play for me. In fact, if you're done, you can get started while I clean up."

"All right." She rose with her plate, but James took it from her hand. "Let me. I can handle this part."

Her stomach fluttered as she moved into the living room and sat down at the piano. It wasn't as if this were a true performance, and he'd already heard her play once. Still, she'd let him talk her into it before. This was offered freely. There was a difference.

She played a few warm-up exercises, eighth notes followed by scales in increasing tempo, until her hands and arms felt warm and fluid. Then she launched into a Chopin mazurka, a moderate piece that fit her cheerful mood. She was surprised to find she didn't stumble over the notes. She usually kept the sheet music by her piano at home, even if she rarely needed to consult it. The mazurka melded into a nocturne she had performed enough times that her fingers remembered the notes even when her brain wasn't so certain.

The clink of plates and rush of water from the kitchen stopped. A few minutes later James entered with two mugs that he set on the side table. The aroma of coffee drifted to her.

He settled onto the bench beside her. "What's this?"

"Chopin. One of my favorites."

"It's beautiful." He leaned in close enough to whisper. "So are you."

"You're trying to distract me."

He brushed aside her hair and stroked the back of her neck. "What about now?"

It took all her control not to squirm on the bench. "Not going to work."

Next it was his lips in the same spot, and her involuntary shiver made her miss an obvious chord. She struggled against a smile. "If you want me to play, stop it. Or go over there."

"I'll behave, I promise." James put his hands in his lap, and she didn't need to look to know he was grinning like a schoolboy. But he kept his word and didn't try to touch her until she finished the piece and lifted her hands from the keys.

"That's one of my greatest regrets, you know." He retrieved the mugs from the table and held one out to her. "My father was such a talented musician. Even Muriel plays the piano. But Serena and I never learned."

Andrea accepted her mug and wrapped both hands around the cup. "It's not too late."

"Maybe not. But you have a gift, Andrea. You amaze me. Really."

The tenderness in his gaze made her believe it. She doubted James recognized his own gift. It had taken her a while to see his caring, nurturing side, but he was thoughtful in all his interactions with his family. He showed his love by cooking for them, sharing his talents when he didn't have to. He had done nothing but ensure Andrea was comfortable, entertained, and treated with respect when she was with him.

Her thoughts must have shown on her face, because his smile faded, replaced with a sort of quiet awareness. "Why did you give up performing?"

She swallowed hard. His eyes remained fixed on her, steady, compassionate, and she realized she did trust him.

"I met my ex-husband during my senior year at NYU," she began. "I roomed with his sister. She played the cello. The first time I met Logan, I fell hard. He was handsome. Charming. So self-assured." She gave James a bare smile. "A little like you, actually."

James grimaced, and somehow the expression gave her the push she needed to keep going. "It all felt like a fairy tale. I was only twenty-two, but I was so innocent. He was twenty-eight. Do you know who Bryan Roberts is?"

James shook his head.

"He's Logan's father. Back then he was a senator. Old money, lots of contacts. The family is like American royalty. Logan worked for his father, and he had all that wealth at his disposal. He gave me lavish gifts, took me on trips. I shouldn't have let myself get seduced by it all. I was raised to know better. But what girl wouldn't get caught up with a man who could take her to Paris for dinner or to the Spanish Riviera for a day at the beach on a whim?"

"Of course you were susceptible," James said. "He was trying to impress you."

"And he succeeded. Things got serious fast, faster than I was ready for. I knew the relationship was wrong, but that deep into it, I didn't know how to slow down or back away. And I thought I loved him.

"When I graduated from college that May, I was already eight weeks pregnant."

She swallowed again, barely daring a glance at his face, but he just waited, unsurprised, not judging. He gave her hand an encouraging squeeze.

"We told his parents first. We knew it would be a scandal, but I still didn't expect his father's reaction." Her voice fell an octave. "He wanted me to have an abortion."

She heard his long, slow exhale and plowed on. "I refused. Senator Roberts then informed us we would be getting married. You see, he was going to be running for president. And for a man who was campaigning on family values, it would be a scandal."

"He sounds like a prize," James said, his tone low, gravelly.

"Well, it wasn't how I'd pictured things going, but I loved Logan. I was going to have a husband and a family. I gave up an offer to play with the New York Philharmonic in order to have the baby."

"You did what you thought was right. You wanted to give your baby a stable home." He rubbed the back of her hand reassuringly.

"We honeymooned in Maui. It was supposed to be romantic, but things were already different between us. Logan was distant. He resented being trapped in a marriage he really didn't want. I was sick half the time we were there, so I stayed in the room while he played golf.

"One day I was feeling a little better, so I went down to the hotel restaurant, and he was having lunch with this pretty blonde. Apparently *golf* was just code for other activities." She dipped her head, the humiliation and pain of the memory hitting her again with full force. "I made a huge scene. Needless to say, the woman was shocked to find out he had a pregnant wife."

Andrea dragged air into her lungs, steeling herself for the next part of the story. "Logan didn't come back to our room that night. Or the next morning. I knew I couldn't stay married to him. If he treated me like that on our honeymoon, life with him would be … Well, I would rather raise the baby on my own than have my child exposed to that kind of marriage. I was booking my plane tickets home when I started to have this terrible pain."

James's patient expression changed, darkening, but he didn't say anything, just clasped her hand tighter.

"I ended up being be rushed to the hospital into emergency surgery. I lost the baby." Her throat burned from the effort of holding back tears. Her memories of that day were blurred, but she would never forget the ultrasound technician's pronouncement that there was no heartbeat. She hurried on with the story before she could change her mind about telling it.

"Logan finally showed up at the hospital the next day. I don't know what I expected. Some sort of reaction, some emotion. I'd lost our baby, and I could have died in the process. But the only thing he said was 'Too bad you couldn't do that a few weeks ago. You could have saved us both a lot of trouble.'"

James put his arms around her and kissed her hair, but she was too locked in the memory to register anything beyond his presence.

She leaned against him and said, "That was the end of my marriage. He went back and filed for an annulment before I could divorce him. He said I'd tricked him into marrying him by getting pregnant and then I'd had an abortion. I was on the front cover of every tabloid. It didn't matter what I said. It was my word against theirs, and Logan came out looking like the victim. Everyone believed him over me. My father, my church—everyone but Becky.

"I was pretty much shunned in New York. No one dared to go against the Roberts family. So I took my mother's maiden name and went back to school. After a while, things died down and people stopped recognizing me. But I couldn't go back to performing. It would dredge up the old scandal, and I couldn't go through it all again. "

James tightened his arms around her. "Andrea. You realize this was not your fault. You were just trying to do what was best for the baby. Logan will have to answer for his actions someday."

"Yeah. I'm still waiting." She closed her eyes, summoning courage for the last part of her story. Even if they were just acquaintances, he deserved to know. Before he got any ideas about what they might be to one another.

Yet when she opened her mouth, the words stuck in her throat. James drew back from her and took her face in his hands, his expression pained but his eyes gentle. "Let it go, Andrea. You've carried it for too long."

Andrea started to tell him she was fine, but the only thing that came out was a choked cry. She fell against him and sobbed.

Chapter Twenty-Five

Emotions warred inside James as Andrea wept against him, her body shaking, her tears soaking his shoulder. He didn't trust his voice in the grip of burning anger toward the man who had wounded her so deeply she'd had to turn her back on everything that was important to her. Instead he just tightened his arms around her and smoothed her hair with his free hand.

It all made sense now, though: her reluctance to let down her guard, her determination to believe he was just another entitled celebrity, her need to reassure herself she wasn't merely a conquest to him. She had carried a terrible burden all these years. She had been pregnant, devastated, and treated cruelly, when she deserved to be protected and cherished.

Like he would do, if given half a chance.

The thought ambushed him and drained the air from the room. His heart thudded so hard in his chest, he was sure it would jolt her from his arms. What exactly was he thinking here? He couldn't possibly be having serious thoughts about a woman he'd known less than a week. It had taken six months of dating Cassandra to admit they were in a committed relationship, and more than two years until he'd worked up the courage to ask her to marry him.

Maybe that should have been an indicator it wasn't meant to be.

Before he could dwell further on those disturbing thoughts, he realized Andrea's body had stilled and her tears had subsided. Still, she clung to him, her head tucked into the spot between his neck and shoulder. Her vulnerability took his breath away.

She pulled back, her gaze sliding past him to the piano. "I'm sorry. I didn't mean …" She moved away from him down the bench, straightening her clothing as she went. She wiped her eyes with the back of her hand, and the stiffness in her body spoke of embarrassment. As much as he ached to see the invisible shield go up around her again, she would never trust him if he forced the issue.

"I'll go reheat our coffee." James straightened his legs, cramped from his awkward position on the piano bench, and collected their coffee mugs. As he took them to the microwave, he heard the tentative notes of the piano begin again. He'd been afraid she would close up to him completely, but the quiet melancholy strains of the piano made him think she was merely gathering her thoughts.

If she'd really turned her back on the woman who'd risked everything on love, she would have given up her music completely, wouldn't she have?

He almost groaned aloud. First, he'd let Ian make him second-guess all his choices, and now he was psychoanalyzing a woman he barely knew, trying to assess her readiness for a relationship he'd spent the last two years insisting he didn't want.

Wasn't that why he'd dated pretty young women who were happy to take what he was willing to give? Because he knew they couldn't tempt him out of a vow of permanent bachelorhood?

He thumped his head against the cabinet, hard. Ian deserved whatever torture James could devise for leading him down a slippery slope of ... self-examination.

Andrea's idle playing had turned into a quiet, moody melody he didn't recognize. He removed their mugs from the microwave and went back to the reception room. He sat back down on the bench, but this time he didn't try to touch her. "What is that?"

"I don't know." Red still rimmed her eyes and tears had dried in faint tracks down her cheeks, but she seemed settled now, if not entirely peaceful. "Do you like it?"

"You're just making that up?" It had the sound of a fully composed piece, not something she was creating on the fly.

"I play when I'm upset." She lifted her hands from the keys, but the chord faded away slowly. "I ... I'm sorry, Jamie. I know you weren't asking for all this. We don't even know each other." She glanced up and fixated on the wet blotch on his shoulder. "I've made a mess of your sweater."

It took everything he had not to take her in his arms again and tell her he wanted to know everything about her, but he stopped himself just in time. He'd already said he was infatuated with her. Any more and he risked looking like a lovesick idiot.

Did he actually just think that?

He threw her a smile instead. "Don't worry. I'm washable."

She struggled for words. "I understand if you ... I mean, I know we ..." She broke off and chewed her bottom lip. "It doesn't matter, does it? I only have one day left here."

"Andrea, nothing you have told me changes the way I see you. If anything, it makes me realize how amazing you really are. You've made a wonderful life for yourself."

"I'm broken," she whispered.

"We're all broken. We're only human. Some wounds only God can mend. If we let Him." He took her hand. "I haven't been so good at that myself. But I've been thinking perhaps I'm ready to try." He brought her fingers to his lips and kissed them gently.

She flinched at his touch, and her abrupt withdrawal made him feel like he was falling off a cliff. He scrambled for purchase on the slippery edge, tasting desperation. He took her by the shoulders and turned her to face him. "I don't know what comes next, Andrea. But I'm willing to figure it out."

Tears sprang to her eyes again, glistening in the dim light. "Jamie, I might not be able to have children."

If he had been falling, now he was jerked to an abrupt stop. Whatever he'd expected, it wasn't this. "Because of the miscarriage?"

She wasn't looking at him again, but she nodded. "They were overaggressive because I could have died. The damage is probably irreversible. No one knows if … It could be difficult. It could be impossible."

And like that, everything else fell into place. The respectable men she could date would want families of their own. The ones who didn't care were the ones who wanted something she wasn't willing to give. No wonder she'd devoted herself to work. Why set herself up for heartbreak?

He moved carefully, not wanting to spook her. This wasn't a discussion anyone had until they'd been dating for months. Not just a few days and a few kisses into an acquaintance that might not have a chance to develop into more. But he didn't have the time to let things unfold naturally. "There is more than one way to build a family, Andrea."

Her tears were back. Before they could spill over, he pulled her onto his lap and kissed her slowly and carefully, handling her like a breakable thing. When she pulled away, her wondering look did terrifying things to his insides.

He clawed back to some sense of normalcy. "What do you say to a quiet movie in tonight? I imagine I could even find us some popcorn to go with it."

"That sounds perfect." She rose from his lap and settled herself a safe distance away on the bench once more.

"My laptop is still down at the cottage. Do you want to stay here and play while I go get it? I won't be long."

"If you don't mind. Jamie?"

"Yes, love?"

She smiled and reached for his hand. "Hurry back."

His heart lifted. He retrieved his keys and quickly exited the front door. Just as he closed it behind him, Andrea's melody started again, this time with a hopeful lilt.

Chapter Twenty-Six

Andrea played with half a mind, teasing out a melody on the piano. It was easier than facing the swell of emotion in her chest. Other than her sister, she'd never told anyone the full story of her relationship with Logan. James hadn't seemed shocked. If anything, her admission had drawn out a tenderness for which she'd never dared to hope.

Telling the story should have made her feel better, but it still didn't completely ease the burden on her heart. She'd thought when he knew how little she could offer him, he'd pull back and make it easier on the both of them. Instead he'd kissed her with such aching gentleness, her insides twisted into knots.

Her fingers stilled on the piano keys. *We're all broken. We're only human. Some wounds only God can mend.*

She sighed. It wasn't that simple. Maybe James could put his problems behind him that easily. Or maybe he hadn't. It wasn't as if he had his life together. He could barely speak to his own brother, and it sounded like he wasn't on the greatest terms with his mother either. Plus there were plenty of issues left over from his broken engagement with Cassandra. He was hardly a model for God's healing grace.

I haven't been so good at that myself. But I've been thinking I'm ready to try.

We're only human.

Maybe it was unfair to expect him to have his own life figured out just because he claimed to have faith. Whatever his faults, he was kind. Funny. Intelligent. He made her smile, and her heart felt light when she was with him. That couldn't be bad, could it?

She went back to the piano, playing simple exercises automatically. She was trying to rationalize something that was patently irrational. James was absolutely wrong for her. His job, his lifestyle, his wealth—all warning flags when it came to men. And still, everything in her strained toward him when he was near, had since the moment she met him.

Tires crunched on gravel outside, and the quiet hum of a motor died. When James entered the front door again, she was midway through the seventh movement of Schumann's "Scenes from Childhood," a lovely, simple piece that fit the wistfulness of her mood. There was a reason it was subtitled "Dreaming."

She didn't look at him, and he stood near the door until she finished. Then he pressed a soft kiss to her cheek and moved into the kitchen, giving her space to think.

She could learn to love this man.

A groan slipped from her mouth. That was definitely enough Schumann for now.

"What's wrong?"

Andrea jumped to her feet and almost knocked over the piano bench. She quickly righted it and moved into the kitchen. James had the popcorn and some oil heating in a heavy, lidded pot on the range.

"Like to do things the old-fashioned way?"

He smiled over his shoulder. "The microwave holds no challenge for me."

"Does anything cooking related hold a challenge for you?"

He held out an arm, and she went to him. He pulled her to his side and squeezed her waist. "Be careful. I might start believing you're fond of me."

"Hard to believe after all the grief I've given you, isn't it?" He was backing off, and she was grateful for it. There had been far too much intensity today. She couldn't handle any more tonight.

James dipped his head to peck her lips. "You've never been any grief. Well, today at least. You were awfully feisty when we met."

Andrea elbowed him, and he chuckled. "Stop! I'll burn the popcorn."

"It's not even popping yet."

On cue, the first kernels snapped in the pan, followed by a cacophony of pops. He gave her a knowing stare. "It's a gift."

"You're always so humble." She grinned, her pensive mood evaporating, and moved away to rummage in the cabinet for a bowl. She set it on the counter beside him.

"Thanks, sweetheart."

Her heart gave a little leap at the absent-minded endearment, and her mind wandered to what it would be like to hear it from his lips every day.

No. Can't go there tonight.

"Butter or margarine?" She laughed at his incredulous look. "Sorry I asked. Butter it is." It took a quick look in the refrigerator to remember the marble crock on the counter where Muriel kept the softened butter.

James seasoned the popcorn, dumped the whole mess into the bowl, and swept a hand toward the living room. "Your movie awaits. If I can remember how to plug in the computer. I don't usually watch on a big screen."

"That one I can handle." She'd done enough presentations to have this kind of technology down pat. Within minutes, Andrea had a cable hooked from the laptop's video output to the TV's input. "What are we watching?"

"It's a surprise. You sit. I can do the rest. My fragile male ego can't handle any more of your extreme competence."

Andrea laughed and went back to the sofa. "Right. Your ego wouldn't suffer from a little deflation."

"Ouch. You don't pull punches." He apparently had the movie set up, because he flipped the light off and hurried back to the sofa as the main titles came up.

Andrea smiled slowly at the familiar opening. "*North by Northwest*?"

"I figured you should have a chance to prove why it's the greatest movie ever made."

"A Hitchcock film starring Cary Grant? I shouldn't have to argue the point. Handsome, charming, and looks great in a suit."

"I'm pretty sure you're talking about Grant and not Hitchcock, but those are pretty big shoes for a man to fill."

Andrea smiled at him. "You stack up pretty well from where I'm sitting."

He grinned and put his arm around her. "In that case, sit a little closer."

Andrea settled in beside him, his arm draped over her shoulder, and let out a sigh of contentment. She wouldn't spoil this moment by thinking about what had to happen next. She couldn't remember the last time she'd spent a quiet night at home watching a movie with a man, free of pressure or expectations. Had she ever? She hadn't been particularly experienced when she met Logan. He'd loved Manhattan's nightlife, and they always had to be seen at the hottest clubs and parties.

Like James.

Still, that didn't feel like the whole truth. She couldn't reconcile the paparazzi hound with the man who made popcorn and streamed her favorite sixty-year-old movie simply to give her a reprieve from the intense emotion of the day. He surprised her time and again with his sensitivity.

The day's emotional roller coaster had taken its toll, and before long her eyes burned from the effort of focusing on the screen. Somewhere after the scene where Cary Grant's character was framed for the murder of the UN delegate, Andrea's eyelids began to drift downward. She shifted against James for a more comfortable position while he traced patterns on her arm in long, lazy strokes.

"Time to wake up, sweetheart." James's soft tone penetrated the fog, and she pried her eyes open. She blinked at the flicker of light from the television, disoriented. The movie was over, and the evening news was playing at a barely audible level. She lay against his side, legs curled up on the sofa beside her. At some point he had apparently covered her with a blanket.

"This is the second time I've fallen asleep with you."

"I'm beginning to think it's my personality."

She smiled and brushed her messy hair from her eyes, enveloped in a pleasant haze. "You make a nice pillow. A little hard, maybe, but warm."

"Are you ready to go, then? Serena and Muriel got home a while ago." James eased himself out from beneath her and stood, then pulled her to her feet and planted a kiss on her forehead.

She should feel self-conscious about the fact his family had seen her curled up on the sofa with him, but she was too sleepy to care. She stifled a yawn. "You may have to carry me to the car."

"Gladly." He helped her with her coat, but she could barely focus through her sleep-drugged brain to coordinate the movement of her arms. She blinked against the grit in her eyes and followed him out to the car, where she huddled into the depths of her coat. After their warm cocoon on the sofa, the cold, damp air sent waves of shivers through her.

When James walked her to the door of her cottage minutes later, he lingered, as if he were reluctant to say good night. Andrea didn't think. She simply slid her arms around his neck and pressed her lips to his. He pulled her close and returned the kiss, slow and sweet and filled with as much tenderness as she'd felt from him.

He pulled away first and touched his forehead to hers. "Good night, Andrea."

She smiled, still sleepy but now thoroughly happy. "Jogging tomorrow?"

"Wouldn't you rather get some rest?"

"It's my last day on Skye. I want to see the sunrise one more time."

"Jogging it is, then. Sleep well, love."

She stepped inside and closed the door behind her. He'd used the address casually before, but now she thought he might truly mean it.

Chapter Twenty-Seven

Andrea woke before dawn, and her heart began racing before she could consciously identify the reason for it. Then the events of the day before came rushing back to her.

She cringed when she recalled how she'd wept on James's shoulder. What must he think of her today? He had been sweet and understanding, but what else would he do when faced with a crying woman? Still, thinking of how she had fallen asleep against him on the sofa and awakened to his touch ignited a deep ache of longing in her. She wanted that sort of companionship so badly it hurt to breathe.

And today was her last day in Skye.

She rolled over and buried her head in her pillow. She was stupid. She had known this was just temporary. She had known it when she let him pierce her armor and see the life she had built was just a shield to protect a heart that couldn't bear to be damaged again. She had risked it knowing full well the consequences, and now she would pay the price.

The idea of dragging herself out of bed for her usual yoga warm-up sounded less and less appealing. Instead she took her phone from where it charged beside the bed and plugged in her earphones. Her favorite Mendelssohn composition flooded out, and she burrowed deeper in the covers, letting the music wash over her.

She woke much later to the glaring spill of sunlight through the windows and squinted at the clock on the nightstand. 10:13. She jerked upright in bed and pulled the earbuds out of her ears. Jogging. James. She'd slept through their morning date. She reached for the room phone and dialed his extension, but the line only rang.

Irrational panic seeped into her chest. What if he'd decided he was completely insane for getting involved with someone as damaged as her? What if he'd had the night to think about what she'd told him and decided he didn't want to deal with her baggage?

She didn't even try to convince herself she didn't care. She swung her legs out of bed, thrust her feet into her slippers, and shuffled to the door. She peered out through the crack. The wagon was still there, but a note was taped to her door.

Andrea pulled it off and unfolded the plain sheet of computer paper. What she assumed was James's handwriting, surprisingly precise and angular, slanted across the page.

Andrea,

I came by this morning, but you didn't answer. I didn't want to wake you. I have business in Portree, but I'll be back this afternoon. I left the keys to the car in case you want to get out. Be sure to stop by my room when you wake up. Door's unlocked.

Love, James

Her eyes lingered on the last words, and the knots in her stomach relaxed a little. That didn't sound like he had fled, only that he couldn't wait around for her to wake up.

She bathed and dressed quickly, too curious about what waited in his cottage to dally. Still, she felt like an intruder when she let herself in.

A smile spread across her face. He had set the kitchen table for one with dishes and flatware and a clutch of wildflowers spilling out of a teacup. A scrap of paper on the plate said, *Look in the fridge. Water for tea and bread for toast are on the counter.*

She opened the small refrigerator with anticipation. A glass of orange juice sat beside a bowl of yogurt and a small dish of fresh berries. She withdrew them with a smile and carried them to the table. Then she made herself a cup of tea from the electric kettle he'd left filled by the range and popped two slices of bread into the toaster.

What could she say about a man who would go to such pains to reassure her she hadn't scared him off? She hesitated for only a second before she found the number James had programmed into her cell phone, then lifted the room's handset and dialed.

He picked up on the third ring. "Good morning, Andy." She could tell by his tone he was smiling. "Did you find your surprise?"

"I did, thank you. I'm sorry I missed our date."

"You deserved some rest. I'm sorry I couldn't stick around. I didn't want you to think—"

"I know. You're sweet for being concerned."

Silence stretched, and Andrea belatedly realized he was probably in the middle of something important. "I didn't mean to interrupt you."

"Not at all. I'll be finished here in about an hour. We can be on our way to Inverness around one. If you're bored, you can drive up to the house. I'm sure Serena would like to see you."

"Sure, thanks. I'll see you soon."

Kind as his family was, Andrea didn't feel like spending the morning up at the house, so after she ate breakfast and washed the dishes, she set off toward the water's edge. The air carried a hint of warmth today, and the clouds that mounded over the mainland and spread erratically over the sound were of the fluffy variety, not the thunderheads that had followed them for the last several days. Regret gnawed at her midsection as she looked out onto the smooth blue waters. She had fought tooth and nail against this place, but it had wound its way into her heart without her noticing. Much like James had stolen into her heart and claimed a piece she had thought was lost forever.

It was ridiculous, impossible even, to have these sorts of feelings for someone she barely knew, but it made them no less real.

She walked along the shore, her feet sinking into the damp sand. She gathered smooth pebbles and bits of driftwood and tossed them into the water, watching them splash and disappear beneath the dark surface. She took out her phone, intending to snap a picture of the scenery, then shoved it back into her pocket. James was right. Whatever images she captured couldn't hope to reproduce how she felt here, standing on the edge of civilization, watching the glimmer of sunlight on the water and feeling the salt breeze on her face.

Tomorrow she would be back in New York amidst the towering skyscrapers of steel, stone, and glass, enveloped in the night sounds of horns and traffic with the drift of exhaust and garbage on the air. Could she ever see the bustle of home the same way again?

She wandered back up to the hotel, and her heart lurched when she saw James's Audi parked beside the Green Monster. Belatedly, she realized she'd never bothered to put on makeup and had barely brushed her hair. She changed course swiftly toward her own room, but she only made it a few steps before James's door opened.

"Going somewhere?"

"I was just …"

He smiled, and her heart skipped a beat. Wordlessly, he moved to her side, pulled her against him, and gave her a lingering kiss that erased all doubts about his feelings. "I've been waiting all morning to do that."

Me, too, she thought, but she was still feeling too shaky to say it aloud. "I should go pack."

He dipped his head and trailed light kisses along her cheek and jaw, raising a shiver on her skin. "Pack later."

She groaned at the effort of extricating herself from his grasp. "Pack now. I want to say good-bye to Serena and Muriel."

James let her pull out of his arms, but the way he watched her put a glow of giddiness into her chest. It faded when she stepped inside the cottage and remembered this was her last morning at the water's edge.

No, she couldn't think about it. She quickly zipped her suits into her garment bag, folding it over the single pair of jeans she could fit into her suitcase. She looked sadly at her gray quilted coat. Leaving the clothes behind felt like abandoning her memories of Skye, but she hadn't spent enough on them to justify buying another suitcase to bring them home.

She shook off her pensive mood, shoved her laptop into its case, and turned her attention to straightening her room. She removed the sheets from the bed and folded them loosely, then added her used towels to the pile. When she came across her scarf still hanging on the back of the bathroom door, she ran her fingers across the fringe and tucked it into the pocket of her wool coat.

James was waiting for her when she finally emerged from the cottage. He wordlessly took her bag and put it in the trunk of the sedan. Andrea worked the cottage's key from her key ring and handed it to him.

His fingers lingered on hers as he took it, her conflict reflected in his expression. It felt like an ending of something they had never defined, and neither of them knew what to do next.

"Shall we go up to the house and say good-bye?" he said finally, dropping her hand. She nodded and climbed into the car.

Serena and the kids were taking advantage of the sunny weather when they arrived. Emmy ran circles around the yard, flapping her arms and pretending to be some sort of flying creature, while Max sat contentedly on a blanket, munching cereal from a small bowl.

Serena waved as James parked a safe distance away. "Off to Inverness?" she asked when they climbed out.

James threw another conflicted glance at Andrea. "Just came to say good-bye."

"Auntie's in the house."

James took the hint and headed up the front steps. Serena linked her arm with Andrea's. "So, what now?"

"We're going to see a band tonight. A friend of the family's? Davy something."

Serena lifted her eyebrows. "That's not what I meant."

"I know it wasn't."

Serena nodded slowly. "I think by now you've figured out my brother is not exactly what he makes himself out to be."

"I've noticed that."

"Then maybe you should ask yourself why he's never with the same woman twice, if it's not for the reason he leads everyone to believe." She squeezed Andrea's arm and abruptly let go as the front door opened again. James emerged with Muriel.

"Andrea, darling." Muriel approached her with open arms and pressed her into a warm embrace. "It was lovely to have met you. I hope you'll consider coming back to visit us."

"Thank you, Muriel. I appreciate your hospitality."

"Emmy, come say good-bye to Andrea!" Serena called.

The little girl changed course immediately and flung herself at Andrea, almost knocking her off her feet. "Don't go! I want to show you how good I've gotten!"

Andrea swallowed hard and bent down so she could look the little girl in the eye. "I'm sorry, sweetie. I have to go home. Keep practicing, though. I'm sure your uncle will tell me all about your progress."

Emmy twisted her T-shirt between her fingers fitfully. "Are you coming back?"

Andrea's throat tightened. "I don't know. But if I do, you will be one of the first to know, okay?"

"Okay." Emmy's lower lip quivered as she threw her arms around her neck. Andrea struggled to breathe as she pressed the little girl to her. Finally she disentangled herself and straightened.

James watched her, holding Max with one arm. He nuzzled the baby and asked, "You want to say good-bye to Andrea, Maxie?"

She ran her hand over Max's downy head with a lurch of her heart, then gave him a kiss on the cheek. "'Bye, little one. Be good for mama. Let her sleep one of these nights, all right?"

Serena laughed, took Max from her brother, and accepted James's quick kiss on the cheek. "If I only thought he would listen to you. Have fun, you two. It was good meeting you, Andrea." She looked at James and then back at Andrea significantly, as if reminding her of their brief conversation.

Andrea's stomach jerked nervously as they climbed back into the car. James turned back down the drive and onto the main road before he asked, "What was that all about?"

"I'm not entirely sure." Had the words come from Ian, Andrea would have thought it was a warning that James would move on from her as quickly as he had with other women. But Serena almost sounded afraid James would be the one to get hurt in this scenario.

James leaned forward and turned on the stereo. Soft jazz spilled from the speakers, filling the silence. Andrea watched the scenery rush by as they headed back to the mainland, the vise around her chest tightening with each passing mile. When they reached the Skye Bridge, she closed her eyes against tears and leaned her head back against the seat.

"I've been thinking of taking some time off to travel," James said.

Andrea opened her eyes and looked at him. "You don't travel enough for work?"

"I've been to Los Angeles and Chicago, but would you believe I've never been to New York?"

Her pulse quickened at the implication. "That's a shame. New York has lots to offer."

"It's just too bad I don't know anyone who lives there. It would be nice to have someone show me around."

"I might know a few people." A slow smile crept over Andrea's face. "I wouldn't recommend going in the summer, though. Fall is much more pleasant."

"I was thinking more like spring." He glanced at her before quickly returning his eyes to the road. "April is already pretty booked, but I'm sure I can find some time in May. It only makes sense if my tour guide is free, though."

"I'll have her check her schedule."

He grinned. "I hope you're joking. Do I need to be more direct?"

"No, I think you got your point across just fine." She sighed, the glow fading a little. "You do realize I have to work. I can't just take off at a moment's notice like you can."

"Why not?"

"Because I don't own my own business. I'm subject to the whims of a very demanding boss, and after the whole London debacle ..."

"Let me ask you this. What do you want out of life?"

His serious tone took her aback. "I don't know. I want to be successful. I want to achieve my goals. I want to feel like I accomplished something when I go home at night. I guess ... I guess I'm happy where I am."

"So there isn't any room for change? No room for someone to share your life with?" James stared straight out the windshield, his muscles tensed, as if he dreaded the answer to his question.

Andrea couldn't breathe against the sudden swell of fear. She wanted to throw caution to the wind, ask him to speak plainly, but the words stuck in her throat. "I don't know. I'd like to believe that someday ..."

"It's okay. Never mind."

"Is that what you're looking for?"

He shrugged, but it didn't seem like a casual gesture. "I'm content with what I've achieved. But yes. I had hoped for other things by this point in my life." She saw his throat work as he swallowed down the rest of his words. "Forget it."

Andrea stared out the window, an ache building in her chest. His unspoken question made her at once giddy, terrified, and desperately sad. He wanted to know if there was a future for them, and she honestly didn't know how to answer.

Chapter Twenty-Eight

James tried not to let Andrea's reticence pierce him too deeply. It had nothing to do with him. This was probably the first relationship in which she'd been involved since Logan, and she wasn't quite sure how to handle the idea.

So this is a relationship now?

He didn't know exactly what this was. Certainly not what he'd intended when this all began. Somewhere he'd gone from wanting to tease her from her professional demeanor to needing to learn everything about her. To make her smile. To soothe her fears. To help her forget the things that made her gaze go distant with regret and pain.

He had glimpsed the woman behind the executive, the one who could play the piano with extraordinary beauty and make a baby squeal with delight. The one who was afraid of heights but wouldn't let it stop her from enjoying a view. The one who was strong enough to pick up the pieces of her broken life and build a new one for herself.

He knew what that all added up to. He tasted the words on his tongue. And he could say nothing, because she wasn't ready to hear it. She wasn't yet willing to believe a relationship could end in anything but heartache.

James felt her retreating from him, and he reached for her hand, trying to draw her back. She flinched, but she interlaced her fingers with his. That was something, at least.

"How much time do I need in order to see New York properly?"

"It all depends on what you want to do. Do you like the theater? Musicals?"

"Sure. I've been to some West End plays. I'd like to see Broadway. I'll even go to an opera if you like."

She made a face. "I can't stand the opera. I didn't mind playing in the orchestra; I just don't like sitting in the audience."

"Okay, we can scratch opera off the list. How about the ballet?"

"You don't have to impress me. This is your vacation, remember?"

"Well, in that case, how about Madison Square Garden?"

"Basketball or boxing?"

He quirked a glance at her. "Now you're trying to impress me."

"I like both," she said with a shrug.

"Aren't you full of surprises? What else don't I know about you?"

She thought for a moment. "I belonged to the chess club in junior high school."

"Wow. I'd never have thought you'd be a chess whiz."

"Why, because I'm a girl?"

"Because you're ... pretty."

That elicited a hearty laugh from her. "You're terrible. I take it you don't play, then?"

"Oh no. I'm quite good." James had spent half his childhood trying to beat his father, who had been an expert tactician. "I'll prove it
to you sometime."

Neither of them wondered aloud when that might be.

They passed the rest of the three-hour drive trading tidbits of their
likes and dislikes as any couple would early in their relationship. He
learned Andrea liked all foods but Mexican, had tried and given up the
violin before she started playing the piano, and read spy novels on the
beach in the summer. He told her he hadn't been joking about wanting
to be a race-car driver as a child, but his mother hadn't considered it a
worthwhile pursuit.

"You've mentioned your mother a few times. What exactly does
she do?"

"She doesn't exactly *do* anything," he said. "She's a Pierce."

"I don't know what that means."

"Heiress to the Pierce fortune. You know, shipping, banking,
commercial development. Anything that makes money."

"Oh. That Pierce family." Andrea nodded thoughtfully. "I bet
it really irritates her you've made a good living doing something as
undignified as cooking."

He grinned. "That it does. An unexpected benefit to the whole
venture." Another reason to like Andrea. Many women would want
to know if he would inherit the family fortune, but she seemed to give
it no more thought beyond what it meant about his relationship with
his mother.

He didn't say anything about their destination, wanting to see her
unguarded reaction. He turned off the A96 onto a well-marked side
road as they moved past Inverness proper and followed a long drive.

"Where are we going?" Andrea asked, frowning at the open land around them.

"Our hotel." James threw her a smile. "Don't spoil my surprise."

A sprawling Georgian mansion loomed up before them, its manicured lawns lush and green even this early in the season. A tasteful sign identified it as the Culloden Manor Hotel.

"Jamie, my company would never approve—"

"This isn't business. I thought your last night in Scotland required something special." She started to protest again, but James cut her off. "Please. Let me do something nice for you. You're a hospitality consultant, surely you've heard of the place."

"I have. And I also know the tariffs. It's too much."

"Andrea, don't make me convince you. You know full well a night here is not a hardship to me."

"I don't suppose I can convince you to let me pay my own way? My shoes cost more than a night here. It's not as if it would completely ruin my budget."

"Not a chance, my dear." He could tell she didn't like the idea of him footing the bill, though from the admiring glance she threw at the country house's exterior, a fierce battle raged inside her. "If you want to go somewhere else, we can. Let me just make a few calls."

She put a hand out and touched his arm. "No. This is lovely. Thank you."

James parked on the side of the circular drive. No sooner had they stepped out of the car than a uniformed staff member emerged from the mansion's massive entry to greet them and carry their bags inside. Andrea followed the man up the red-carpeted front steps into the hotel's stunning front hall.

James smiled as Andrea took in the details of the manor. He'd stayed here dozens of times, and he still couldn't help but be impressed. Archways with original plaster detailing spanned the space, and elaborate cornices decorated the soaring ceiling. Marble fireplaces and crystal chandeliers added a luxurious touch to the reception area.

"Lovely," Andrea said, but she wasn't gaping as an uninitiated visitor might. He'd bet she was cataloging the architectural details, mentally dating them in her mind as if learning the mansion's history from the layers of renovations and restorations.

"Mr. MacDonald!" Henry Black, the hotel's manager, strode across the room, his smile bright and his hand extended. "It's good to have you back with us."

Black was a portly man, bald as a billiard ball but impeccably dressed in suit and tie, gold cufflinks winking at his wrists. James shook his hand warmly. "It's always a pleasure. Mr. Black, this is my colleague, Andrea Sullivan."

Andrea smiled and shook his hand as well. "Quite a lovely hotel, Mr. Black. I was just admiring the plasterwork. Original to the current structure, I'd think. Mid- to late-eighteenth century?"

"Indeed. You have a good eye, Ms. Sullivan."

"Andrea's a hospitality consultant," James said. "She's an expert in British architecture."

"Hardly an expert." Andrea threw him a glance, but the fact she didn't color at the compliment made him think she was just being humble.

"Let me get your keys, and Donovan can show you to your rooms." Mr. Black gave them what almost looked like a bow, then disappeared behind the reception desk half-hidden by columns in the corner.

Andrea looked at James with raised eyebrows. "Your colleague?"

"I thought you'd be more comfortable with that introduction." And he couldn't properly explain their relationship to someone else when he couldn't define it himself. "I made your reservation under your name."

"Thank you. That was thoughtful."

Mr. Black returned with their keys, mechanical ones with old-fashioned brass key tags that bore the hotel's thistle logo. "I've put you in room eleven, and Mr. MacDonald, you are down the hall in fourteen."

They took their keys, said their farewells to the hotel manager, and followed the young bellhop, Donovan, up the sweeping staircase to the first floor. As grand as the structure appeared, James had always enjoyed the comfortable atmosphere of the hotel—much more like staying with friends at a country house than checking into a sterile, anonymous hotel with well-trained but impersonal staff. It was the kind of feeling he imagined for the hotel on Skye, though their place was not nearly so luxurious.

"Your mother's family has a Georgian estate in England, if I'm not mistaken," Andrea said.

"In Yorkshire, yes." He shouldn't be surprised she knew that, given her architectural background. "Designed by Robert Adam as well."

"No wonder you like this hotel. It must remind you of it."

"Actually I spent very little time there. My mother favored London, and of course, I preferred Scotland."

"Your room, Ms. Sullivan." Donovan stopped before a polished wooden door with a brass number placard and took the key from Andrea's hand. James waited as the young man placed her suitcase inside on the folding rack and orientated her to the room's features. She tipped him discreetly and paused in the doorway.

"We have dinner reservations downstairs at half past six," James said. "Shall I come by for you a few minutes before?"

"I'll be ready."

James followed Donovan a few steps down the hall to a room on the opposite side. He dismissed the bellhop before he could go through the same routine with him. The room was less opulently decorated than the hotel's common areas, but it was still expansive and tasteful. James spent a few minutes hanging the evening's clothing in the wardrobe and then sank into an overstuffed wingback.

It was his last night with Andrea. The thought put a queasy feeling in his stomach. Even the prospect of visiting her in New York didn't ease the ache of knowing he'd have to put her on a plane tomorrow and watch her fly out of his life.

What was to say she wouldn't return home to New York, fall back into her routine, and realize this had all been a diversion, merely a pleasant interruption from the stresses and demands of a high-powered career? Meanwhile James would be left behind in Scotland, suffering another heartbreak he should have been smart enough to avoid.

No, he couldn't accept that. Somehow he had to do something, and he had to do it tonight, before she walked away from him forever.

Chapter Twenty-Nine

Andrea took her time getting ready for dinner, applying her makeup with a practiced hand and blowing her hair out straight and sleek, glad to have a blow-dryer again at her disposal. Then she pulled on her remaining pair of slim-fitting jeans and thrust her feet into stiletto peep-toes while she wavered on whether to wear the blouse hanging on the wardrobe's handle. She always packed one dressy item in case she got pressed into an evening event outside of office hours, but the ombré sequined design seemed better suited to London than Inverness.

She shimmied into it and turned a critical eye on herself in the mirror. It wasn't revealing exactly. In fact, the high-necked blouse only showed off her toned arms and her collarbone, but it flowed over her curves like a metallic waterfall. Maybe she should put something over it so it didn't seem so flashy. She slipped on her tailored black suit jacket and then shrugged it back off.

This was idiotic. She never agonized this much over her appearance. Still, if this was to be her last night with James, she wanted to be sure he would remember how she looked. With an irritated shake of her head, she turned from the mirror and put the jacket back on.

A knock came at the door at twenty past six. Andrea opened it to find James standing in the hallway, dressed casually in dark jeans and an untucked button-down shirt. He looked her up and down, smiling, and for a moment she lost the power of speech. Somehow she always seemed to forget the effect that expression had on her.

She glanced down at herself. "Too much? Or too little?"

"You look …" He broke off and shook his head.

"I'll take speechless as a compliment, then."

"Oh, it is." He moved in to kiss her cheek, pausing to inhale her perfume. "I'd kiss you, but I don't think you'd thank me for mussing your makeup this early in the evening."

She swayed toward him and had to place a hand on his chest to steady herself. "Isn't our table waiting?"

He pulled back and grinned. "It is. Shall we go?"

She took his offered arm and grabbed her purse from the table by the door before letting it fall shut behind her. Wearing heels again, she was almost as tall as he was, and the height gave her confidence even though the shoes made her rubbery legs feel even more unsteady.

They were woefully underdressed for the hotel's dining room— Scots tended to be more formal about their dress for dinner than Americans—but James didn't seem concerned when the maître d' showed them to their table. She didn't object when he ordered wine for them, and she took his suggestion on her meal.

"You eat here often?"

"When I stay in Inverness. The food is excellent."

"High praise coming from you. Tell me, what was the business that interfered with our morning run?"

"If I recall, you were the one who slept in. I came by at six, but the lights were still off. I didn't have the heart to wake you."

"I can't remember the last time I slept in," she admitted. "I must have needed it."

"You've more than earned it. But in answer to your question, I was at the bank, making arrangements for Kyle and his family."

Andrea's eyebrows lifted. One more task she thought he'd delegate, but in which he'd taken a personal interest instead. She certainly hadn't expected him to pay for the move from his personal accounts. "How is he?"

"He's been moved out of ICU. And they've arrested the shooter."

"That's great news! Isn't it?"

"Kyle's refusing to talk. There were witnesses, but it doesn't seem likely they'll testify either. They'll probably have to let the suspect go."

Andrea reached for his hand across the table and gripped it hard. "What happens now?"

"I talked to a friend of mine who owns a restaurant in Essex. Kyle has all the basics down, so Rob's willing to take him on as a kitchen assistant."

"What about Kyle's family?"

"His mum has had enough. She just wants her children out of London. We'll help them get moved to Chelmsford. The mother's a hard-working woman. The family's just hit a spot of trouble."

Andrea studied him for a long moment. "They're lucky to have you."

James brushed off the compliment with a shrug. "It's not like I can't spare the money. What good is it if I can't help someone who really needs it?"

"I'm not talking about the money," she said. "I'm talking about your time, your effort. The fact you really care about the boy."

"You make time for what's important," he said, holding her gaze. "People come first."

They were no longer talking about Kyle and his family. She moistened her lips and looked away. His sudden intensity hummed along her nerves and made her heart do a double step. There was none of his usual playfulness in evidence tonight. Part of her waited breathlessly to hear what he might say, but the other part was afraid he would make a declaration she couldn't return.

No matter what feelings he elicited in her, this week had been a diversion, an aberration. Nothing more. She would be foolish to make it into something it wasn't.

Fortunately he kept the conversation light throughout the meal, which was indeed very good, traditional yet elegant. It couldn't beat James's cooking, but she was admittedly biased. Half her enjoyment of his food was in watching him work.

At the end of the meal, James signed the check to his room and glanced at his watch. "It's almost eight. Are you ready to go?"

"Absolutely. It was a lovely meal, thank you."

"What did I tell you? Scotland is full of surprises."

"I'm willing to concede the point."

James took her hand as they left the restaurant and went outside to where he had parked on the drive. Fog had already settled over the city, and a damp wind ruffled her hair. He opened the car door for her, but before she could get in, he captured her around the waist and turned her toward him.

"Jamie, we're in full view of the hotel."

"There's no one around. Besides, I'm not doing anything scandalous." His words were light, but his serious expression made her heart thud dully against her rib cage. Whatever he meant to say, she wasn't ready to hear it.

"We're going to be late, aren't we?"

"Yeah." He dropped a quick kiss on her lips and stepped back so she could climb into the car.

The concert venue wasn't far from the hotel, back toward town and located in a surprisingly residential-looking district. From the outside, it looked like just another traditional whitewashed croft house, but a line of people already snaked through the door and spilled out onto the sidewalk. James found parking in a large adjacent lot, and they headed for the hall. This time when he took her hand, she didn't try to dissuade him, despite the fact they were bound to draw attention.

A wall of noise and heat struck her when they finally made their way into the crowded building. The room was painted in dark colors and dimly lit, accented by a glass-and-metal bar that ran the length of the back wall. Semicircular booths with large round tables lined the room, cabaret style, with an open space near the curtained stage for standing room. Above them stretched a tiered balcony with more tables.

"Good turnout." James pulled her closer, releasing her hand in favor of an arm around her waist.

"Interesting crowd." Andrea looked over the concertgoers, a cross section of Scottish society. Some of the women were dressed like her, in heels and even more revealing tops, while others looked like they were headed for a casual night at the pub. A man brushed by her, his head studded with almost as much metal as his leather jacket.

"It's not your typical cèilidh band," James said. "Look, I see a couple of chairs over there."

He took her hand again and led her through the crowd with practiced ease. Curious glances fell on them as they passed.

"I don't know how you get used this," she murmured beneath the din.

He looked around in surprise and broke into a grin. "They're not looking at me, love. You are stunning tonight."

She was saved from answering when a stocky blond man stopped in their path. "Jamie MacDonald! Is it really you?"

"Alec!" James shook the other man's hand heartily. "Good to see you, mate. I didn't realize you were back in Inverness."

"I'm not really. The wife and I live in Sterling, but we heard Davy was playing, so we made the drive. How are you?"

"Excellent." James drew Andrea forward a little and said, "Alec is an old friend of mine. He and Davy and I went to grammar school together. Alec, this is Andrea."

Andrea reached forward and shook the man's hand. "It's a pleasure, Alec."

"The pleasure is mine. You're American?"

"Here on business," Andrea said. "Jamie has been showing me around."

"I see." Alec's eyes flicked mischievously to James, but he smiled at her. "Come join us. There's space at our table. Lila and Cameron are here too."

"Don't worry," James whispered in her ear as they followed Alec to a booth in the corner, already crowded with people. "You'll like them."

James and Andrea slid into the booth, and Alec introduced her to the others at the table. His wife, Maura, was a plump woman with cropped brown hair and a sprinkling of freckles across her nose. Lila, on the other hand, looked like a model, with long blonde hair and a slim figure clad in a slinky dress. Her husband, Cameron—Cam, he insisted—was her polar opposite: dark, pierced, and extensively tattooed. It was an odd mix of characters, but they conversed with the familiarity of long acquaintance.

"I'll get our drinks," James said in her ear. "What do you want?"

"Just a soda, please." The heat and the noise already made her dizzy. She didn't need to add alcohol to the mix.

"A fizzy for Andrea. Anyone else?" When there were no takers, he slid back out of the booth and pushed his way to the bar. Andrea watched him admiringly, but she didn't realize her thoughts were written on her face until she saw Alec grinning at her. Her cheeks heated, which seemed to be their permanent condition when it came to James.

"How long you known Jimmy-boy?"

She grinned at the nickname, and her embarrassment faded. "Long enough to know he'd hate being called Jimmy-boy."

Alec chuckled. "Right about that. Seem to remember him giving me a good thrashing for it."

"You're such a liar, Alec," Maura said, giving her husband a nudge. "These boys were like brothers. Inseparable. Until Jamie left, that is. He came back for our wedding, but that was ten years ago."

James returned with their drinks and slid in next to her. Ale for himself, soda for her. She raised the glass. *"Slàinte."*

The others lifted their own glasses and echoed her. She took a drink. It wasn't the Coca-Cola she had expected, but some carbonated currant-flavored thing. "Good choice. I like it."

"See, I know you better than you think," he murmured, his lips brushing her ear.

"Behave," she warned.

James grinned. For that matter, so did the rest of the group.

Before the flush could take up residence in her cheeks again, the lights in the hall dimmed, and the spotlights came up on the stage. Patrons found spots at tables, the bars, even standing around the corners of the room, as the musicians emerged with their instruments. They filed onto the stage, and the room burst into spontaneous applause. James draped his arm casually over Andrea's shoulder, and she settled against him for a better view.

A pretty woman with purple streaks in her short black hair stepped to the microphone, a fiddle held beneath one arm. "Wow. And here I always remembered Inverness having more sheep than people."

The crowd chuckled, and she smiled. "I'm Davy McWilliams. This is my band. I hope you enjoy the show."

She stepped back and raised the fiddle, then drew the bow across the strings. The notes of a mournful, traditional ballad filled the room, played with so much emotion that gooseflesh rose on Andrea's arms. Then the drums, keyboard, and guitar came in with a driving dance beat, and the room went wild as the Scottish melody transitioned into a catchy rock riff. Andrea laughed out loud, and James's arm tightened around her. The musicians were incredible, and he was right—she had never quite heard anything like it before.

The next song had more of a jazz vibe. She sipped her soda and relaxed against James, letting the music wash over her. He kissed her temple and laid his cheek against the side of her head. It was getting difficult to tell herself she didn't want this, that she didn't long for the kind of affection he seemed to take for granted. He had the ability to make her feel like it was just the two of them, even surrounded by his oldest friends. How could she not fall in love with a man like that, at least a little?

No, no, no. She would not go down this path. She could not.

James must have felt her tension, because he whispered, "Relax. You're still on holiday, remember?" But the damage was done. The sweet moments of relaxation in his arms fled, leaving only the queasy tendrils of anxiety in their place.

Halfway through the set, the band took a break and the floor turned into a churning sea of people once again, hundreds of voices sending up a dull roar. Maura excused herself to the loo, and Cam slid over in the booth so he could talk to Andrea more easily.

"So, Andrea, where do you live?"

"New York City."

"Oh? What do you do there?"

"I'm a hospitality consultant." When he looked at her blankly, she said, "Basically I get to tell people like Jamie what to do."

Everyone at the table laughed, and Cam grinned. "He doesn't look too upset about it."

Lila propped her chin on her hand and frowned. "So how does that work exactly, with you in New York and Jamie in London?"

Andrea's stomach clenched. "Um, well, we're not—"

"We haven't quite figured that out yet," James said smoothly. "Right now it's just looking like a lot of travel for the both of us."

He squeezed her closer, rubbing her shoulder, but it changed nothing. No matter what he said, their schedules didn't allow for a long-distance relationship. She had to resign herself to the idea this was all there was. Five days in Skye had upended her world, and now she would be going home trying to piece it back together again. Alone.

"Jamie! Andrea! You made it!"

Andrea jerked her head up and found Bree standing at the edge of the table, looking down at them. She had squeezed her voluptuous figure into a short, tight black dress that left little to the imagination, and she held a sequined clutch under one arm.

James's tone remained calm and impeccably polite. "Hello, Bree."

She waited, clearly expecting to be invited to sit down, but nobody said a word. They just looked back at her. She tried again. "This is such a nice little reunion. Why don't we get a picture?" She dug a digital camera from her purse and held it up to view the screen.

Andrea became uncomfortably aware of James's arm around her, the press of his body alongside hers. She nudged him aside so she could slide from the booth. "Since this is a Skye reunion, I'll excuse myself. Lila, where's the ladies' room?"

"Back behind the bar to the right. Do you want me to show you?"

"No, I'll be fine." Andrea felt a little wobbly as she stood, and she saw a few concerned glances fly her direction. She must be pale, if her dizziness was any indication.

"She doesn't like having her picture taken," James explained.

Andrea hurried away from the table, but not before she heard Cam's incredulous reply. "I can't imagine why when she looks like that. Nicely done, Jamie."

She pressed her hands to her face as she pushed her way through the crowd. Her heart beat too fast in her chest, though she didn't know which made her feel more panicky—the threat of being photographed with James or the thoughts Bree had interrupted.

The ladies' room was crowded, but most of the activity was pressed around the mirror, so Andrea slipped into an unoccupied cubicle and shut the door. She was too practical to let her feelings get this out of control. She was making far too much of the situation. James hadn't said anything about any future intentions, and what she felt now was merely infatuation. He was a good-looking, charismatic man, and she'd allowed herself to fall a little too deeply under his spell. When she went back to New York, he would pick up where he left off with some twenty-year-old actress, and Andrea would be forgotten as a temporary distraction. Hadn't Ian warned her as much?

She was a grown woman with a successful career and a satisfying, well-ordered life. She would be fine. She gathered herself, breathing deeply until she felt some semblance of calm returning. Just as she was about to open the door, she heard an unfamiliar voice outside.

"Did you see the woman with Jamie MacDonald tonight?"

A second woman answered, her tone knowing. "Just his type. Thin, gorgeous, disposable ..."

The first woman laughed maliciously. "She's pulling out all the stops, isn't she?"

"You know Jamie. He's always had a weakness for a pretty face. Too bad he never keeps them around long."

"Mmm. This one is American. Convenient, that."

Humiliation flooded through Andrea. James's conquests, real or not, were well known. They probably thought she'd been spending the last week in his bed, even though he'd been scrupulously careful not to cross any boundaries.

"Well," the other girl said, "I suppose she's getting what she wants out of the deal, isn't she?"

Anger snuffed out humiliation in an instant. Andrea threw open the door and strode out of the stall toward the two women standing in front of the mirror. To her shock, one of them was Gail, the hostess from the seafood restaurant on Skye. The woman's eyes widened.

Andrea stepped up beside her, pleased she towered over the other woman in her heels. She took her lipstick from her purse and applied a light coat, then winked at Gail in the mirror. "I admit, there are perks to my job. Have a nice evening, ladies."

She managed to smile as she left the restroom, strutting back toward the stage. At least she hadn't let them see how their words had shaken her. Halfway there, she stopped. She couldn't face the scrutiny of James's friends, couldn't pretend as though everything was fine. No matter what she told herself, fine felt far out of reach.

Chapter Thirty

James glanced at his watch as the lights lowered in preparation for the band's return to the stage. Andrea had been gone at least ten minutes. Surely the ladies' room wasn't as crowded as that? He excused himself from the table and made his way back through the throng, scanning the room as he went. He peeked down the hallway where the restrooms lay, but there wasn't a line outside the door. Frowning, he pushed down the packed corridor and out the front door.

Andrea stood by the entrance, arms wrapped around herself, staring into the dark.

"Andrea, what are you doing out here? What's wrong?"

She started at his voice. "I just needed to escape the crowd."

"I thought you were having a good time."

"I was," she said brightly. "But now I'd just like to go back to the hotel if that's okay."

"Of course."

She thrust her hands in her coat pockets, a sure sign she didn't want him to touch her, so he kept his distance as they walked back toward the car park. Just a few minutes ago she had been relaxing in his arms, enjoying the show, charming his friends. Then Bree came along with her camera, and Andrea panicked. He supposed he couldn't blame her. After what she'd been through with Logan, exposing herself to scrutiny here was already a challenge.

"We should talk."

She shook her head. "It's okay, James. You don't have to say anything."

The use of his given name hit him like a punch in the gut. She was pulling back from him, distancing herself. "I don't think you understand."

She favored him with a small, chilly smile. "I understand just fine. Don't worry. I'm a big girl. This was fun."

"Fun? You think I was just passing the time?"

"Weren't you? You didn't want me here in the first place. You thought it would be amusing to seduce the consultant Ian foisted on you."

He grabbed her arm and jerked her to a stop. "When have I ever given you any reason to believe my intentions were less than honorable? When have I ever treated you with anything but respect?"

She glared at him. "Let go of me."

He released her arm, and she picked up her pace again, hurrying toward the car. She yanked the door handle, but James reached around her and held the door shut. "Andrea, I'm in love with you."

Her eyes flew to his face, shocked. His heart rose into his throat. This was not how he'd imagined this happening. He'd wanted to tell her in some romantic way, not in the middle of a car park.

"That's impossible. You can't be. We've known each other for five days."

"Possible or not, it's how I feel."

"I can't do this. I can't.... I won't."

James had no choice but to press forward. "You won't what? You won't take a chance? You won't let yourself feel something?"

"I won't let you make me forget everything I've worked for. I've made a life for myself. I've sacrificed for it."

"And exactly what did you have to sacrifice?"

Her eyes flashed. "What are you implying?"

"Not what you're inferring, I'm sure. Tell me, what are you going to do when you get home tomorrow?"

She frowned. "Pack for my trip to Toronto. It's been planned for weeks. What are you getting at?"

"It's easy to sacrifice when there's nothing to give up, when you live your life in one-week increments so you don't have to get attached to anyone or anything. That's not living, Andrea; that's existing. There's a difference."

"You fly all over the UK to check on your restaurants and your business deals. How is that any different?"

"It's different because I take chances. They may not work out, but at least I don't live my life by the lowest common denominator. Take a risk, actually feel something for a change."

Before she could react, he slid his hand behind her back and pulled her to him. In the past, he had kissed her playfully or seductively; now his mouth came down hard and insistent on hers, his body pressing her back against the car. She resisted for a moment and then softened against him, her arms going around his neck, her fingers sliding into his hair. He felt a flash of triumph as she pulled him more tightly against her, returning his kiss with a passion he hadn't dared to imagine.

"Say *cheese*," a saccharine voice called just before the flash of a camera cut through the dark.

Andrea jerked away from James, too stunned by the kiss to understand what had happened. Then she saw Bree holding her digital camera, a brilliant, malicious smile on her face.

A wave of panic crashed over Andrea. There could be no denying the situation. She was still pinned between James and his car, every inch of their bodies touching, her hands in his hair. She struggled away from him, sparks bursting in her vision. She was only a breath away from passing out.

James swore. "I've thought you were a lot of things, Bree, but spiteful was never one of them."

Bree smirked. "I'm not the one snogging his newest conquest in public. Good night, Jamie. Good night, Andrea. Enjoy your evening."

Her poisonous tone only increased Andrea's dread. "Let's go before we draw any more attention to ourselves," she pleaded in a low voice.

He opened the door for her, and she slid in, happy to be enveloped in the dark, away from Bree's malicious gaze. The woman couldn't possibly do anything with the photo, could she? Surely she was just trying to get a rise out of them.

She pressed her fingertips to her eyes. Somehow, Bree seemed like the least of her worries. James wasn't playing fair. He knew the

effect he had on her, and he was using it against her. She had been
here before, though. She had refused to recognize lust masquerad-
ing as love when it had come to Logan. She had been seduced into
a relationship that was completely wrong, and she'd paid the price.

Never mind the fact James had gone to great lengths to be sure
they wouldn't be tempted into doing something they'd regret. It was
not his motivations that worried her. It was hers. She could not deny
the powerful attraction between them, how she lost the will to resist
anytime he touched her. But that was not love. Maybe she couldn't
feel love.

What could she offer him anyway? He might think she was
enough right now, but she saw the way he loved his niece and
nephew, how he doted on his aunt. He knew how to fill a home with
warmth. He deserved a woman who could give him children of his
own, who wouldn't always regret how her past decisions had robbed
them of their own family.

"Andrea." James reached for her hand, but she shook it off. This
had to end now. If she let him touch her again, her resolve would
weaken. She would let him convince her that what she offered was
enough, and then she would spend the rest of her life making him
unhappy. That was something she couldn't do to him.

The silence during the short ride back to the hotel lay thick
with tension. After they parked, he opened her car door as he
always did, but he didn't try to touch her. They walked side by side
up the front steps and across the foyer, but they may as well have
been miles apart.

When they stopped in front of her room, James reached for her.

"Don't," she whispered.

He dropped his hands. "If you need time, I'll give you time. Go home, take your trip to Toronto. I'll clear my schedule. You can show me around New York."

"We both know that can't happen, James." She recoiled at the look of anguish in his eyes, but she forced herself to kiss him softly on the cheek. "Good-bye."

Then she put the key in the door and stepped inside, trying not to see the look of hurt on his face as she shut the door.

James stared at the brass number plate on Andrea's door, unable to draw a breath beneath the iron band that constricted his chest. He could barely pull his thoughts together enough to turn away and return to his own room down the hall.

He had lost her.

He only had himself to blame. She wasn't ready to be truthful about her feelings for him, let alone accept that he loved her. He'd thought their mutual attraction was the way to break through her defenses, to get her to open up the possibility of more, but maybe it went no further than that.

He let himself into his room with numb efficiency. How could he have messed this up so badly? Just today they had been planning his trip to New York, thinking about the future, and now she wouldn't speak to him.

He pulled off his jacket and tossed it on the bed. Then he sank down onto the edge and put his head in his hands.

I don't understand, Lord. Was I wrong about her? Was I wrong about this?

He'd loved Cassandra, but his trust had been misplaced. She had never been content to just be with him and enjoy his company. It had all been about leveraging their combined celebrity to further their careers. Their relationship had just been a slight of hand, smoke and mirrors. He'd even begun to doubt his judgment, his own heart, when it came to women.

Yet everything in him told him Andrea and the feelings she stirred were real.

James exhaled heavily and fell back on the bed. Maybe once she slept on the matter, he could get through to her. He couldn't let her go with things standing like this between them.

Andrea marked the passing of the night by the change of the glowing red numbers on the hotel room's clock. Every time she shut her eyes, she could see the shock and hurt on James's face as she'd closed the door. He had meant it when he said he was in love with her.

He hadn't actually said, "I love you." That was different, wasn't it? She would leave, and he would move on, and it would be like she had never come.

That was splitting hairs, and she knew it.

She lifted the receiver of the hotel phone, then glanced at the clock. 4:00 a.m. She put it back in the cradle. She wouldn't wake him yet.

When 6:00 a.m. rolled by without a single minute of sleep, she wandered into the bathroom and splashed water on her face. When she came back out, she picked up her cell phone from habit and saw she had an email waiting. What could be coming through at this time on a Saturday morning?

Andrea opened her email app. It was an Internet alert. What scandal had one of her clients gotten himself involved in this time? Rich men seemed to spend as much time in the tabloids and gossip columns for their escapades with women, controlled substances, and law enforcement as for their business deals. She tapped the screen to follow the link to a popular UK gossip site.

The browser opened to a photo, and the air whooshed out of her lungs. Front and center was a photo of her and James kissing in the parking lot, their arms wrapped around each other. She sank to the bed on unsteady legs. It had been a private moment never meant for public consumption, and now it was posted on the Internet for all to see.

Her face burned with humiliation and fury as she read the headline: "Who Is Jamie's Tasty New Dish?" She couldn't even read the short blurb below it—her hands trembled too hard to steady the screen.

She wrapped her arms around herself, swallowing bile. *This can't be happening. Thousands of people will see that. Hundreds of thousands. My sister. My colleagues. Michael.*

She dropped the phone and fled to the bathroom in time to empty her stomach into the toilet. She wiped her mouth with the back of a shaky hand and gripped the porcelain until the nausea subsided and she was sure she could stand under her own power.

She brushed her teeth numbly and forced herself to push down the part of her that wanted to curl into a ball and sob. Damage control. She needed to get in front of this. Her name wasn't listed. She could call Michael first, and things would be fine.

It was just after 1:00 a.m. in New York, but she would be unlikely to catch Michael at home on a Friday night. She dialed his cell number instead. He picked up on the fifth ring.

"Andrea?" Noise in the background suggested a club or a bar.

"Yeah, Michael, it's me. I didn't mean to interrupt your evening."

He laughed. "I'd ask you how yours was, but I have a feeling I already know."

Her cheeks burned with shame, but she managed to keep her voice steady. "You saw the picture, I take it."

"I saw it. Did you get it?"

"What?"

"Did you get the contract?"

This wasn't how Andrea had expected the conversation to go. "Uh, not yet."

"Get on it, then. Hate for all your hard work to be for nothing."

"So … you're not upset?"

"I was a bit surprised after what happened in London, but I guess I should have known you'd come through in the end."

A new wave of nausea roiled in her stomach. He couldn't be saying what it sounded like. "I don't sleep with clients."

"Of course not," Michael said. "At least not the unattractive ones."

The room spun around her, and the whoosh of blood in her ears made her miss Michael's next comment. "What did you say?"

"I said, your new business cards are already on order, and the nameplate is screwed on the office door. I'd suggest you do whatever it takes to close this deal."

He had said the same thing many times before, but now they took on a new meaning. She wanted to vomit again. "Right," she heard herself say from a distance. "I'll see you soon."

She hung up and stared dully at the phone. She had worked her tail off, hustling accounts, staying on the road twice as much as everyone else, just to prove she was more than a pretty face. All the times Michael had assured her they valued her capabilities and told her to ignore the office gossip, he had been making the same vile assumptions about her as his employees were.

She should be happy. She had feared for her job should this—whatever it was—come to light, but Michael didn't seem to care. She should be happy. All she had to do was call James and ask him to sign the contract. She had no doubt that he would, and VP of Sales would be hers.

She wandered into the bathroom, enveloped in a bubble of shock. Finally she stripped off her pajamas and climbed into the shower. The hot water beat down on her, soaking her hair, running down her face in rivulets and mingling with her tears.

What was she going to do? She leaned her forehead against the tile wall, feeling the life she had built for herself crumbling around her.

The room phone was ringing when she finally climbed out of the shower. She wrapped a towel around herself and rushed to pick it up.

"Andrea."

Her heart leaped into her throat at the sound of James's voice. "We don't have anything to talk about. I'm sorry." She hung up on him.

In a daze, Andrea dried her hair, put on her makeup, and dressed in her gray suit. She was just beginning to pack when someone rapped at her door.

She peeked through the peephole and saw James standing there, again dressed in jeans and his leather jacket, his hair wet from the shower. She leaned her forehead against the door and sucked in a deep breath for strength.

"Open up, Andrea. I know you're still there."

She blanked her expression and yanked open the door. "What do you want?"

"I'm sorry. I should've thought of how you'd feel. I didn't know this was going to happen."

So he'd seen the picture too. She sighed and leaned against the door frame. "It's not your fault. I just … I can't do this. I've been here before, and I thought I could handle it, but I won't ever be able to get used to this kind of life. I'm sorry."

"So that's it? It's over? You're giving up on us?"

"James," she said softly, "there never was an *us*."

She shut the door and leaned against it, biting her lip to keep the tears from coming again. It was for the best. Even if she were inspired to try to make whatever this was work, she couldn't live wondering when her face would show up on a website or in the newspaper. And she wouldn't ask him to change his life for her.

Andrea folded her clothes into her suitcase with shaking hands. She'd just managed to convince herself she could simulate some level of calm when the room phone rang.

She stared at the red light flashing with each ring, her heart in her throat, until the phone went silent again. She couldn't move for a full minute. Then her cell phone trilled.

She turned away, not wanting to see James's name on the screen. A beep indicated the call had been sent to voice mail. It didn't ring again.

Pushing down unreasonable disappointment, she lifted the room phone's receiver and dialed the front desk. "Could you please call me a taxi to the airport?"

"Mr. MacDonald already requested a car to take you," the clerk said. "Shall I notify you when it arrives?"

"Please do," she managed to choke out. She hung up the phone.

Andrea made one last sweep of the hotel room, checking for forgotten items. When the bellman rapped lightly on the door, she was perched on the edge of the bed, her hands folded neatly in her lap.

The young man's name tag said *Liam*. She started at it blankly until he held out a large, white envelope. "This was outside your door."

She knew what was inside before she slid open the flap and withdrew the contract. Her breath caught at the sight of James's neat signature on the last page, above Ian's. Of course, he wouldn't let her leave without wrapping up this last detail. Too bad she didn't know if she'd gotten the contract because of her professional expertise or his personal feelings for her.

And Michael would always think she'd closed the deal because she slept with James.

She tore the contract in half before she knew she was going to do it, then tore those pieces in half again for good measure. She shoved the ripped papers back into their envelope, ignoring Liam's puzzled look, and strode down the hallway with a purposefulness she didn't feel.

Liam took her single bag and followed her down the hall to the sweeping staircase. They'd barely set foot on the bottom step when a dark-haired clerk skirted the reception desk and approached. "Ms. Sullivan!"

Andrea faltered, cursing the overly efficient staff member for remembering her. She couldn't very well ignore her, though. She paused and waited until the woman joined her and held out an envelope, her scarlet-painted nails a stark contrast to the creamy hotel stationery. "For you, Ms. Sullivan."

Andrea didn't need to look at her name scrawled across the front to know it was from James. She shoved it in her purse and handed the contract envelope to the clerk. "Could you leave this for Mr. MacDonald, please?"

The woman took it. "Of course. Thank you for staying with us."

Andrea nodded numbly and walked through the front doors where a sedan waited for her at the bottom of the steps.

She barely saw her surroundings through the car's dark-tinted windows, too focused on keeping her breath moving steadily in and out of her lungs. This was just another business trip. She wouldn't think about what it might have become.

Only years of travel helped her maintain her composure through the security lines and the long wait at the gate. She managed an impressive semblance of control while she marched up the stairs into the plane, shoved her bag into the overhead compartment, and flopped into her window seat.

Then she reached into her pocket to switch off her phone for takeoff and touched something warm and buttery soft instead.

The scarf. She rubbed the patterned lamb's wool between her fingers and draped it around her neck. Then she leaned her head against the window and poured out her pain in great gulping sobs.

Chapter Thirty-One

James resisted the urge to look out the window of his room to see if the car he'd requested for Andrea had arrived. The fact she'd ignored a dozen of his calls proved it was the only gesture she would accept from him. She was sticking resolutely to her decision, and forcing a confrontation would only make matters worse.

Worse. He barked out a harsh laugh. As if leaving him with no intention of having any contact with him again could get any worse.

James took his time packing his bag and vacating the hotel room. He still had three more days in Skye before he left for Glasgow. He momentarily considered flying directly there since he was already in Inverness, but he couldn't abide the city right now. He wanted the familiar, beloved scenery of the island. It was the perfect place to brood and curse himself for his own daftness.

He checked out of the hotel, shoving the envelope the desk clerk gave him into his laptop case, then threw his suitcase into the back of his car and pointed himself back toward home. He drove automatically, cataloguing the reasons he should move on with his life and forget Andrea completely. He failed miserably. How could he have let her get into him so deeply he could no longer imagine life without her?

He should have listened to Ian. Not that his brother had been right about his intentions, but if he had've been smart enough to let her go, he would never have noticed the gaping emptiness she'd exposed in his life.

He was so engrossed in his own musings as he turned down the road leading onto Sleat that he didn't see the scattering of sheep until it was almost too late. He jammed on the brakes with a squeal of tires and lurched to a stop just before he would have flattened one of the stupid creatures into the asphalt. It lifted its head and looked straight at him, then lay down in the middle of the road. James laid on the horn, but instead of hurrying out of the road, half the flock decided a nap was a cracking idea and joined it.

James threw his head back against the headrest and stifled the cry of frustration in his throat. Perfect. All he wanted to do was get home and wallow in self-pity, and he couldn't even manage that because of a flock of mindless animals. Could this day possibly get any worse?

They lay in wait for cars and just fling themselves into the road. He'd been trying to make Andrea laugh. It just figured that he'd get a personal demonstration today of all days.

Beside him on the passenger seat, his phone buzzed, indicating a message. He snatched it up, his heart thrumming as if he'd run a marathon. Only one bar, but a miracle all the same. He dialed his voice mail, where the robotic voice told him he had two messages.

"James, it's Alice. Call me immediately."

Disappointment spiked through him when he heard his publicist's voice and not Andrea's. What could be so urgent to warrant a call on Saturday? He played the next message.

"For heaven's sake, James. Will you call me back? Or at least check your email."

That didn't sound good. He deleted Alice's second message and opened his email. The photo that came up knocked the wind out of him: him and Andrea last night, locked in a passionate embrace.

He threw his phone into the passenger seat and reached for the envelope the desk clerk had given him. He'd assumed it held the second copy of the signed contract, but when he opened it, a handful of ragged scraps fell into his lap.

Andrea had left him, and now she'd probably lose her job too.

He had managed to single-handedly ruin her life.

James held his head in his hands. He hadn't understood before, but he did now. He'd thought when she said she couldn't handle this type of life, she'd just been trying to say she didn't want him. If he'd known about the photo ...

"It wouldn't have made a difference." Heaviness settled over him like an oppressive fog. That was part of his life. He was in the public eye, and the public liked gossip. With his reputation, he was surprised she'd ever entertained getting involved with him at all. He'd been a fool to think otherwise.

After what could have been minutes or hours, the sheep decided to meander off the road. He put the car in gear and drove numbly back to Isleornsay. He only debated for a moment before heading to Muriel's house. His aunt wouldn't press him. If he were lucky, she'd have a bottle of Scotch stashed in one of the cabinets. If he weren't so lucky, he could take out his frustrations on the ingredients for dinner. He'd come up with more than a few new recipes after Cassie left.

He didn't think it was possible to feel any worse until he saw Ian's car in Muriel's driveway.

"Brilliant." He wasn't going to back down today or let his brother run him off. He slammed the gear shift into park, shut off the engine, and threw open the car door.

When he entered, Ian sat on the sofa, reading a book with the television turned on low in the background. He took off his reading glasses and set them aside when James stormed into the house.

"She's gone?"

James ignored the question and passed through the living room to the kitchen. He rummaged in a cabinet and finally found a mostly full bottle of single-malt Scotch in the back. Ian watched him from the doorway as he pulled out the cork and poured a dram into an old-fashioned glass.

"So you're just going to drink yourself into a stupor?"

"That's the plan. You here to stop me?"

Ian shrugged, retrieved another glass from the cabinet, and took the bottle.

"What are you doing? You don't drink."

"I do when the occasion calls for it." Ian poured a finger of Scotch for himself. "I think the occasion calls for it."

James threw back his whiskey with a defiant look at Ian and blinked at the burn down his throat. It had been years since he'd had anything stronger than wine or ale. "Go ahead and say it. I want to be sober enough for you to enjoy it." When Ian stared blankly at him, James said, "You told me so."

"I don't understand."

"You told me I never thought of anyone but myself. Well, congratulations. You were right. My reputation came back and bit me." He pulled his mobile from his pocket, brought up the photo, and shoved the phone across the island. "Go ahead."

Ian looked at the photo and sighed. "I'm sorry, Jamie."

James blinked. "I thought you'd be pleased to know that, once again, you were right, and I was wrong."

"I've always loved you, no matter what you think."

"You have an odd way of showing it. When you moved to London with Mum, we no longer existed to you. You had your exclusive school, your rowing. You never looked back."

"Did you ever wonder what it was like to have to go to London with Mum so she wouldn't be alone? You and Serena wouldn't leave Dad."

"That's right. Always so self-sacrificing." James reached for the bottle and poured himself another glass, daring Ian to interfere. "Perfect student. Perfect athlete. If only I could live up to your example."

"And yet Mum always loved you best."

James laughed humorlessly. "Right. That's why she left us."

"She was unhappy, Jamie." Ian's expression turned sorrowful. "She never wanted to live in Scotland. Dad promised her it would be only for a few years. A couple years turned into twenty. She got tired of waiting."

"If she loved us, she would have stayed."

"And if he had loved her, he would have seen how miserable she was and gone with her. Instead he put everything else ahead of her. The hotel. His students."

"So that's why you didn't tell me he was sick," James said quietly. "Out of spite."

"Don't be daft." Ian downed his whiskey and thwacked the glass down on the counter. "He needed his will amended, and Mum knows practically every lawyer in London. He didn't want you two to feel sorry for him."

"Then why go to you?"

Ian met his eyes, and for the first time, James saw the full force of the bitterness his brother carried with him. "Because he figured I wouldn't have any sympathy to spare for him. After all, I was the son who abandoned him."

James pressed his fingers to his eyes. How could things have been so convoluted and he had never known? "You should have told me. I could have said good-bye."

"Yeah. I should have told you. But he was the one who didn't want you to know. How could you forgive him for that and not forgive me?"

"Why did you hold on to your share of the hotel, then? Why not sell out your portion like Serena?"

"Because of you." Ian's eyes darkened. "I didn't just lose my father; I lost you and Serena too. I thought maybe, finally, here was something we could do together. But you wouldn't see past what you thought was my betrayal. You're just like Dad. Anyone who doesn't do it your way, you walk away from. You did it with us. And now you're doing it with Andrea."

"No. Andrea left me." James lifted his glass to drink, then set it down again. All he'd gain from getting drunk was a headache. It wouldn't ease the ache in his heart.

Ian's anger faded. "Do you love her?"

"Doesn't matter. She doesn't feel the same way."

"For heaven's sake, how blind could you be? Every single one of us could see she was head over heels for you."

James put his head in his hands and dug his fingers into his hair. "If she doesn't want me, I'm not going to chase her."

"Jamie, men in this family are rubbish at relationships. We fall in love, then we let them walk away from us without a fight. Don't make the same mistakes Dad and I did."

"Cassandra—"

"Wasn't worth fighting for. Andrea is. Unless I'm wrong. Unless this really was just some game to you."

James hung his head and stared into his glass. He could try to convince himself otherwise, but he loved Andrea. More than his life in Scotland. More than his pride. Drinking himself blind and stupid wouldn't change matters.

He pushed away from the counter and lifted the bottle. "You done with this?" He recorked it and replaced it in the cabinet, significantly fuller than he'd intended to leave it.

"I'm sorry, Ian," he said quietly, afraid to turn. "I was unfair. I didn't understand."

"Yeah, me too." Ian clapped a hand on his shoulder. "I'm driving back to London tomorrow. Come with me. I'll drop you in Glasgow."

"A road trip?" James shot him a frown, but there was no heat behind it. "Why would I want to be stuck in a car for five hours with you?"

Ian smiled. "Because it will give us time to figure out how you're going to get Andrea back."

Chapter Thirty-Two

Andrea cried through the entire flight back to London, ignoring the flight attendants' attempts to speak to her until they finally gave up and left her alone. She disembarked at Gatwick, her eyes swollen and her face blotchy, but her tears finally spent, leaving only a blank calmness in their place.

She barely noticed the concerned looks people gave her as she dragged her suitcase through the airport toward the airline's customer service desk. The polite young agent shot nervous looks at her tear-stained face, but quickly switched her flight from New York to Dayton. It cost her an extra four hundred dollars and added a stop in Chicago, but at this point Andrea didn't care. She couldn't go back to New York. Ohio was the only place she had left.

She clutched her new boarding passes and found a quiet spot by a bank of pay phones. It took her a moment to work up her courage to dial Michael's number.

"Give me some good news," he said teasingly.

Andrea swallowed and stared at the pitted airport floor beneath her feet. "I didn't get the contract."

Silence stretched so long, she checked her phone to see if they were still connected. Then he said, his tone chilly, "That's unfortunate. You realize you've put me in an awkward position here, Andrea."

"I know. I'm sorry."

"I don't think sorry will cut it this time. The board had doubts about approving you for the vice president position, and I went to bat for you. Now … I'm afraid I'm going to have to let you go."

Andrea's mouth dropped open. She'd said she needed this deal to save her job, but somehow she'd never really thought he'd fire her. "You're letting me go because I failed to close two deals? After the millions—"

"Not because of your performance, Andrea," he said. "Because of your actions. Or don't you remember your contract stipulates a certain standard of professional behavior while on company business?"

"I haven't done anything wrong!"

"It doesn't matter what happened. Just how it looks. You know that."

For a minute, Andrea couldn't speak or even breathe. Then she started to laugh.

"Andrea?"

"Oh, Michael …" She reined in her laughter long enough to speak, aware it had taken on a hysterical tinge. "I'd tell you what you could do with your VP position, but it's not worth the effort. Tell accounting to send my final check to my home, and I expect a letter of recommendation from you along with it."

"Why would I do that?"

"Because it will look very bad for you when my lawyer delivers an affidavit to the board of directors stating I was fired for defending myself against a client and for not sleeping with another like you implied I should."

Now Michael sounded nervous. "You'll never be able to prove that happened."

"It doesn't matter if it happened. Just how it looks. Isn't that right, Michael?" She waited for an answer, but the line remained silent. "Just be glad I'm only asking for a recommendation. Juries don't take kindly to accusations of sexual harassment these days."

She rode the satisfaction of having the last word through her short wait at the gate lounge, but as she boarded her plane to Chicago, the sinking feeling crept back into her gut.

She'd just lost her job.

Because of a man.

She swallowed down nausea as she found her seat by the window. She texted her arrival information to her sister, then shut off her cell phone. She didn't have the emotional wherewithal to explain why she was coming home. She didn't want to explain why she had nowhere else to go.

Andrea slept on the plane ride from London to Chicago and woke with a pounding headache as soon as the wheels touched the tarmac. She fumbled with her carry-on bag and walked zombie-like toward her connecting gate while she flipped on her cell phone. Two messages.

The first was from Becky. She sounded worried about the abrupt change of plans, but she assured Andrea she would pick her up in Dayton.

The second was from James.

Andrea's throat constricted again with unshed tears. She deleted the message before she could hear more than "Hi, Andrea, it's James."

She couldn't. Not when she desperately needed to keep it together. She boarded her plane to Dayton and refused to let herself think of what he might have said.

She passed the short flight to Ohio in a daze and walked through Dayton's stark steel-and-glass airport wrapped in a blur of exhaustion and jet lag. She could barely keep herself moving in a straight line as she made her way down to the ground transportation exit. Becky waited by the first baggage carousel as promised, dressed in sweatpants and a T-shirt, her long dark hair bound in a ponytail at the nape of her neck. She chewed her nails fitfully as she scanned the passengers. Her expression shifted when she saw Andrea, changing first to relief, then wariness.

Andrea dropped her bag and went straight into Becky's waiting embrace.

"Oh, honey," Becky whispered, holding her tight. "What happened?"

Andrea blinked back tears. "Can we just go?"

"Of course we can." Becky grabbed the handle of her bag and pulled it along behind her, linking her arm with her sister's as they headed for the parking lot.

"Where are the kids?"

"At home with Dan. It's nine o'clock."

"Right." Andrea rubbed her eyes. "I'm jet-lagged. I don't even know what day it is. I hope it's not too much of an inconvenience—"

"Shh. I'm always happy to see you, no matter the reason."

Becky led her to a white Mercury sedan and popped the trunk with the remote fob. Andrea walked to the left side of the car before she remembered she was back in the States and circled around to the passenger side. She climbed in and leaned back against the headrest with a long sigh.

Becky slipped into the driver's seat and stuck the key in the ignition. Then she touched Andrea's arm. "Andy, what happened?"

"I lost my job."

Becky blinked in surprise. "Why? Does this have something to do with James?"

"He said he was in love with me."

Despite the fact Andrea thought she couldn't cry any more, the tears slid down her face and didn't stop on the short ride back to her sister's home.

Becky didn't try to pry the story out of Andrea on the way back to her rambling brick ranch a few minutes outside of Dayton, for which Andrea was inexpressibly grateful. She followed Becky numbly up the front steps, the porch light blinding her gritty eyes while her sister unlocked the front door.

Becky's husband lay on the overstuffed sofa in the front room, watching the news. His lanky build and messy blond hair contrasted with Becky's dark, exotic looks. When they came in, he immediately rose and gave Andrea a warm hug.

"Hi, Dan," she said hoarsely. "Sorry to intrude on you without notice."

"It's never an intrusion." Dan released her and looked at his wife. "I made up the sofa bed in the basement."

"Thanks, sweetheart." Becky put an arm around her husband's waist and lifted her face to accept his kiss. "Kids asleep?"

"For a while now."

Andrea looked away from the affectionate couple, loneliness stabbing at her chest. The house looked like it always did: comfortable furniture, hardwood floors, toys and books strewn across most surfaces. She wandered toward the kitchen, where Becky had framed and hung the children's artwork over the breakfast table. Every inch of it screamed *home*.

She'd thought going back to her empty apartment would be more painful, but now, surrounded by the trappings of her sister's happy life, she wasn't so sure.

"Are you hungry?" Becky asked from the doorway. "I can make you something."

"No, thanks. I'd really just like to go to bed if you don't mind."

"Come on, then," Becky said. "I'll show you to your room."

Andrea followed her sister down a flight of stairs to the basement, wondering what kind of scene awaited her. The last time she'd seen it, the lower level had just been an empty, cavernous space.

"Dan finished it last month." Becky flipped a switch, flooding the space with light. "He did an amazing job, didn't he?"

"Yes, he did." It was now a cozy, carpeted rec room painted a buttery yellow, with built-in cabinetry for books, and a large TV. The upright piano that had once been in the living room—Andrea's piano from their old home—now had a place of honor along one wall. She dragged her eyes away from it to the sofa bed, already pulled out and made up with clean sheets and a coverlet.

"Is that Mom's quilt?"

"Yeah. I guess Dan thought you could use it."

Andrea blinked away tears. "That was nice of him."

"Andy … you sure you're okay?"

"I'm fine. I just need to get away from my life for a while. Sort things out." Andrea put her arms around her sister and squeezed her tight. "We'll talk in the morning?"

"All right. You know where I am if you need me. Bathroom's through the door over there."

"Thanks, Becks. I'll be fine."

Her sister cast a final concerned look at her before leaving her alone. Andrea placed her suitcase on a coffee table that had been pushed out of the way of the fold-out bed and traded her suit for pajamas. Then she flicked off the light, climbed beneath their mother's old quilt, and closed her eyes to the tears that slowly seeped from beneath her lashes.

Andrea woke hours later, disoriented, and fumbled for her phone on the side table. In the windowless basement, she couldn't tell if it was midnight or noon. She squinted in the glare from the screen and tried to make out the numbers. Ten in the morning? Surely that couldn't be right.

She flipped on the lamp beside the bed, her heart pounding. Then she remembered James. The photo. Her job. She sucked in a breath and rode out the wave of panic. What had she been thinking? What had she done? Eight years of work, thrown away. For nothing.

Becky thumped down the basement stairs, a mug in one hand. "You're awake!"

"Sort of. Is that for me?"

Becky handed her the cup. "Of course. I checked on you a couple hours ago, but you were out. I didn't have the heart to disturb you. If the kids didn't manage to wake you up with their racket, you must have really needed the sleep."

Andrea sipped the coffee with a sigh. "A few more of these and I might feel human again."

"Take your time. When you're ready, get dressed and come up. I'll make you breakfast. Dan took the kids to church, so it's just you and me."

"Thanks, Becks." She was grateful for what her sister left unsaid. Becky had cleared the house so Andrea could spill her story uninterrupted.

She took her time getting ready, not anxious to tell the story even though she knew she had no choice. She took a shower in the small basement bathroom, blew her hair dry, put on some mascara and lip gloss. Then she pulled on the single pair of jeans she had brought from Scotland and a long-sleeved blouse and trudged up the stairs.

To her credit, Becky just asked casually, "You hungry?"

"Bowl of cereal maybe. I've probably gained ten pounds eating James's cooking this past week." The words spilled out so naturally the spike of pain that came with them took her by surprise. Somehow even the three flights from Inverness to Dayton hadn't driven home the realization she would never see James again. She sank into a chair on suddenly shaky legs.

"So you spent a lot of time together." Becky set a bowl in front of Andrea, followed by the milk carton and a box of cornflakes. "What happened?"

Andrea poured the cereal and milk, glad to have her hands busy. "I tried. I really did. I just … Maybe there are some of us who aren't meant for the whole domestic scene."

Becky pulled out a chair and sat across from her. "You didn't tell me he asked you to marry him."

"What? No! He didn't."

"So what's the problem, then? You like him. He obviously likes you, more than a little. You fly to London all the time. Why can't you just see where things go?"

"You don't understand," Andrea said miserably. "He's not … He …"

"He makes you want more than that."

Andrea pressed her fingertips to her eyes. "He wants more than that. And I don't know if I can give it, should it come down to it."

Becky reached across the table and grabbed Andrea's free hand. "You were not meant to carry this burden for the rest of your life. Let it go."

Andrea stared at her cornflakes. "That's what he said."

"You told him? About Logan and the baby?"

Andrea nodded.

Becky sat back in the chair. "Why him? Why now?"

"I don't know."

"You thought it would scare him off. Did it?"

Andrea met her sister's eyes. "No."

"I think none of this was any accident. I think you were supposed to go to Skye for this very reason."

"To meet him, you mean."

"No, sweetie. To make you see all you were missing. To make you think about what your life could be like if you'd just give it all up to God. This sorrow was never part of His plan." Becky rose and gave Andrea a hug. "I'll let you think about that. I'm going to go get dressed."

Andrea ate her cornflakes automatically. Becky made it seem so simple. As if she could just decide to be done with it and move on. As if she could just throw off the guilt and the pain and live her life as if none of it had ever happened.

Why not? Why do you keep punishing yourself?

Wherever the thought came from, it raised gooseflesh on her arms.

Because it was my fault. Because Mom would have been ashamed of me, letting power and money seduce me into doing things I knew were wrong. If I hadn't made bad choices, none of it would have happened. I could have a husband and family now.

I could have James.

She put her cereal bowl in the dishwasher and wandered toward the living room, which had been straightened up since last night. She bent to pick up a tiny doll and placed it on the end table. Tears pricked her eyes as she remembered playing with Emmy at the coffee table while James cooked. It was too easy to imagine a life like that for herself, even though it was impossible.

She wiped her eyes with the back of her hand and headed for the basement stairs. She should at least check her email. When she reached the bottom, though, it wasn't her laptop that drew her. It was the piano.

She strode across the carpeted room, seated herself at the bench, and pushed back the fall board. As she started her warm-up exercises, she realized it had been tuned recently. Were the kids taking piano lessons now? Or had Becky just had it tuned for her when they moved it to the basement? It would be just like her sister to do something so thoughtful when all Andrea had done was reject opportunities to come back to Ohio.

When she passed the point of warm and still kept playing scales, she knew she was just avoiding matters. Her feelings had a tendency to spill out into the music. She started with Schumann, but somehow the song morphed and changed into the melody with which she'd experimented the day she'd told James her story. The day she'd kissed him for the first time. The day she'd finally begun to admit her feelings for him.

Three days ago. How could it have only been three days?

She couldn't think about that. Instead she played. The music shifted, ebbed and flowed. It seemed to suggest the soft tempo of time on Skye, the lap of waves along the shore, the swift movements of clouds across the sky.

We're all broken. We're only human. Some wounds only God can mend.

She had rejected James's words because they had hinted at something she couldn't accept. But now ...

She didn't realize she was crying until the tears fell on the keyboard. She played until she couldn't see the keys and then wrapped her arms around herself while choked sobs burst from her mouth.

Life should be more than just a catalog of business deals and signed contracts. She wanted to love and be loved. She wanted to be whole again.

She needed to believe there was something greater to hold onto.

"I'm sorry," she prayed, her voice barely more than a whisper. "I lost my way. I've made so many mistakes. I've been chasing the wrong things, trying to prove I was worth something. Please … just … please …"

If she expected a rush of awareness or a light from heaven, she would have been disappointed. God's presence flowed into her gently, filling the empty spaces that had lain barren for so long. It suffused her body like the quiet trill of birdsong, the lap of waves along the shore, the soft scatter of light along the water through the clouds overhead. She recognized those quiet moments of peace she had found in Skye, realized God had been with her there, bringing her to this moment. She braced her elbows on her knees and let her hair fall forward as the tears streamed down her face, taking with them the buried pain and loneliness of the past eight years.

When the tears finally subsided, she was free.

Chapter Thirty-Three

"I don't know about this." Andrea looked at herself doubtfully in the mirror. The red-and-white flowered sundress was the last thing she would have chosen for herself, but it was one of the few items from her sister's closet that fit her. It seemed silly to shop for clothes when she would be returning to New York in few days. The past two weeks in Ohio had been a blessed escape from reality, but it was time to return home and make a decision about her future.

"You look beautiful," Becky said.

"I look like June Cleaver." Andrea didn't really mind, though. Becky said she'd feel out of place wearing a suit in their casual church, but she couldn't quite bring herself to throw on jeans in the house of God. She thrust her feet into her red Jimmy Choos and slipped on a white cardigan, also purloined from her sister's closet.

"I'm glad you're coming." Becky slipped an arm around Andrea's waist and leaned her head on her shoulder. "It will almost be like old times, when we used to go to church with Mom."

"Almost," Andrea said. "I wish she was still here. I miss her."

They piled into two cars, Dan driving the kids in their SUV, Becky taking Andrea in the white sedan. As soon as they pulled onto the tree-lined street, Becky asked, "What are you going to do now?"

"I've been thinking I might go out on my own. My clients know what I can do. They'll give me recommendations. I can be up and running in a few months."

"So you're really going back to New York?"

"For now." She knew what Becky was thinking, but James hadn't called since leaving the voice mail she'd deleted. She spent every evening with her cell phone in hand, his number on the dialer. She would run her fingers over the scarf he'd given her and allow herself to remember what it felt like to be in his arms, convinced she'd made a terrible mistake in leaving. Somehow, though, she couldn't bring herself to push the call button. She'd forced him away, refused him in no uncertain terms. She wouldn't blame him for never wanting to see her again. The measure of peace she had found amidst a life still in upheaval was too tenuous to risk.

She realized Becky was waiting for her to finish her answer, so she said, "I still like New York. I'll have to sell my apartment, but I can find something affordable while I build my business. Brooklyn, maybe. Or New Jersey."

Becky looked so horrified that Andrea laughed. "Or maybe upstate. I don't know, Becky. I'll see where the Lord takes me."

Her sister reached across the console and rubbed her arm. "You realize I never thought I would hear those words come out of your mouth."

"Me neither. I'm sorry I gave you such a hard time over the last few years."

"Call it a reminder to continue praying. I never lost hope."

"I know you didn't. Thank you, Becks." Andrea reached into her purse for her lipstick, but instead of the metal tube, her fingers touched the sharp edge of an envelope. Frowning, she drew it out.

The square of cream-colored vellum bore the thistle stamp of the Culloden Manor Hotel.

Blood whooshed in her ears. How could she have forgotten about this? She had gone through her purse countless times and had never seen the note, shoved forgotten into an inside pocket.

"What's that?" Becky asked.

"Nothing." Andrea quickly slipped it back into her purse with trembling hands, but she'd have had better luck ignoring a signal beacon now that she remembered it was there.

The community church lay on the edge of town, a white clapboard building with a spire that reminded Andrea of the country churches in every old movie she'd seen. Green lawn spread around it, and churchgoers already stood in clusters along the walkways and on the steps.

A sudden burst of panic overcame her as Becky parked next to her husband in the small lot. "I don't know if I can do this."

Becky put a steadying hand on her shoulder. "It's okay, Andy. No one's going to judge you. No one even cares about what happened back then, if they even remember."

Andrea swallowed down the lump in her throat and gathered her courage before she climbed out of the car.

Becky and Dan each took one of the three-year-old twins—David and Hannah—from their car seats, leaving nine-year-old Casey to Andrea. She held the door open for the boy while he hopped down, and he slipped his hand into hers.

"Don't be afraid, Aunt Andy," he said. "Church is fun."

"Am I that obvious?"

His smile made him look like small version of Dan. "Mom said your old church was mean to you. Everyone's nice here. You'll like them."

"Well, how could I be afraid with that kind of reassurance?" Andrea squeezed Casey's shoulder. "Why don't you show me where we have to go."

They made their way to the sanctuary in fits and starts, stopped by clusters of people that knew Becky's family. Becky introduced Andrea as her sister, and no one showed anything but pure welcome as they shook her hand. Gradually, some of the tension eased from her shoulders.

"I'll take the kids to Sunday school," Dan said. "Why don't you and Andrea find seats?"

Andrea smiled at Dan's departing back as he led the twins away, Casey trailing behind. "You've got a good one there."

"I absolutely do." Becky walked her down the center aisle of the small church. She chose a pew near the back and slid in. Not long after, the rest of the seats began to fill. Dan reappeared and sat on the other side of Andrea. They were flanking her for protection, determined that no one do anything to scare her away. Or maybe they were just blocking the exits so she couldn't make a run for it.

Andrea joined in the worship songs, but once the pastor took the pulpit, her mind began to wander to the envelope in her purse again. She drew her attention back to the sermon, which was based on the story of the prodigal son. She bowed her head and smiled. Of all the services she could have attended after coming back to her faith, it was a story of how God rejoiced when lost souls were restored to him. Becky reached for her hand and squeezed it tightly.

Then they were back on their feet, singing the closing song, and Becky slipped her arm around Andrea's waist. "Thanks for coming, sis."

"Thanks for bringing me."

Their exit was just like their entrance. More people who knew Becky and Dan, more friendly introductions. When they finally made it to the walkway, Andrea slipped away from them and reached into her purse for the envelope.

Was she ready to see what it said? Her pulse raced, and fear spiked through her middle. She slid her finger beneath the seal and broke it with a crack.

"You're a difficult woman to track down, Andrea Sullivan. Or should I say, Andrea da Silva?"

Andrea froze at the distinctly Scottish voice behind her. A chill rippled through her body. She shoved the note back into her purse and took a deep breath before she turned. James stood several steps behind her, his hands resting casually in his pockets and looking so handsome she momentarily forgot to breathe.

He walked toward her with the boyish grin that always made her knees go weak. "Do you know how many art deco movie houses there are in Ohio?"

"How many?" Even to her own ears, her voice sounded breathless.

"Thirteen. And every single one of those towns now has a stoplight." His blue eyes bored into hers, and for a minute, she forgot she was standing in a crowd of people. "But I did tell you I enjoyed a challenge."

Before she could say anything, he looked past her, and his smile reappeared. "You must be Becky. I'm James." He brushed past Andrea and took Becky's hands, then kissed her on the cheek.

Andrea stared at Becky in amazement. "You knew?"

"He called a couple days ago," she said sheepishly. "He wanted to make sure you were here before he flew in from London."

"May I steal your sister for a little while?" James asked.

"Have her home before dark." Becky beamed at Andrea, and she wondered how her sister had ever managed to keep the secret for the past few days.

James reached for her hand. "Take a walk with me?"

Andrea hesitated, but the minute her fingers intertwined with his, her world shifted with a satisfying finality, like the pieces of a puzzle clicking into place. "A walk would be nice."

She felt eyes on them as they walked hand in hand down the front path, but she was far too stunned by the presence of the man next to her to care what anyone thought. They moved down the street toward the park in silence until Andrea finally found her voice.

"What are you doing here?"

"You promised me a tour. Where else would I go for a spring holiday but Ohio?"

"Be serious." Her pulse raced so frantically she thought she might faint onto the sidewalk.

"All right, seriously, then." James stopped abruptly and tugged her into his arms right there on the street, so close she could feel the pounding of his heart. "I'm here because I've not been able to stop thinking about you since you left. I've called myself every name I know for letting you go. I wasn't looking for this, but now that I've met you, I can't imagine my life without you."

"Jamie, I—"

"Don't say anything. I know it's fast. I know after all you've been through, you're afraid of making a mistake, and the idea of being in the public eye is the last thing you want. If it bothers you so much, I just won't renew my contract with the network. I don't need the program. I'm busy enough with my restaurants and the hotel. And if I can't convince you to come back to Scotland with me, then … I guess we'll work something out."

Andrea stared at him, stunned speechless. He was offering to give up his TV show for her, without any assurance of her love, without any plans for the future. "Why would you do that?"

He brushed the hair away from her face as he had done that night outside the door of her cottage. "Because now I know what's important to me. I love you."

She stared at him in amazement and waited for panic to rush in at the words. Instead the glow of certainty flowed into her, warming her body like sunlight on a cold day. "I love you too."

Then his lips were on hers, sweet and warm and filled with the promise of the future. She twined her arms around his neck and held him close, not caring who saw them or what they thought. She had resisted this for so long, thinking herself unworthy of love, unworthy of forgiveness. And now all she'd ever wanted stretched out before her for the taking. She kissed him back with abandon, pouring every last bit of her joy into her touch, until her head spun and the only thing keeping her on her feet was his arms around her.

When they parted, James laughed, a low throaty sound in her ear. "If you keep kissing me like that, I won't be able to get you to the altar soon enough."

Andrea stiffened, alarm flaring in her head. "Jamie ... I can't. I love you, but I can't marry you. Not yet. We need time to get to know each other first. Get used to being a couple. Just ... make sure. Can you understand that?"

To her relief, he only smiled. "I think you better read the note, then."

She retrieved the envelope from her purse. Her hands quivered as she bent back the flap and withdrew a folded sheet of paper. Tears pooled in her eyes, but this time she didn't try to wipe them away. A smile came to her lips as she read the single line on the page.

I love you, Andrea. I can wait.

... a little more ...

When a delightful concert comes to an end,

the orchestra might offer an encore.

When a fine meal comes to an end,

it's always nice to savor a bit of dessert.

When a great story comes to an end,

we think you may want to linger.

And so, we offer ...

AfterWords—just a little something more after you

have finished a David C Cook novel.

We invite you to stay awhile in the story.

Thanks for reading!

Turn the page for ...

- **Great Questions**
- **A Sneak Peek at Book Two**
- **About the Author**

Great Questions

for Individual Reflection and/or Group Discussion

1. The story opens with a mistaken-identity meeting straight out of one of Andrea's favorite old movies. Both Andrea and James "stick to the script," acting in expected ways because of the setting. Are there situations in which you behave according to others' expectations? If so, why?

2. James allows other people to believe his playboy reputation is deserved, even though he's technically not doing anything immoral or un-Christian. Is it wrong for him to allow other people to believe the worst? How much responsibility do we have for the way others perceive us?

3. Andrea says she'd rather be a heathen than a hypocrite, which makes James regret the fact that he's been a bad example of a Christian man. How do you reconcile living freely under grace with the need to act as a good witness?

4. Andrea has been subjected to certain assumptions about her business sense because she is an attractive woman. Do you think that there is still a double standard for women in business? Do you think that women have to work harder to prove their capability than their male counterparts?

5. Andrea is expected to do whatever it takes to get the contract. Have you ever been in a situation where your personal beliefs conflicted with the requirements of your job or school? How did you resolve that conflict? In hindsight, do you believe you made the right choice?

6. Andrea dismisses her feelings toward James as merely physical because she no longer trusts her own judgment. How do you regain confidence in your own ability to make good choices after you've made a significant error in judgment?

7. At the end of the book, Andrea realizes that not only does she need to ask God's forgiveness for her past mistakes, she needs to truly accept that she can be free from the past. Why do you think this is so essential to her ability to love again and accept love in return? How do your feelings about your own past influence how you approach the future?

A Sneak Peek at Book Two:

LONDON TIDES

Chapter One

She shouldn't be here.

Grace Brennan snapped several pictures of the fog-shrouded river, forcing down the tide of anxiety that threatened to rise up and engulf her. Chances were he wouldn't be here either. People changed in ten years. She certainly had. What kind of man stuck to such a rigid schedule for over a decade?

She ambled down the cement embankment to where the muddy waters of the Thames lapped the bank and raised her camera once more. Even in the dim morning light, her telephoto lens captured every detail of the boats rowing against the ebb tide, from the markings on the shells to the club crests on the rowers' kit. Grace had photographed enough regattas in her career to recognize the different clubs and schools by their colors, to distinguish the casuals from the competitive rowers. To know from a distance she hadn't seen him yet.

It was a mad impulse that brought her here anyhow. Her regrets should have stayed in the past where they belonged, with the rest of her mistakes. Back then her fears had clouded her judgment, skewed her perspective. And no matter how far she'd come, there might always be parts of her that were broken. What would coming back here do but remind her of what she'd given up?

She was about ready to move on to some street-level shots when a sleek, red eight glided with precision toward the bank on which she stood. Again the camera came up to focus on the crew, and her heart rose into her throat when her gaze landed on the man in the stroke seat nearest the stern.

His dark hair was short now, thick waves cropped into submission, but she would have recognized him anywhere. He radiated capability and confidence with an oar in hand, and even his rowing waterproofs couldn't hide a physique that was as lean and muscular as a decade before. Clearly she'd had good reason to believe things hadn't changed.

Grace's hand tightened convulsively around the column of the thick lens as she let the neck strap take the camera's weight. Her muscles tensed, her heart pounding. Should she call to him? Would he even speak to her?

Then he turned her way and stopped, the oar frozen in mid-air. He saw her, no mistake. She held her breath, waiting to see what he would do.

Just as quickly he turned away, his movements brusque and businesslike as he removed his oar from the lock. Her hopes rushed away as quickly as the tide.

Ten years wondering how she'd feel if she saw him again. Ten years convincing herself that time and distance would change things. Pure rubbish, all of it.

She still loved him. And he still hadn't forgiven her.

Grace wound her way into the Regency Café, ignoring the irritated looks from waiting patrons. Even at eight in the morning, the greasy spoon was packed with diners, the queue stretching out the door, voices raised in a hum just short of deafening. She scanned the crowded room until her gaze landed on a beautiful Indian woman staking out a corner table.

Asha held up her arm and pointed to her wristwatch with raised eyebrows.

"I know, I know, I'm late." Grace grimaced as she approached the table, but Asha squeezed her into a bone-crushing hug before she could get out the rest of her apology.

"Only by about two years! When did you arrive in London? Before you called this morning, I didn't even know you were coming."

"Landed last night." The tightness in Grace's chest eased as she slid into a chair and placed her gear bag between her feet. "It was a last-minute decision. Did you order for us?"

"Of course. I didn't queue for an hour for tea. I got your usual. It *is* your usual, right? You didn't go vegan on me or anything …"

Grace laughed. "Absolutely not. I live on bacon. Besides, Paris hasn't been as much fun since they stopped sautéing everything in a kilo of butter. You know you're in trouble when even the French turn health conscious."

Asha laughed too, her expression radiating happiness. Since they'd met on a medical mission in Jaipur twelve years ago, Dr. Asha

Issar had become her close friend and confidante. Grace had no doubt that her joy was genuine.

"So tell me, why *are* you back in London?"

"To see you, of course." At Asha's disbelieving look, Grace laughed again and amended, "It was time, Ash. I couldn't avoid an entire country forever. I'm considering moving back."

"I'd love that. But you said you'd never leave the field. What happened?" Asha's attention settled on Grace's right arm, where it rested on the table. "Does it have something to do with the new tattoo?"

Grace touched the tiny green dragon that curled around her wrist like a bracelet, melding seamlessly into the design of colored flowers and wrought iron above it. It was good work—artistic work—but she should have known Asha would understand this was no more a whim than the other tattoos that covered her right arm to the shoulder.

"Brian is dead."

"Oh, Grace, I'm so sorry. What happened?"

Grace swallowed hard while she brought her voice under control. "You hear about the incident in Syria?"

"That was him?" Understanding dawned on Asha's face. "That was you. You were the other photographer who survived the blast. Grace, why didn't you tell me?"

Because she hadn't told anyone. Because the grief was too fresh. And deep down she felt responsible.

Sure, she'd not been the one to fire the grenade. She'd warned Brian that their position was too exposed, had been trying to get them out. But he was so young and eager to get the shot, and it had been her responsibility to rein in that reckless enthusiasm, just as her own mentor Jean-Auguste had done for her.

She'd failed miserably.

"So that's why I'm here," Grace said at last. "I'm supposed to be in Aleppo, but I couldn't get on the plane."

Asha reached for her hand across the table and squeezed it hard. "I understand; I really do. But you love the work. Surely you don't want to quit."

"Come on, Ash. You know shooting conflicts was supposed to be a short-term plan, not the past ten years of my life. Everyone with half a brain is out, onto something safer."

"But you've worked for this since you were nineteen!"

"And look where it's gotten me."

"Achieving a level of success most people never imagine. *Newsweek* and *National Geographic* have you on speed dial. You were listed as one of the most influential photographers of the decade, for heaven's sake."

"One of the most influential photographers of the decade." Grace gave a short, humorless laugh. "Had I died along with Brian, would anyone have missed me besides you and Jean-Auguste? I'm thirty-four, Ash. I can pack up my entire life in three cases and a duffel bag. My parents don't talk to me anymore, and the only person to send me a birthday card was the president of my photo agency."

Asha's gaze drilled into her. "You're back for Ian."

"When you say it that way, I sound completely pathetic."

"Not *completely* pathetic. Just a little bit."

"It was daft," Grace said. "If you could have seen the look on his face—"

"You saw him? What did you do? What did he say?"

"I don't know. I didn't stick around to find out."

"Grace—"

"I know, I know. But what do you say in that situation? 'Hi, I'm sorry I ran out on you six months before our wedding. How have you been?' Besides, for all I know, he's married and has half a dozen kids now."

"He's not married."

The pronouncement stunned Grace into momentary silence. "You've seen him?"

"He and Jake go out for a pint on occasion. He dates, but as far as I can tell, nothing serious. It leads one to believe he's waiting for something. Or someone."

Grace's heart jolted at the words, but she shook her head. However much she might want to put things right, what she had done to him was unforgivable. What kind of woman left the man she loved without a proper good-bye? What kind of man forgave that kind of betrayal?

"You should talk to him, Grace. Even if it's just to put him behind you."

As Grace opened her mouth to reply, the woman behind the counter shouted a familiar order. "That us?"

"Yeah. I'll get it." Asha pushed back the chair.

"Bacon, egg, mushrooms, tomatoes, two toasts! You comin' to get it, or you want me to fax it to ya?"

Grace chuckled. "Let me. Least I can do after you saved me the hour wait."

She pushed her way to the counter, relieved to escape her friend's scrutiny. Maybe Asha was right, but she'd been trying to put Ian behind her for ten years. What made either of them think she'd be any more successful now?

By the time Grace returned with their breakfasts, she'd steeled herself for more analysis, but Asha didn't bring up the subject again. Instead she asked, "Where are you staying?"

"Hotel."

Asha reached into her handbag and slid a key across the table to her. "You know the address."

"Ash, I couldn't—"

"Nonsense. Of course you could. How long will you be here?"

"At least through the end of August. A friend is putting together a showing of my portraits at his gallery in Putney. After that, I'm not sure."

"You just got here, and you're already looking for an excuse to leave." A smile softened Asha's words, though, and she reached out to squeeze Grace's hand. "I'm glad you're back."

"Me too." To stave off further discussion, Grace dug into her breakfast and barely stifled a groan of pleasure. Paris might be the culinary center of Europe, but nothing beat an old-fashioned fry-up from this landmark diner. She allowed herself to savor a few more bites before she shot a stern look at Asha. "So. Jake. Don't think you're going to slip that one by me. Did you finally say yes?"

Asha shrugged. "After five years of asking me out, it seemed only fair to give the bloke a chance."

"It's about time. I've always thought you two would make a great couple."

She laughed. "It had crossed my mind over the years. But one or both of us were always seeing someone else. He was busy with work;

I was splitting my time between here and India … It wasn't the right time for a relationship."

If anyone understood that, it was Grace. Still, after Asha had broken off a tumultuous romance with a fellow physician, Grace had wondered if she would ever take a chance on another man. "We should have dinner, then, the three of us. I haven't seen him in ages."

"You haven't seen anyone in ages," Asha countered, but it was without heat. She glanced at her watch and grimaced. "I have to go or I'll be late for my shift. Move your things to the flat, yeah? I'll be back later tonight."

"Thanks, Ash. It means a lot to me." Grace gave her a quick hug, then watched her stride from the restaurant. Of all her friends, Asha was the most dependable, the most understanding. But then she had a better perspective on what Grace did for a living, having spent much of her early career in conflict zones herself. It took firsthand experience to understand how it felt to live day to day in varying degrees of danger.

She turned back to her plate, but her mind returned to Ian. She should have stuck around and talked to him, told him the conclusions she'd reached in the three months since Brian's death. After all these years, he deserved to know why she had run away. Deserved to know it hadn't been because she'd stopped loving him.

And maybe he deserved to know that leaving him had been the biggest mistake of her life.

ABOUT THE AUTHOR

Carla Laureano is the author of the RITA* award-winning romance *Five Days in Skye* as well as the Celtic fantasy series The Song of Seare (as C. E. Laureano). A graduate of Pepperdine University, she worked as a sales and marketing executive for nearly a decade before leaving corporate life behind to write fiction full-time. She currently lives in Denver with her husband and two sons.

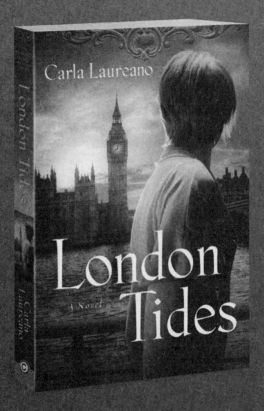

A Second Chance at First Love

Can Irish photojournalist Grace Brennan and Scottish
businessman Ian MacDonald change the course of their futures
together—or will life's tides once again tear them apart?

David C Cook

transforming lives together

Coming Summer 2016, book three of
the MacDonald Family Trilogy …

Under
Scottish
Stars